TRUE HISTORY DECRYPTED

FULL TEXT AND COMMENTARY OF LUCIAN'S *TRUE HISTORY*

CONTENTS

True History Decrypted: Full text and Commentary of Lucian's *True History*

Edited by Frank Redmond
Notes by C. S. Jarram, Thomas Francklin, Christopher Wieland, and Frank Redmond
True History text translated by H.W. and F.G. Fowler

First Edition (1.0), 2013
Second Edition (2.0), 2015
Second Edition Updated (2.2), 2016

**I do not claim originality for this work, for it is intended to be a reference book compiled from sources found in the public domain.

Mênin Web and Print Publishing
http://meninpublishing.org/
Chicago, Illinois, United States of America

Citations

The Works of Lucian from the Greek. Thomas Francklin. London. Printed for T. Cadell in the Strand. 1780.

Lucian. With an English translation by A. M. Harmon of Princeton University. London. William Heinemann; New York: The Macmillan Co. 1913.

Luciani Vera Historia. Edited with Introduction and Notes for the Use of Middle Forms in Schools. C. S. Jarram, M.A. Oxford at the Clarendon Press. 1879.

Lucian of Samosata from the Greek with the Comments and Illustrations of Wieland and Others. William Tooke, F.R.S. London. 1820.

Chattering Courtesans and Other Sardonic Sketches. Translated with and Introduction and Notes by Keith Sidwell. Penguin Books. 2004.

Book Cover Image by Aubrey Beardsley:

Lucian's True History. Translated by Francis Hickes. Illustrated by William Strang, J.B. Clark, and Aubrey Beardsley with an introduction by Charles Whibley, 1902.

INTRODUCTION

One of the translators of Lucian, Thomas Francklin, bemoaned in his introduction to *True History*, "We cannot but lament that the humour of many of the references has been lost to us; therefore, Lucian's *True History* cannot be half as pleasurable as when it was first written, but there are enough remaining allusions which we understand to secure it from being unrelatable." This work, *True History Decrypted*, attempts to take those "remaining allusions" and make them relatable to the modern reader. Modern audiences rarely have the background to fully understand all of the allusions made in *True History* and classical texts in general. It would be unfortunate if there were not a book that could help guide the reader through each section and provide the necessary background to fully enjoy the work.

This book takes a two-tiered approach to understanding *True History*: (1) provide extensive commentary section-by-section, addressing the main themes and ideas of the work as the reader goes along (all material is found in the public domain); (2) provide an Appendix of works that Lucian may have been acclimated to and used as a basis for the parody found in *True History*. With these two eyes, the *True History* becomes a great deal more enjoyable and easier to comprehend (likewise, found in the public domain)

There is no doubt that *True History* is Lucian's most famous and influential work. It has influenced works like More's *Utopia* and Swift's *Gulliver's Travels*. *True History* masquerades as a clinical account of the travels of the narrator and his companions. The style, tone, and approach of *True History* is exceptionally true to the travel genre; however, it is with the content where

Lucian makes his satirical intent manifest. The narrator travels to the moon and back, to different islands like the Island of Cheese and Island of the Damned; he meets a cast of strange, twisted characters throughout, some more fanciful than others. Underneath it all, Lucian is really questioning the idea of truth found in factual, non-fiction writing. On a meta level, Lucian is trying to show the impossibility of absolute truth in writing. If the purpose of satire is improve the condition of a certain aspect of society, then Lucian is trying to call out some of the more grossly inaccurate worldly depictions in order to improve, all around, truth in literature, history, and entertainment.

Frank Redmond – 2013 (1st Edition; 1.0)
Frank Redmond – 2015 (2nd Edition; 2.0)
Frank Redmond – 2016 (2nd Edition; 2.2)
2nd Edition (2015) modifications – Patched Introduction; fixed minor content bugs; added additional notes to Lucian text.
2nd Edition (2016) modifications – Standardized citations; style updates.

TRUE HISTORY TEXT AND COMMENTARY

PREFACE

SECTION 1

Athletes and physical trainers do not limit their attention to the questions of perfect condition and exercise [1]; they say there is a time for relaxation also — which indeed they represent as the most important element in training. I hold it equally true for literary men that after severe study [2] they should unbend the intellect, if it is to come perfectly efficient to its next task.

[1] Exercise | The advantages arising from the athletic exercises practiced in Greece and sometimes their downsides are set forth Lucian's dialogue *Anacharsis*.

[2] Severe study | Such severe literary study can be glimpsed from Lucian's work *On How to Write History* 5: "There might as well be an art of talking, seeing, or eating; history-writing is perfectly easy, comes natural, is a universal gift; all that is necessary is the faculty of translating your thoughts into words. But the truth is — you know it without my telling, old friend —, it is not a task to be lightly undertaken, or carried through without effort; no, it needs as much care as any sort of composition whatever, if one means to create 'a possession forever,' as Thucydides calls it."[i]

SECTION 2

The rest they want will best be found in a course of

literature which does not offer entertainment pure and simple, depending on mere wit or felicity, but is also capable of stirring an educated curiosity [1] — in a way which I hope will be exemplified in the following pages. They are intended to have an attraction independent of any originality of subject, any happiness of general design, and any authenticity in the piling up of fictions. This attraction is in the veiled reference underlying all the details of my narrative; they parody the rooster-and-bull stories [2] of ancient poets, historians, and philosophers; I have only refrained from adding a key [3] because I could rely upon you to recognize as you read. [4]

[1] Capable of stirring an educated curiosity | Not only amuses by a narrative of marvelous adventures, but engages the literary or critical facility by imitating the accounts of professed poets and historians.

[2] Rooster-and-bull stories | A rooster and bull story is a false account or tall tale.

[3] A key | Lucian wants his audience to look for the clues in his work for he is not going to explicitly identify any subjects.

[4] Rely upon you to recognize as you read | An object of Old Comedy was to openly attack subjects and topics, but Lucian is taking a different approach by hiding the key and allowing the audience to investigate the sources of ridicule themselves.

SECTION 3

Ctesias [1], son of Ctesiochus of Cnidus, in his work on India and its characteristics, gives details for which he had neither the evidence of his eyes nor of hearsay. Iambulus's *Oceanica* [2] is full of marvels; the whole thing is a manifest fiction, but at the same time pleasant reading. Many other writers have adopted the same plan, professing to relate their own

travels, and describing monstrous beasts, savages, and strange ways of life [3]. The fount and inspiration of their humor is the Homeric Odysseus, entertaining Alcinous's court with his prisoned winds, his men one-eyed or wild or cannibal, his beasts with many heads, and his metamorphosed comrades; the Phaeacians were simple folk, and he fooled them to the top of their bent [4].

[1] Ctesias | He wrote also thirty books of the Persian History. He lived in the time of Artaxerxes. Fragments of Ctesias' *History of India* are preserved in the *Bibliotheca* of Photius. Many of the wonders he relates are distortions of fact, e.g. the 'talking birds' and the black dog headed men with long teeth and nails, who have a voice like a bark and make gestures and grimaces.

[2] Iambulus's *Oceanica* | Nothing is directly left of the works of Iambulus. Diodorus Siculus is supposed to have copied from Iambulus in his description of a journey through Ethiopia to the Island of the Sun. Very fantastical.

[3] Many other writers have adopted the same plan, professing to relate their own travels, and describing monstrous beasts, savages, and strange ways of life | Perhaps an allusion to Herodotus.

[4] Fooled them to the top of their bent | Allusion to Homer's *Odyssey* 9-12. The tales of Odysseus at the court of Alcinous, about the Cyclops, the bag in which the winds were confined, the enchantments of Circe, etc.

SECTION 4

When I come across a writer of this sort, I do not much mind his lying; the practice is much too well established for that, even with professed philosophers [1]; I am only surprised at his expecting to escape detection. Now I am myself vain enough to cherish

the hope of bequeathing something to posterity; I see no reason for resigning my right to that inventive freedom which others enjoy; and, as I have no truth to put on record, having lived a very humdrum life, I fall back on falsehood — but falsehood of a more consistent variety; for I now make the only true statement you are to expect — that I am a liar [2]. This confession is, I consider, a full defense against all imputations. My subject is, then, what I have neither seen, experienced, nor been told, what neither exists nor could conceivably do so. I humbly solicit my readers' incredulity.

[1] Professed philosophers | Seems to be an allusion to Plato's myths, especially the one that concludes the *Republic*, the Myth of Er.

[2] I am a liar | Lucian is playing with the philosophical idea of the "liar's paradox". In philosophy and logic, the "liar's paradox" (*pseudomenon* in Ancient Greek) is the statement "this sentence is false." Trying to assign to this statement a classical binary truth value leads to a contradiction. If "this sentence is false" is true, then the sentence is false, which is a contradiction. Conversely, if "this sentence is false" is false, then the sentence is true, which is also a contradiction.

BOOK I

SECTION 5

[1] Starting on a certain date from the Pillars of Heracles [2], I sailed with a fair wind into the Atlantic. The motives of my voyage were a certain intellectual restlessness, a passion for novelty, a curiosity about the limits of the ocean and the peoples who might dwell beyond it. This being my design, I provisioned and watered my ship on a generous scale. My crew amounted to fifty, all men whose interests, as well as their years, corresponded with my own. I had further provided a good supply of arms, secured the best navigator to be had for money, and had the ship — a pinnace [3] — specially strengthened for a long and arduous voyage.

[1] Starting... | Here the history begins. The previous four sections must be considered a preface even though it is not labeled as such in the original.

[2] Pillar of Heracles | The Pillars of Heracles were Mount Abyla in Mauritania and Calpe in Spain, one on either side of the Fretum Gaditanam, now the Straits of Gibraltar. According to legend they were once a continuous mountain, which Heracles rent asunder. Outside these straits lay the Western Ocean, a tract almost unknown, except possibly to some bolder Phoenician adventurers. The term *Oceanus* was originally applied to the fabled river which was believe to encircle the world; but as geographical knowledge advanced it was used to designate the great outside expanse waters, especially the Atlantic, as distinguished from the Mediterranean or inner sea.

[3] Pinnace | A light craft. Lucian provides the reader with a very specific type of vessel.

SECTION 6

For a day and a night we were carried quietly along by the breeze, with land still in sight. But with the next day's dawn the wind rose to a gale, with a heavy sea and a dark sky; we found ourselves unable to take in sail. We surrendered ourselves to the elements, let her run, and were storm-driven for more than eleven weeks. On the eightieth day the sun came out quite suddenly, and we found ourselves close to a lofty wooded island, round which the waves were murmuring gently, the sea having almost fallen by this time. We brought her to land, disembarked, and after our long tossing lay a considerable time idle on shore; we at last made a start, however, and leaving thirty of our number to guard the ship I took the other twenty on a tour of inspection.

SECTION 7

We had advanced half a mile inland through woods, when we came upon a brazen pillar, inscribed in Greek characters — which however were worn and dim —'Heracles and Dionysus reached this point.' Not far off were two footprints on rock [1]; one might have been an acre in area, the other being smaller; and I conjecture that the latter was Dionysus's, and the other Heracles'; we did obeisance, and proceeded. Before we had gone far, we found ourselves on a river which ran wine; it was very like Chian [2]; the stream full and copious, even navigable in parts. This evidence of Dionysus's sojourn was enough to convince us [3] that the inscription on the pillar was authentic. Resolving to find the source, I followed the river up, and

discovered, instead of a fountain, a number of huge vines covered with grapes; from the root of each there issued a trickle of perfectly clear wine, the joining of which made the river. It was well stocked with great fish, resembling wine both in color and taste; catching and eating some, we at once found ourselves intoxicated; and indeed when opened the fish were full of wine-lees; presently it occurred to us to mix them with ordinary water fish, thus diluting the strength of our spirituous food. [4]

[1] Two foot prints on the rock | Passage is probably a parody of Herodotus 4.82, "One thing, however, shall be mentioned which it has to show, and which is worthy of wonder even besides the rivers and the greatness of the plain, that is to say, they point out a footprint of Heracles in the rock by the bank of the river Tyras, which in shape is like the mark of a man's foot but in size is two cubits long."[ii]

[2] Chian | Among the Greek wines, so much admired by ancient connoisseurs, those of the islands of the Archipelago were the most celebrated, and of these the Chian wine, the product of Chios, was by far the most supreme. This was particularly true of that which was made from vines growing on the mountain Arevisia. The double superlative adds a rarity to the statement.

[3] Enough to convince us | Lit. "Entered our minds" or "we were induced".

[4] Diluting the strength of our spirituous food | The Greeks mixed wine with water in the Krater prior to drinking. A Krater is a large vase which was used to mix wine and water. At a Greek symposium, Kraters were placed in the center of the room. They were quite large, so they were not easily portable when filled. Thus, the wine-water mixture would be withdrawn from the Krater with other vessels. What makes this passage peculiar is the use of solid fish-water with solid fish-wine to mix

the two. Sort of like a mash of solids.

SECTION 8

We now crossed the river by a ford, and came to some vines of a most extraordinary kind. Out of the ground came a thick well-grown stem; but the upper part was a woman, complete from the loins upward. They were like our painters' representations of Daphne in the act of turning into a tree just as Apollo overtakes her [1]. From the finger-tips sprang vine twigs, all loaded with grapes; the hair of their heads was tendrils, leaves, and grape-clusters. They greeted us and welcomed our approach, talking Lydian, Indian, and Greek, most of them the last. They went so far as to kiss us on the mouth; and whoever was kissed staggered like a drunken man. But they would not permit us to pluck their fruit, meeting the attempt with cries of pain. [2] Some of them made further amorous advances; and two of my comrades who yielded to these solicitations found it impossible to extricate themselves again from their embraces; the man became one plant with the vine, striking root beside it; his fingers turned to vine twigs, the tendrils were all round him, and embryo grape-clusters were already visible on him. [3]

[1] Daphne in the act of turning into a tree just as Apollo overtakes her | There are several versions of the myth, but the general narrative is that because of her beauty, Daphne attracted the attention and ardor of the god Apollo (Phoebus). Apollo pursued her and just before being overtaken, Daphne pleaded to her mother Gaia (or Ge) to be rescued. Gaia then swallowed her in the earth, and subsequently created the laurel tree (*Laurus nobilis*) tree to console Apollo's grief.

[2] Some early translators left off the last few sentences of section 8 deeming them too racy.

[3] ... visible on him | Episode is a possible allusion to Virgil's story of Polydorus and the groaning cornel-tree, *Aeneid* Book 3. The story goes that Aeneas lands in Thrace hoping to establish a colony for his people. The land is overgrown with various plants, and as Aeneas begins to uproot them, they begin to spout blood. The plant begins to speak and explains that it is Polydorus - the spears that were used to kill him stuck into the ground and took root, transforming into plants.

SECTION 9

We left them there and hurried back to the ship, where we told our tale, including our friends' experiment in viticulture [1]. Then after taking some casks ashore and filling them with wine and water we bivouacked near the beach, and next morning set sail before a gentle breeze. But about midday, when we were out of sight of the island, a waterspout [2] suddenly came upon us, which swept the ship round and up to a height of some three hundred and fifty miles above the earth. She did not fall back into the sea, but was suspended [3] aloft, and at the same time carried along by a wind which struck and filled the sails.

[1] Viticulture | Especially the part about having sexual intercourse with vines.

[2] A waterspout | Epicurus in his *Letter to Pythocles* explains the etiology of waterspouts: "Fiery whirlwinds are due to the descent of a cloud forced downwards like a pillar by the wind in full force and carried by a gale round and round, while at the same time the outside wind gives the cloud a lateral thrust; or it may be due to a change of the wind which veers to all points of the compass as a current of air from above helps to force it to move; or it may be that a strong eddy of winds has been started and is unable to burst through laterally

because the air around is closely condensed. And when they descend upon land, they cause what are called tornadoes, in accordance with the various ways in which they are produced through the force of the wind; and when let down upon the sea, they cause waterspouts."[iii]

[3] Suspended | In the same manner as Gulliver's island of Laputa, a kingdom devoted to the arts of music and mathematics that was suspended in the sky; from this passage it is not improbable that Swift borrowed the idea.

SECTION 10

For a whole week we pursued our airy course, and on the eighth day descried land; it was an island with air for sea, glistening, spherical, and bathed in light. We reached it, cast anchor, and landed; inspection soon showed that it was inhabited and cultivated. In the daytime nothing could be discerned outside of it; but night revealed many neighboring islands, some larger and some smaller than ours; there was also another land below us containing cities, rivers, seas, forests, and mountains; and this we concluded to be our Earth [1].

[1] Our Earth | At this point, Lucian and his comrades have left the atmosphere and are looking down on the planet.

SECTION 11

We were intending to continue our voyage, when we were discovered and detained by the Horse-vultures [1], as they are called. These are men mounted on huge vultures, which they ride like horses; the great birds have ordinarily three heads. It will give you some idea of their size if I state that each of their quill-feathers is longer and thicker than the mast of a

large merchantman. This corps is charged with the duty of patrolling the land, and bringing any strangers it may find to the king; this was what was now done with us. The king surveyed us, and, forming his conclusions from our dress, 'Strangers,' said he, 'you are Greeks, are you not?' we assented. 'And how did you traverse this vast space of air?' In answer we gave a full account of ourselves, to which he at once replied with his own history. It seemed he too was a mortal, named Endymion [2], who had been conveyed up from our Earth in his sleep, and after his arrival had become king of the country; this was, he told us, what we knew on our Earth as the moon [3]. He bade us be of good cheer and entertain no apprehensions; all our needs should be supplied.

[1] Horse-vultures | Literally *Hippogypi* from *hippos*, horse, and *gyps*, vulture.

[2] Endymion | Lucian has founded his history on some common legend. Endymion was a king of Elis, though some consider him a shepherd. Shepherd or king, however, he was so physically attractive, that the moon, who saw him leaping on mount Latmos, fell in love with him. This was a common pagan story, one in which Lucian probably doubted. Lucian makes ample amends in his history by making Endymion the emperor of the moon.

[3] Earth as the moon | Modern astronomy states that we are to the moon just the same as how the moon is to the Earth. Lucian agreed with that assessment.

SECTION 12

'And if I am victorious,' he added, 'in the campaign which I am now commencing against the inhabitants of the Sun, I promise you an extremely pleasant life at my court.' We asked about the enemy, and the quarrel. 'Phaethon,' he replied, 'king of the Sun

(which is inhabited [1], like the Moon), has long been at war with us. The occasion was this: I wished at one time to collect the poorest of my subjects and send them as a colony to Lucifer, which is uninhabited. Phaethon took umbrage at this, met the emigrants half way with a troop of Horse-ants [2], and forbade them to proceed. On that occasion, being in inferior force, we were worsted and had to retreat; but I now intend to take the offensive and send my colony. I shall be glad if you will participate; I will provide your equipment and mount you on vultures from the royal coops; the expedition starts tomorrow.' I expressed our readiness to do his pleasure. [3]

[1] Inhabited | Unlike the moon which is potentially habitable, the sun is definitely inhabitable.

[2] Horse-ants | Literally *Hippomyrmices* from *hippos*, horse, and *myrmex*, ant.

[3] I expressed our readiness to do his pleasure | This is an instance of Lucian's art in making impossibilities seem natural. The newcomers undertake the management of their vulture-steeds at a day's notice, as quite an ordinary affair.

SECTION 13

That day we were entertained by the king; in the morning we took our place in the ranks as soon as we were up, our scouts having announced the approach of the enemy. Our army numbered 100,000 (exclusive of camp-followers, engineers, infantry, and allies), the Horse-vultures amounting to 80,000, and the remaining 20,000 being mounted on Salad-wings [1]. These latter are also enormous birds, fledged with various herbs, and with quill-feathers resembling lettuce leaves. Next these were the Millet-throwers [2] and the Garlic-men [3]. Endymion had also a contingent from the North of 30,000 Flea-archers [4]

and 50,000 Wind-coursers [5]. The former have their name from the great fleas, each of the bulk of a dozen elephants, which they ride. The Wind-coursers are infantry, moving through the air without wings; they affect this by so girding their shirts, which reach to the ankle, that they hold the wind like a sail and propel their wearers' ship-fashion. These troops are usually employed as skirmishers [6]. 70,000 Ostrich-slingers [7] and 50,000 Horse-cranes [8] were said to be on their way from the stars over Cappadocia [9]. But as they failed to arrive I did not actually see them; and a description from hearsay I am not prepared to give, as the marvels related of them put some strain on belief.

[1] Salad-wings | Literally *Lachanopteri* from *lakhanos*, any kind of herb, and *pteros*, wing.

[2] Millet-throwers | Literally *Cinchroboli*; *millii jaculatores*, darters of millet (millet is a type of small grain).

[3] Garlic-men | Literally *Schorodomachi, alliis pugnantes*, garlic fighters. The supposition is that these fighters threw garlic at the enemy, which served as a sort of stinkbomb.

[4] Flea-archers | Literally *Pfllotoxotoe, pulici sagittarii,* Flea-archers.

[5] Wind-coursers | Literally *Anemodromi, venti cursores,* Wind-coursers.

[6] Skirmishers | Also known as peltasts, a sort of light-armed foot soldier, who principally harassed the enemy by their agility.

[7] Ostrich-slingers | Literally *Strathobalani, passeres glandium*, or Acorn-sparrows.

[8] Horse-cranes | Literally *Hippogerani, equi grues,* Horse-cranes.

[9] Cappadocia | Probably because Cappadocia was famous for its breed of horses. Lucian would have known it well as it bordered on his native district of Commagene.

SECTION 14

Such was Endymion's force. They were all armed alike; their helmets were made of beans, which grow there of great size and hardness; the breastplates were of overlapping lupine-husks sewn together, these husks being as tough as horn; as to shields and swords, they were of the Greek type.

SECTION 15

When the time came, the array was as follows: on the right were the Horse-vultures, and the King with the *elite* of his forces, including ourselves. The Salad-wings held the left, and in the center were the various allies. The infantry were in round numbers 60,000,000 [1]; they were enabled to fall in thus: there are in the Moon great numbers of gigantic spiders, considerably larger than an average Aegean island; these were instructed to stretch webs across from the Moon to Lucifer; as soon as the work was done, the King drew up his infantry on this artificial plain, entrusting the command to Nightbat, son of Fairweather, with two lieutenants.

[1] 60,000,000 | What follows is probably a parody on actual descriptions by authors, such as that of the Battle of Cunaxa in Xenophon's *Anabasis* or the battle in *Cyropaedia*, 7.1. In Herodotus, he lists Xerxes army to be 1,700,000 men strong (7.60).

SECTION 16

On the enemy's side, Phaethon occupied the left with his Horse-ants; they are great winged animals resembling our ants except in size; but the largest of them would measure a couple of acres. The fighting was done not only by their riders; they used their horns also; their numbers were stated at 50,000. On their right was about an equal force of Sky-gnats [1] — archers mounted on great gnats; and next them the Sky-pirouetters [2], light-armed infantry only, but of some military value; they slung monstrous radishes at long range, a wound from which was almost immediately fatal, turning to gangrene at once; they were supposed to anoint their missiles with mallow juice. Next came the Stalk-fungi [3], 10,000 heavy-armed troops for close quarters; the explanation of their name is that their shields are mushrooms, and their spears asparagus stalks. Their neighbors were the Dog-acorns [4], Phaethon's contingent from Sirius. These were 5,000 in number, dog-faced men fighting on winged acorns. It was reported that Phaethon too was disappointed of the slingers whom he had summoned from the Milky Way, and of the Cloud-centaurs [5]. These latter, however, arrived, most unfortunately for us [6], after the battle was decided; the slingers failed altogether, and are said to have felt the resentment of Phaethon, who wasted their territory with fire. Such was the force brought by the enemy.

[1] Sky-gnats | Literally *Acroconopes*, Air-flies.

[2] Sky-pirouetters | Literally *Acrocoraces*, Gr. *Akrokorakes*, air-crows.

[3] Stalk-fungi | Literally *Caulomycetes*, Gr. *Kaulamyketes*, *Caulo fungi*, stalk and mushroom men.

[4] Dog-acorns | Literally *Cynobalani*, Gr. *Kynobalanoi*, cani *glandacii*, acorn-dogs.

[5] Cloud-centaurs | Literally *Nephelocentauri*, Gr.

Nephelokentau, nubicentauri, cloud-centaurs.

[6] Most unfortunately for us | The reason for this misfortune is given a little further in the history.

SECTION 17

As soon as the standards were raised and the asses on both sides (their trumpeters) had brayed, the engagement commenced. The Sunite left at once broke without awaiting the onset of the Horse-vultures, and we pursued, slaying them. On the other hand, their right had the better of our left, the Sky-gnats pressing on right up to our infantry. When these joined in, however, they turned and fled, chiefly owing to the moral effect of our success on the other flank. The rout became decisive, great numbers were taken and slain, and blood flowed in great quantities on to the clouds, staining them as red as we see them at sunset; much of it also dropped earthwards, and suggested to me that it was possibly some ancient event of the same kind which persuaded Homer that Zeus had rained blood at the death of Sarpedon [1].

[1] Rained blood at the death of Sarpedon | *Iliad* 16.458: "Hera spoke. The father of gods and men agreed. But he shed blood rain down upon the ground, tribute to his dear son Patroclus was about to kill in fertile Troy, far from his native land. "[iv]

SECTION 18

Relinquishing the pursuit, we set up two trophies [1], one for the infantry engagement on the spiders' webs, and one on the clouds for the air-battle. It was while we were thus engaged that our scouts announced the approach of the Cloud-centaurs, whom Phaethon had expected in time for the battle. They were indeed close upon us, and a strange sight, being compounded

of winged horses and men; the human part, from the middle upwards, was as tall as the Colossus of Rhodes [2], and the equine the size of a large merchantman. Their number I cannot bring myself to write down, for fear of exciting incredulity. They were commanded by Sagittarius [3]. Finding their friends defeated, they sent a messenger after Phaethon to bring him back, and, themselves in perfect order, charged the disarrayed Moonites [4], who had left their ranks and were scattered in pursuit or pillage; they routed the whole of them, chased the King home, and killed the greater part of his birds; they tore up the trophies, and overran the woven plain; I myself was taken, with two of my comrades. Phaethon now arrived, and trophies were erected on the enemy's part. We were taken off to the Sun the same day, our hands tied behind with a piece of the cobweb.

[1] Two trophies | Originally the word trophy, derived from the Greek *tropaion*, referred to arms, standards, other property, or human captives and body parts (e.g. headhunting) captured in battle. These war trophies commemorated the military victories of a state, army or individual combatant.

[2] Colossus of Rhodes | The Colossus of Rhodes was more than 100 feet high. The huge bronze statue was said to have bestridden the harbor at Rhodes.

[3] Sagittarius | In Greek mythology, Sagittarius is identified as a centaur: half human, half horse. In some legends, the Centaur Chiron was the son of Philyra and Saturn, who was said to have changed himself into a horse to escape his jealous wife, Rhea. Chiron was eventually immortalized in the constellation of Centaurus or in some version, Sagittarius.

[4] Moonites | Or Selenites, the inhabitants of the moon.

SECTION 19

They decided not to lay siege to the city; but after their return they constructed a wall across the intervening space, cutting off the Sun's rays from the Moon. This wall was double, and built of clouds; the consequence was total eclipse of the Moon, which experienced a continuous night. This severity forced Endymion to negotiate. He entreated that the wall might be taken down, and his kingdom released from this life of darkness; he offered to pay tribute, conclude an alliance, abstain from hostilities in future, and give hostages for these engagements. The Sunites [1] held two assemblies on the question, in the first of which they refused all concessions; on the second day, however, they relented, and peace was concluded on the following terms. [2]

[1] Sunites | Or Heliots, or inhabitants of the sun.

[2] Refused all concessions ... relented and peace was concluded | Possibly an allusion to the reversal by the Athenians of their cruel decree against the Mitylenaeans after the revolt of that town. One faction, led by Cleon, advocated executing all of the men in the city and enslaving the women and children, while another faction (one spokesman was Diodotus) preferred more moderate treatment in which only men who had been identified as ringleaders would be executed. The Athenian assembly wavered; an order for mass execution was issued on the first day of debate but countermanded on the next. In the end, the city as a whole was spared.

SECTION 20

[1] Articles of peace between the Sunites and their allies of the one part, and the Moonites and their allies of the other part.

1. The Sunites shall demolish the party-wall, shall

make no further incursion into the Moon, and shall hold their captives to ransom at a fixed rate.

2. The Moonites shall restore to the other stars their autonomy, shall not bear arms against the Sunites, and shall conclude with them a mutual defensive alliance.

3. The King of the Moonites shall pay to the King of the Sunites, annually, a tribute of ten thousand jars of dew, and give ten thousand hostages of his subjects.

4. The high contracting parties shall found the colony of Lucifer in common, and shall permit persons of any other nationality to join the same.

5. These articles shall be engraved on a pillar of electrum [2], which shall be set up on the border in mid-air.

Sworn to on behalf of the Sun by [3] Firebrace, Heaton, and Flashman; and on behalf of the Moon by Nightwell, Monday, and Shimmer.

[1] Articles of peace... | A good caricature on the usual form and style of a treaty.

[2] Pillar of electrum | Electrum is a naturally occurring alloy of gold and silver, with trace amounts of copper and other metals. It has also been produced artificially, and is often known as green gold. The ancient Greeks called it 'gold' or 'white gold', as opposed to 'refined gold'. Its color ranges from pale to bright yellow, depending on the proportions of gold and silver.

[3] Firebrace... | Gr. *Pyronides*, *ignes*, fiery; Gr. *Phlogios*, flaming; Gr. *Nyktop*, nocturnal, nightly; Gr. *Menios*, *menstruus*, monthly; Gr. *Polylamtes*, *multilucius*, many lights. These all make good proper names in Greek, but do not translate well into English.

SECTION 21

Peace concluded; the removal of the wall and restoration of captives at once followed. As we reached the Moon, we were met and welcomed by our comrades and King Endymion, all weeping for joy. The King wished us to remain and take part in founding the colony [1], and, women not existing in the Moon, offered me his son in marriage. I refused, asking that we might be sent down to the sea again; and finding that he could not prevail, he entertained us for a week, and then sent us on our way.

[1] Colony | Colonies in antiquity were city-states founded from a mother-city (its "metropolis"), not from a territory-at-large. Bonds between a colony and its metropolis remained often close, and took specific forms. However, unlike in the period of European colonialism during the early and late modern era, ancient colonies were usually sovereign and self-governing from their inception.

SECTION 22

I am now to put on record the novelties and singularities which attracted my notice during our stay in the Moon. In the first place there is the fact that they are not born of women but of men: they marry men and do not even know the word woman at all! Up to the age of twenty-five each is a wife, and thereafter a husband. They carry their children in the calf of the leg [1] instead of the belly. When conception takes place the calf begins to swell. In course of time they cut it open and deliver the child dead, and then they bring it to life by putting it in the wind with its mouth open. It seems to me that the term "belly of the leg" [2] came to us Greeks from there, since the leg performs the function of a belly with them. But I will tell you something else, still

more wonderful. They have a kind of men whom they call the Arboreals, who are brought into the world as follows: Cutting a man's right genital gland, they plant it in the ground. From it grows a very large tree of one calf of the leg, flesh, resembling the emblem of Priapus: it has branches and leaves, and its fruit is acorns a cubit thick. When these ripen, they harvest them and shell out the men. Another thing, they have artificial parts that are sometimes of ivory and sometimes, with the poor, of wood, and make use of them in their intercourse [3].

[1] Calf of the Leg | cf. Zeus rescued the fetal Dionysus by sewing him into his thigh.

[2] "Belly of the leg" | Gr. *Gastronymia.*

[3] Intercourse | The insinuation of the use of sexual objects was omitted from some early modern editions of Lucian.

SECTION 23

When a man becomes old, he does not die, but dissolves in smoke into the air. There is one universal diet; they light a fire, and in the embers roast frogs, great numbers of which are always flying in the air; they then sit round as at table, snuffing up the fumes [1] which rise and serve them for food; their drink is air compressed in a cup till it gives off a moisture resembling dew. Beauty with them consists in a bald head and hairless body; a good crop of hair is an abomination. On the comets [2], as I was told by some of their inhabitants who were there on a visit, this is reversed. They have beards, however, just above the knee; no toe-nails, and but one toe on each foot. They are all tailed, the tail being a large cabbage of an evergreen kind, which does not break if they fall upon it.

[1] Snuffing up the fumes | Herodotus (4.74) says that the Scythians were accustomed to regale themselves by a particular mode of intoxication, caused by the inhalation of hemp-seed. "The Scythians then take the seed of this hemp and creep under the felt coverings, and then they throw the seed upon the stones which have been heated red-hot: and it burns like incense and produces a vapor so thick that no vapor-bath in Hellas would surpass it: and the Scythians being delighted with the vapor-bath howl like wolves."[v]

[2] Comets | Comet meant "long-haired" in Ancient Greek.

SECTION 24

Their mucus is a pungent honey; and after hard work or exercise they sweat milk all over, which a drop or two of the honey curdles into cheese [1]. The oil which they make from onions is very rich, and as fragrant as balsam. They have an abundance of water-producing vines, the stones of which resemble hailstones; and my own belief is that it is the shaking of these vines by hurricanes, and the consequent bursting of the grapes, that results in our hailstorms. They use the belly as a pouch in which to keep necessaries, being able to open and shut it. It contains no intestines or liver, only a soft hairy lining; their young, indeed, creep into it for protection from cold [2].

[1] Cheese | Only for exportation, seeing that the Selenites do not feed upon a coarse diet.

[2] Protection from cold | Lucian, when he originally thought of this idea, probably did not realize that nature had already beat him to the idea, and that there was a kangaroo that is provided with the convenient ability of carrying its young in the belly. Lucian was unaware of the continent of Australia.

SECTION 25

The clothing of the wealthy is soft glass, and of the poor, woven brass; the land is very rich in brass, which they work like wool after steeping it in water. It is with some hesitation that I describe their eyes, the thing being incredible enough to bring doubt upon my veracity. But the fact is that these organs are removable [1]; any one can take out his eyes and do without till he wants them; then he has merely to put them in; I have known many cases of people losing their own and borrowing at need; and some — the rich, naturally — keep a large stock. Their ears are plane-leaves, except with the breed raised from acorns; theirs being of wood.

[1] Organs are removable | Perhaps an allusion to Thucydides. He describes the gold with which the statue of Athena in the Parthenon was overlaid. Thucydides 2.13: "If they were reduced to the last extremity they could even take off the plates of gold with which the image of the goddess was overlaid; these, as he pointed out, weighed forty talents, and were of refined gold, which was all removable." [vi]

SECTION 26

Another marvel [1] I saw in the palace. There is a large mirror suspended over a well of no great depth; any one going down the well can hear every word spoken on our Earth; and if he looks at the mirror, he sees every city and nation as plainly as though he were standing close above each. The time I was there, I surveyed my own people and the whole of my native country; whether they saw me also, I cannot say for certain. [2] Anyone who doubts the truth of this statement has only to go there himself, to be assured of my veracity.

[1] Marvel | This interlude into "marvels" has parallels with Herodotus when he tangentially speaks on various topics.

[2] The time I was there, I surveyed my own people and the whole of my native country; whether they saw me also, I cannot say for certain | Possibly an allusion to the theory of Empedocles, which represented birth as a mingling of elements and death as a separation of the mingled. In essence, the vision of the mirror mingles together elements to make a lifescene and when it dissolves the lifescene disappears.

SECTION 27

When the time came, we took our leave of King and court, got on board, and weighed anchor. Endymion's parting gifts to me were two glass shirts, five of brass, and a suit of lupine armor, all of which, however, I afterwards left in the whale's belly [1]; he also sent, as our escort for the first fifty miles, a thousand of his Horse-vultures.

[1] Whale's belly | Will become an important part of the story in the coming sections.

SECTION 28

We passed on our way many countries, and actually landed on Lucifer, now in process of settlement, to water. We then entered the Zodiac and passed the Sun on the left, coasting close by it. My crew was very desirous of landing, but the wind would not allow of this. We had a good view of the country, however, and found it covered with vegetation, rich, well-watered, and full of all good things. The Cloud-centaurs, now in Phaethon's pay, espied us and pounced upon the ship, but left us alone when they learned that we were parties to the treaty.

SECTION 29

By this time our escort had gone home. We now took a downward course, and twenty-four hours' sailing brought us to Lampton [1]. This lies between the atmospheres of the Pleiades [2] and the Hyades [3], though in point of altitude it is considerably lower than the Zodiac [4]. When we landed, we found no human beings, but numberless lamps bustling about or spending their time in the market-place and harbor; some were small, and might represent the lower classes, while a few, the great and powerful, were exceedingly bright and conspicuous. They all had their own homes or lodgings, and their individual names, like us; we heard them speak, and they did us no harm, offering us entertainment, on the contrary; but we were under some apprehension, and none of us accepted either food or bed. There is a Government House in the middle of the city, where the Governor sits all night long calling the roll-call; any one not answering to his name is capitally punished as a deserter; that is to say, he is extinguished. We were present and witnessed the proceedings, and heard lamps defending their conduct and advancing reasons for their lateness. I there recognized our own house lamp, accosted him, and asked for news of my friends, in which he satisfied me. We stayed there that night, set sail next morning, and found ourselves sailing, now, nearly as low as the clouds. Here we were surprised to find Cloud-cuckoo-land [5]; we were prevented from landing by the direction of the wind, but learned that the King's name was Crookbeak, son of Fitz–Ousel. I bethought me of Aristophanes [6], the learned and veracious poet whose statements had met with unmerited incredulity. Three days more, and we had a distinct view of the Ocean, though there was no land visible except the islands suspended in air; and

these had now assumed a brilliant fiery hue. About noon on the fourth day the wind slackened and fell, and we were deposited upon the sea.

[1] Lampton | Gr. *Lyknopolis*, the city of the Lamps. Perhaps suggested by Herodotus (2.62) of the Feast of Lanterns at Sais in Egypt: "At the times when they gather together at the city of Saïs for their sacrifices, on a certain night they all kindle lamps many in number in the open air round about the houses; now the lamps are saucers full of salt and oil mixed, and the wick floats by itself on the surface, and this burns during the whole night; and to the festival is given the name *Lychnocaia* (the lighting of the lamps). Moreover those of the Egyptians who have not come to this solemn assembly observe the night of the festival and themselves also light lamps all of them, and thus not in Saïs alone are they lighted, but overall Egypt: and as to the reason why light and honor are allotted to this night."[vii]

[2] Pleiades | Open cluster of stars in the constellation Taurus.

[3] Hyades | A cluster of stars, the Hyades, set in the head of Taurus.

[4] Zodiac | The zodiac is a circle of twelve 30° divisions of celestial longitude that are centered upon the ecliptic: the apparent path of the Sun across the celestial sphere over the course of the year.

[5] Cloud-cuckoo-land | Gr. *Nephelokokkygia*, the cloud-cuckoo.

[6] Aristophanes | *Nephelokokkygia* is a fantastical place mentioned in Aristophanes' *Birds*.

SECTION 30

The joy and delight with which the touch of water

affected us is indescribable; transported at our good fortune, we flung ourselves overboard and swam, the weather being calm and the sea smooth. Alas, how often is a change for the better no more than the beginning of disaster! We had but two days' delightful sail, and by the rising sun of the third we beheld a crowd of whales and marine monsters, and among them one far larger than the rest — some two hundred miles in length [1]. It came on open-mouthed, agitating the sea far in front, bathed in foam, and exhibiting teeth whose length much surpassed the height of our great phallic images [2], all pointed like sharp stakes and white as elephants' tusks. We gave each other a last greeting, took a last embrace, and so awaited our doom. The monster was upon us; it sucked us in; it swallowed ship and crew entire. We escaped being ground by its teeth, the ship gliding in through the interstices.

[1] Two hundred miles in length | Equivalent to fifteen hundred stadia long.

[2] Phallic images | If the teeth of this monster were only in proportion to his whole bodily circumference, we can here admit no smaller phalli than the colossal ones of which mention is made in the *Syrian Goddess*, which by the most reasonable measure, were thirty fathom or 180 feet high, and yet can come into no comparison with the teeth of a Caschelottan, which were 930,000 feet in length.

SECTION 31

Inside, all was darkness at first, in which we could distinguish nothing; but when it next opened its mouth, an enormous cavern was revealed, of great extent and height; a city of ten thousand inhabitants might have had room in it. Strewn about were small fish, the *disjecta membra* of many kinds of animal,

ships' masts and anchors, human bones, and merchandise; in the center was land with hillocks upon it, the alluvial deposit, I supposed, from what the whale swallowed. This was wooded with trees of all kinds, and vegetables were growing with all the appearance of cultivation. The coast might have measured thirty miles round [1]. Sea-birds, such as gulls and halcyons [2], nested on the trees.

[1] Thirty miles round | Two hundred and forty stadia.

[2] Gulls and halcyons | Gulls and halcyons do not build nests in trees.

SECTION 32

We spent some time weeping, but at last got our men up and had the ship made fast, while we rubbed wood to get a fire and prepared a meal out of the plentiful materials around us; there were fragments of various fish, and the water we had taken in at Lucifer was unexhausted. Upon getting up next day, we caught glimpses, as often as the whale opened his mouth, of land, of mountains, it might be of the sky alone, or often of islands; we realized that he was dashing at a great rate to every part of the sea. We grew accustomed to our condition in time, and I then took seven of my comrades and entered the wood in search of information. I had scarcely gone half a mile when I came upon a shrine, which its inscription showed to have been raised to Poseidon; a little further were a number of graves with pillars upon them, and close by a spring of clear water; we also heard a dog bark, saw some distant smoke, and conjectured that there must be a habitation.

SECTION 33

We accordingly pressed on, and found ourselves in

presence of an old man and a younger one, who were working hard at a plot of ground and watering it by a channel from the spring. We stood still, divided between fear and delight. They were standing speechless, no doubt with much the same feelings. At length the old man spoke:—'What are you, strangers; are you spirits of the sea, or unfortunate mortals like ourselves? As for us, we are men, bred on land; but now we have suffered a sea change, and swim about in this containing monster, scarce knowing how to describe our state; reason tells us we are dead, but instinct that we live.' This loosed my tongue in turn. 'We too, father,' I said, 'are men, just arrived; it is but a day or two since we were swallowed with our ship. And now we have come forth to explore the forest; for we saw that it was vast and dense. Methinks some heavenly guide has brought us to the sight of you, to the knowledge that we are not prisoned all alone in this monster. I pray you, let us know your tale, who you are and how you entered.' Then he said that, before he asked or answered questions, he must give us such entertainment as he could; so saying, he brought us to his house — a sufficient dwelling furnished with beds and what else he might need —, and set before us green-stuff and nuts and fish, with wine for drink. When we had eaten our fill, he asked for our story. I told him all as it had passed, the storm, the island, the airy voyage, the war, and so to our descent into the whale.

SECTION 34

It was very strange, he said, and then gave us his history in return. 'I am a Cyprian, gentlemen. I left my native land on a trading voyage with my son here and a number of servants. We had a fine ship, with a mixed cargo for Italy; you may have seen the

wreckage in the whale's mouth. We had a fair voyage to Sicily, but on leaving it were caught in a gale, and carried in three days out to the Atlantic, where we fell in with the whale and were swallowed, ship and crew; of the latter we two alone survived. We buried our men, built a temple to Poseidon, and now live this life, cultivating our garden, and feeding on fish and nuts. It is a great wood, as you see, and in it are vines in plenty, from which we get delicious wine; our spring you may have noticed; its water is of the purest and coldest. We use leaves for bedding, keep a good fire, snare the birds that fly in, and catch living fish by going out on the monster's gills; it is there also that we take our bath when we are disposed. There is moreover at no great distance a salt lake two or three miles round, producing all sorts of fish; in this we swim and sail, in a little boat of my building. It is now seven and twenty years since we were swallowed.

SECTION 35

'Our lot might have been endurable enough, but we have bad and troublesome neighbors, unfriendly savages all.' 'What,' said I, 'are there other inhabitants?' 'A great many,' he replied, 'inhospitable and abhorrent to the sight. The western part of the wood (so to name the caudal region) is occupied by the Stockfish tribe [1]; they have eels' eyes and lobster faces, are bold warriors, and eat their meat raw. Of the sides of the cavern, the right belongs to the Tritonomendetes [2], who from the waist upwards are human, and weasels below; their notions of justice are slightly less rudimentary than the others'. The left is in possession of the Crabhands [3] and the Tunnyheads [4], two tribes in close alliance. The central part is inhabited by the Crays [5] and the Flounderfoots [6], the latter warlike and

extremely swift. As to this district near the mouth, the East, as it were, it is in great part desert, owing to the frequent inundations. I hold it of the Flounderfoots, paying an annual tribute of five hundred oysters. [7]

[1] Stockfish tribe | Gr. *Tarichanes*, salt-fish-men.

[2] *Tritonomendetes* | triton-weasels.

[3] Crabhands | Gr. *Karkinokhires*, cancri-mani, crab's hands.

[4] Tunnyheads | Gr. *Thynnokephali*, tunny-heads, i.e. men with heads like those of the tunnyfish.

[5] Crays | Gr. *Paguarde*, crabmen.

[6] Flounderfoots | Gr. *Psittopodes*, sparrow-footed from passer marinus.

[7] These descriptions are reminiscent of the meeting of Greek colonists with the native peoples.

SECTION 36

[1] 'Such is the land; and now it is for you to consider how we may make head against all these tribes, and what shall be our manner of life.' 'What may their numbers be, all told?' I asked. 'More than a thousand.' 'And how armed?' 'They have no arms but fishbones.' 'Why then,' I said, 'let us fight them by all means; we are armed, and they are not; and, if we win, we shall live secure.' We agreed on this course, and returned to the ship to make our preparations. The pretext for war was to be non-payment of the tribute, which was on the point of falling due. Messengers, in fact, shortly came to demand it, but the old man sent them about their business with an insolent answer. The Flounderfoots and Crays were enraged and commenced operations with a tumultuous inroad upon Scintharus — this

was our old man's name.

[1] Begins an interlude with no annotations.

SECTION 37

Expecting this, we were awaiting the attack in full armor. We had put five and twenty men in ambush, with directions to fall on the enemy's rear as soon as they had passed; they executed their orders, and came on from behind cutting them down, while the rest of us — five and twenty also, including Scintharus and his son — met them face to face with a spirited and resolute attack. It was risky work, but in the end we routed and chased them to their dens. They left one hundred and seventy dead, while we lost only our navigating officer, stabbed in the back with a mullet rib, and one other.

SECTION 38

We held the battlefield for the rest of that day and the night following, and erected a trophy consisting of a dolphin's backbone upright. Next day the news brought the other tribes out, with the Stockfish under a general called Slimer on the right, the Tunnyheads on the left, and the Crabhands in the center; the Tritonomendetes stayed at home, preferring neutrality. We did not wait to be attacked, but charged them near Poseidon's temple with loud shouts, which echoed as in a subterranean cave. Their want of armor gave us the victory; we pursued them to the wood, and were henceforth masters.

SECTION 39

Soon after, they sent heralds to treat for recovery of their dead, and for peace. But we decided to make no

terms with them, and marching out next day exterminated the whole, with the exception of the Tritonomendetes. These too, when they saw what was going on, made a rush for the gills, and cast themselves into the sea. We went over the country, now clear of enemies, and occupied it from that time in security. Our usual employments were exercise, hunting, vine-dressing, and fruit-gathering; we were in the position of men in a vast prison from which escape is out of the question, but within which they have luxury and freedom of movement. This manner of life lasted for a year and eight months.

SECTION 40

It was on the fifth of the next month, about the second gape (the whale, I should say, gaped regularly once an hour, and we reckoned time that way)—about the second gape, then, a sudden shouting and tumult became audible; it sounded like boatswains giving the time and oars beating. Much excited, we crept right out into our monster's mouth, stood inside the teeth, and beheld the most extraordinary spectacle I ever looked upon — giants of a hundred yards in height rowing great islands as we do triremes. I am aware that what I am to relate must sound improbable; but I cannot help it. Very long islands they were, but of no great height; the circumference of each would be about eleven miles; and its complement of giants was some hundred and twenty. Of these some sat along each side of the island, rowing with big cypresses, from which the branches and leaves were not stripped; in the stern, so to speak, was a considerable hillock, on which stood the helmsman with his hand on a brazen steering-oar of half a mile in length; and on the deck forward were forty in armor, the combatants; they resembled men except in their hair, which was

flaming fire, so that they could dispense with helmets. The work of sails was done by the abundant forest on all the islands, which so caught and held the wind that it drove them where the steersman wished; there was a boatswain timing the stroke, and the islands jumped to it like great galleys.

SECTION 41

[1] We had seen only two or three at first; but there appeared afterwards as many as six hundred, which formed in two lines and commenced an action. Many crashed into each other stem to stem, many were rammed and sunk, and others grappled, fought an obstinate duel, and could hardly get clear after it. Great courage was shown by the troops on deck, who boarded and dealt destruction, giving no quarter. Instead of grappling-irons, they used huge captive squids [2], which they swung out on to the hostile island; these grappled the wood and so held the island fast. Their missiles, effective enough, were oysters the size of wagons, and sponges which might cover an acre. Aeolocentaur and Thalassopot [3] were the names of the rival chiefs; and the question between them was one of plunder; Thalassopot was supposed to have driven off several herds of dolphins, the other's property; we could hear them vociferating the charge and calling out their Kings' names. Aeolocentaur's fleet finally won, sinking one hundred and fifty of the enemy's islands and capturing three with their crews; the remainder backed away, turned and fled. The victors pursued some way, but, as it was now evening, returned to the disabled ones, secured most of the enemy's, and recovered their own, of which as many as eighty had been sunk. As a trophy of victory they slung one of the enemy's islands to a stake which they planted in our whale's head. They lay moored round him that

night, attaching cables to him or anchoring hard by; they had vast glass anchors, very strong. Next morning they sacrificed on the whale's back, buried their dead there, and sailed off rejoicing, with something corresponding to our paean. So ended the battle of the islands. [4]

[1] Here Lucian gives a very fair mockery of descriptions of naval engagements such as that in Thucydides at Naupactus 2.83-92 or the sea-fight in the harbor of Sicily 7.70-71.

[2] Huge captive squids | Aelian, *Varia Historia*, Chapter 1, described the habits of the polypus (squid) and its mode of lying in wait for and catching its prey: "Of the Polypus. The Polypusses are so ravenous that they devour all they light on; so that many times they abstain not even from one another. The lesser taken by the greater, and falling into his stronger nets, (which are usually called the hairs or grasps of the Fish) becometh his prey. They also betray Fishes in this manner; lurking under the Rocks they change themselves to their color, and seem to be all one with the Rock itself. When therefore the Fishes swim to the Rocks, and so to the Polypus, they entangle them in their nets, or grasps."[viii] Pliny, *Natural History* 9.29, mentions an enormous one with feelers thirty feet long, which is doubtless and exaggeration of fact as it appears from the actual size of an octopus.[ix] See endnote for detail.

[3] Aeolocentaur and Thalassopot | It is supposed these creatures were Leviathan-like. *Thalassopotes* is Greek for "the drinker of the sea".

[4] So ended the battle of the islands | Lucian is mirroring the language used at the end of Sicilian Expedition in Thucydides. Lucian possibly intended for this last section to be a parody of Thucydides' work. Thucydides, in grand language, 7.87: "This was the greatest Hellenic achievement of any in this war, or, in

my opinion, in Hellenic history; at once most glorious to the victors, and most calamitous to the conquered. They were beaten at all points and altogether; all that they suffered was great; they were destroyed, as the saying is, with a total destruction, their fleet, their army, everything was destroyed, and few out of many returned home. Such were the events in Sicily."[x]

BOOK II

SECTION 1

I now began to find life in the whale unendurable; I was tired to death of it, and concentrated my thoughts on plans of escape. Our first idea was to excavate a passage through the beast's right side, and go out through it. We actually began boring, but gave it up when we had penetrated half a mile without getting through. We then determined to set fire to the forest, our object being the death of the whale, which would remove all difficulties. We started burning from the tail end; but for a whole week he made no sign; on the eighth and ninth days it was apparent that he was unwell; his jaws opened only languidly, and each time closed again very soon. On the tenth and eleventh days mortification had set in, evidenced by a horrible stench; on the twelfth, it occurred to us, just in time, that we must take the next occasion of the mouth's being open to insert props between the upper and lower molars, and so prevent his closing it; else we should be imprisoned and perish in the dead body. We successfully used great beams for the purpose, and then got the ship ready with all the water and provisions we could manage. Scintharus was to navigate her. Next day the whale was dead. [1]

[1] The whale episode is not particular to Lucian, but has hints of other traditions throughout the Mediterranean, most notably being the story of Jonah. In an interesting letter from Augustine of Hippo to Deogratias (Letter CII, Section 30), he is skeptical of the tale of the survival in a whale's belly showing credulity on all accounts: "The last question proposed is concerning Jonah, and it is put

as if it were not from Porphyry, but as being a standing subject of ridicule among the Pagans; for his words are: "In the next place, what are we to believe concerning Jonah, who is said to have been three days in a whale's belly? The thing is utterly improbable and incredible, that a man swallowed with his clothes on should have existed in the inside of a fish. If, however, the story is figurative, be pleased to explain it. Again, what is meant by the story that a gourd sprang up above the head of Jonah after he was vomited by the fish? What was the cause of this gourd's growth? Questions such as these I have seen discussed by Pagans amidst loud laughter, and with great scorn."[xi]

SECTION 2

We hauled the vessel up, brought her through one of the gaps, slung her to the teeth, and so let her gently down to the water. We then ascended the back, where we sacrificed to Poseidon by the side of the trophy, and, as there was no wind, encamped there for three days. On the fourth day we were able to start. We found and came into contact with many corpses, the relics of the sea-fight, and our wonder was heightened when we measured them. For some days we enjoyed a moderate breeze, after which a violent north wind rose, bringing hard frost; the whole sea was frozen [1] — not merely crusted over, but solidified to four hundred fathoms' depth; we got out and walked about. The continuance of the wind making life intolerable, we adopted the plan, suggested by Scintharus, of hewing an extensive cavern in the ice, in which we stayed a month, lighting fires and feeding on fish [2]; we had only to dig these out. In the end, however, provisions ran short, and we came out; the ship was frozen in, but we got her free; we then hoisted sail, and were

carried along as well as if we had been afloat, gliding smoothly and easily over the ice. After five days more the temperature rose, a thaw set in, and all was water again.

[1] The whole sea was frozen | Perhaps an allusion to Herodotus 4.28 concerning the sea freezing on Palus Moeotis so that wagons are driven over ice. Lucian presumably knew nothing of a real frozen sea and thought that lighting a fire on the ice an impossibility. Herodotus 4.28: "This whole land which has been described is so exceedingly severe in climate, that for eight months of the year there is frost so hard as to be intolerable; and during these if you pour out water you will not be able to make mud, but only if you kindle a fire can you make it; and the sea is frozen and the whole of the Kimmerian Bosphorus, so that the Scythians who are settled within the trench make expeditions and drive their wagons over into the country of the Sindians. Thus it continues to be winter for eight months, and even for the remaining four it is cold in those parts. This winter is distinguished in its character from all the winters which come in other parts of the world; for in it there is no rain to speak of at the usual season for rain, whereas in summer it rains continually; and thunder does not come at the time when it comes in other countries, but is very frequent, in the summer; and if thunder comes in winter, it is marveled at as a prodigy: just so, if an earthquake happens, whether in summer or in winter, it is accounted a prodigy in Scythia. Horses are able to endure this winter, but neither mules nor asses can endure it at all, whereas in other countries horses if they stand in frost lose their limbs by mortification, while asses and mules endure it."[xii]

[2] A scholiast was angry with the shear inbelievability of this fictional account as if there were other parts of the *True History* that were more believable. Lucian obviously wishes to carry the marvelous tale to its

extreme degree of absurdity. The scholiast missed the memo that the *True History* is composed of lies and hyperbole.

SECTION 3

A stretch of five and thirty miles brought us to a small desert isle, where we got water — of which we were now in want —, and shot two wild bulls before we departed. These animals had their horns not on the top of the head, but, as Momus [1] recommended, below the eyes. Not long after this, we entered a sea of milk, in which we observed an island, white in color, and full of vines. The island was one great cheese, quite firm, as we afterwards ascertained by eating it, and three miles round. The vines were covered with fruit, but the drink we squeezed from it was milk instead of wine. In the center of the island was a temple to Galatea the Nereid [2], as the inscription informed us. During our stay there, the ground itself served us for bread and meat, and the vine-milk for drink. We learned that the queen of these regions was Tyro [3], daughter of Salmoneus, on whom Poseidon had conferred this dignity at her decease. [4]

[1] Momus | The god of mockery, censorious criticism, and according to Hesiod a son of Night. This piece of ridicule about the bull's horns is referred by Lucian in his dialogue *Nigrinus* 32: "One observation of his in the same spirit fairly caps the famous censure of Momus. Momus found fault with the divine artificer for not putting his bull's horns in front of the eyes."[xiii]

[2] Galatea the Nereid | One of the fifty Nereids, or Sea-Nymphs; so-called on account of the fairness of their skin. Etymology from *gala*, milk. She was from a milky island; therefore, she was naturally the presiding deity.

[3] Tyro | According to Homer, Tyro fell in love with the

famous river Enipeus and was always wandering on his banks where Poseidon found her and he covered with her waves. Throwing her in a deep sleep; he supplied for her the place of Enipeus. Lucian has made her amends by naming one of his imaginary kingdoms for her. Lucian's part of the story though is fanciful.

[4] Galatea and Tyro | Galatea and Tyro recall the Greek words for "milk", *gala*, and "cheese", *tyros*.

SECTION 4

After spending five days there we started again with a gentle breeze and a rippling sea. A few days later, when we had emerged from the milk into blue salt water, we saw numbers of men walking on the sea; they were like ourselves in shape and stature, with the one exception of the feet, which were of cork; whence, no doubt, their name of Corksoles [1]. It struck us as curious that they did not sink in, but travelled quite comfortably clear of the water. Some of them came up and hailed us in Greek, saying that they were making their way to their native land of Cork. They ran alongside for some distance, and then turned off and went their own way, wishing us a pleasant voyage. A little further we saw several islands; close to us on the left was Cork, our friends' destination, consisting of a city founded on a vast round cork; at a greater distance, and a little to the right, were five others of considerable size and high out of the water, with great flames rising from them.

[1] Corksoles | Gr. *Phellopodes*, cork-footed.

SECTION 5

There was also a broad low one, as much as sixty miles in length, and straight in our course. As we drew near it, a marvelous air was wafted to us,

exquisitely fragrant, like the scent which Herodotus describes as coming from Arabia Felix [1]. Its sweetness seemed compounded of rose, narcissus, hyacinth, lilies and violets, myrtle and bay and flowering vine. Ravished with the perfume, and hoping for reward of our long toils, we drew slowly near. Then were unfolded to us haven after haven, spacious and sheltered, and crystal rivers flowing placidly to the sea. There were meadows and groves and sweet birds, some singing on the shore, some on the branches; the whole bathed in limpid balmy air. Sweet zephyrs just stirred the woods with their breath, and brought whispering melody, delicious, incessant, from the swaying branches; it was like Pan-pipes heard in a desert place [2]. And with it all there mingled a volume of human sound, a sound not of tumult, but rather of revels where some flute, and some praise the fluting, and some clap their hands commending flute or harp.

[1] Arabia Felix | Herodotus 3.113: "Let what we have said suffice with regard to spices; and from the land of Arabia there blows a scent of them most marvelously sweet."[xiv]

[2] Pan-pipes | It appears to have been a common practice with the shepherds who had won some prize on the seven-holed flute, to hang it up in honor of Pan in some solitary open place in the border of their pastures, in such manner that the wind (somewhat as with the Aeolian harp) produced from it a melodious murmuring strain.

SECTION 6

Drawn by the spell of it we came to land, moored the ship, and left her, in charge of Scintharus and two others. Taking our way through flowery meadows we came upon the guardians of the peace, who bound us

with rose-garlands — their strongest fetters — and brought us to the governor. As we went they told us this was the island called of the Blest [1], and its governor the Cretan Rhadamanthus [2]. When we reached the court, we found there were three cases to be taken before our turn would come.

[1] Island called of the Blest | This description of Elysium, or the Island of the Blest, is well drawn, and abounds in fanciful and picturesque imagery, interspersed with strokes of humor and satire. Pindar's "Second Olympic Ode", 2.73-83, appears to be alluded to in the text by Lucian: "Those who have persevered three times, on either side, to keep their souls free from all wrongdoing, follow Zeus' road to the end, to the tower of Cronus, where ocean breezes blow around the island of the blessed, and flowers of gold are blazing, some from splendid trees on land, while water nurtures others. With these wreaths and garlands of flowers they entwine their hands according to the righteous counsels of Rhadamanthys, whom the great father, the husband of Rhea whose throne is above all others, keeps close beside him as his partner. Peleus and Cadmus are counted among them, and Achilles who was brought there by his mother, when she had persuaded the heart of Zeus with her prayers — Achilles, who laid low Hector, the irresistible, unswerving pillar of Troy, and who consigned to death Memnon the Ethiopian, son of the Dawn."[xv]

[2] Cretan Rhadamanthus | In Greek mythology, Rhadamanthus was a wise king, the son of Zeus and Europa. Later accounts even make him out to be one of the judges of the dead. His brothers were Sarpedon and Minos (also a king and later a judge of the dead).

SECTION 7

The first was that of Ajax [1], son of Telamon, and

the question was whether he was to be admitted to the company of Heroes [2]; it was objected that he had been mad and taken his own life. After long pleadings Rhadamanthus gave his decision: he was to be put under the charge of Hippocrates the physician of Cos [3] for the hellebore treatment [4], and, when he had recovered his wits, to be made free of the table.

[1] Ajax | Lucian degrades him from the character of a hero, and gives him hellebore as a madman. Upon being defeated by Odysseus in a contest for the arms of Achilles, Ajax was seized by madness and began to slaughter the sheep of the Greek army under the impression that they were his enemies.

[2] Company of Heroes | The inhabitants of Elysium, or the Island of the Blessed, consist of two classes, the heroes and the demigods, and the wise and good men, who lived subsequent to the heroic age.

[3] Hippocrates the physician of Cos | Hippocrates was an ancient Greek physician of the Age of Pericles (Classical Greece), and is considered one of the most outstanding figures in the history of medicine. He is referred to as the father of western medicine in recognition of his lasting contributions to the field as the founder of the Hippocratic School of Medicine. This intellectual school revolutionized medicine in ancient Greece, establishing it as a discipline distinct from other fields that it had traditionally been associated with (notably theurgy and philosophy), thus establishing medicine as a profession.

[4] Hellebore treatment | Hellebore was used by the ancients as a treatment for paralysis, gout, and other diseases, but most particularly for insanity.

SECTION 8

The second was a matrimonial case, the parties Theseus and Menelaus, and the issue possession of Helen. Rhadamanthus gave it in favor of Menelaus, on the ground of the great toils and dangers the match had cost him — added to the fact that Theseus was provided with other wives in the Amazon queen and the daughters of Minos. [1]

[1] Helen | In her youth, Helen of Troy was carried off to Athens by Theseus and his friend Pirithous, but was rescued by her brothers Castor and Pollux, and afterwards chose Menelaus out of numerous noble suitors to be her husband. The story of her subsequent abduction from Menelaus by Paris, son of Priam, and the Trojan War, is well known.

SECTION 9

The third was a dispute for precedence between Alexander son of Philip and Hannibal the Carthaginian; it was won by the former [1], who had a seat assigned him next to Cyrus the elder.

[1] Lucian wrote a dialogue in the *Dialogues of the Dead* on this topic. In the dialogue, Alexander comes first, then Scipio, and finally Hannibal. See endnote for the full dialogue. [xvi]

SECTION 10

It was now our turn. The judge asked by what right we set foot on this holy ground while yet alive. In answer we related our story. He then had us removed while he held a long consultation with his numerous assessors, among whom was the Athenian Aristides the Just [1]. He finally reached a conclusion and gave judgment: on the charges of curiosity and travelling we were remanded till the date of our deaths; for the present we were to stay in the island, with admission

to the Heroic society, for a fixed term, after which we must depart. The limit he appointed for our stay was seven months.

[1] Aristides the Just | Aristides was an ancient Athenian statesman. Nicknamed "the Just", he flourished in the early quarter of Athens' Classical period and is remembered for his generalship in the Persian War.

SECTION 11

Our rose-chains now fell off of their own accord [1], we were released and taken into the city, and to the Table of the Blest. The whole of this city is built of gold [2], and the enclosing wall of emerald. It has seven gates, each made of a single cinnamon plank. The foundations of the houses, and all ground inside the wall, are ivory; temples are built of beryl, and each contains an altar of one amethyst block, on which they offer hecatombs. Round the city flows a river of the finest perfume [3], a hundred royal cubits in breadth, and fifty deep, so that there is good swimming. The baths, supplied with warm dew instead of ordinary water, are in great crystal domes heated with cinnamon wood.

[1] Rose-chains now fell off of their own accord | A close imitation, perhaps a parody, of Xenophon's dream in *Anabasis* 4.3.8: "But Xenophon had a dream. In his sleep he thought that he was bound in fetters, but these, of their own accord, fell from off him, so that he was loosed, and could stretch his legs as freely as he wished."[xvii]

[2] Of gold | It is not improbable that Voltaire's El Dorado, in his *Candide*, might have been suggested to him by this passage.

[3] Perfume | Lucian is very particular about the type of perfume that is flowing in the river, for it is not an

ointment, salve, or any other such material. An "essence" would be the most proper way to describe the term. One translator says it is an "oil of roses".

SECTION 12

Their raiment is fine cobweb, purple in color. They have no bodies, but are intangible and unsubstantial — mere form without matter; but, though incorporeal, they stand and move, think and speak; in short, each is a naked soul, but carries about the semblance of body [1]; one who did not touch them would never know that what he looked at was not substantial; they are shadows, but upright [2], and colored. [3] A man there does not grow old, but stays at whatever age he brought with him. There is no night, nor yet bright day; the morning twilight, just before sunrise, gives the best idea of the light that prevails. They have also but one season, perpetual spring, and the wind is always in the west.

[1] Semblance of body | In order to make sense of this sentence, it is presumed that someone who only needs to throw off a single garment (semblance) presents himself in "natural purity", or, according to the common phraseology of the Greeks, naked. This must be supposed in order to make sense of the sentence.

[2] Shadows but upright | i.e. their appearance is exactly like those of shadows made by the sun at noon day, with this only difference, that one lies flat on the ground, the other is erect, and the one is dark, the other light, even diaphanous. Our common notion of ghosts, especially in regard to their not being tangible, corresponds with that of Lucian's.

[3] And colored … | Lucian has been supposed to be ridiculing Plato's theories concerning the nature of the soul as set forth in the *Phaedo* and elsewhere. But Plato distinguishes between good and bad souls; only the latter

retain the form of the body and are contaminated by it, while the former become pure and immaterial. The satire is directed rather at the popular notion of the spirits of the dead as shadowy human forms, according to the descriptions in Homer and Virgil.

SECTION 13

The country abounds in every kind of flower, in shrubs and garden herbs. There are twelve vintages in the year, the grapes ripening every month; and they told us that pomegranates, apples, and other fruits were gathered thirteen times, the trees producing twice in their month Minous [1]. Instead of grain, the corn develops loaves, shaped like mushrooms, at the top of the stalks. Round the city are 365 springs of water, the same of honey, and 500, less in volume however, of perfume. There are also seven rivers of milk and eight of wine.

[1] Minous | Minous, formed by the analogy of Asiatic names of months (with which Lucian must have been familiar), e.g. Hermaeus, Metrous, etc. in Bithynia, Aphrodisius, Caesarius, etc. in Cyprus. The Athenian months were not, except Poseideon, named after the gods or heroes, but marked the seasons for various occupations, as Gamelion, Elaphebolion, etc. The whole description reads like an exaggeration of Homer's account of the gardens of Alcinous, *Odyssey* 7.114, where fruits of all kinds grew in never-failing succession, ripened by a perpetual west-wind at all seasons of the year. *Odyssey* 7.114: "Of these the fruit perishes not nor fails in winter or in summer, but lasts throughout the year; and ever does the west wind, as it blows, quicken to life some fruits, and ripen others."[xviii]

SECTION 14

[1] The banqueting-place is arranged outside the city in the Elysian Plain. It is a fair lawn closed in with thick-grown trees of every kind, in the shadow of which the guests recline, on cushions of flowers. The waiting and handing is done by the winds, except only the filling of the wine-cup. That is a service not required; for all round stand great trees of pellucid crystal, whose fruit is drinking-cups of every shape and size. A guest arriving plucks a cup or two and sets them at his place, where they at once fill with wine. So for their drink; and instead of garlands, the nightingales and other singing birds pick flowers with their beaks from the meadows round, and fly over snowing the petals down and singing the while. Nor is perfume forgotten; thick clouds draw it up from the springs and river, and hanging overhead are gently squeezed by the winds till they spray it down in fine dew.

[1] The banqueting-place ... | A symposia often was attended by sensuous pleasures like perfumes and garlands.

SECTION 15

During the meal there is music and song [1]. In the latter kind, Homer's verse is the favorite; he is himself a member of the festal company, reclining next above Odysseus [2]. The choirs are of boys and girls, conducted and led by Eunomus the Locrian [3], Arion of Lesbos [4], Anacreon [5] and Stesichorus [6]; this last had made his peace with Helen, and I saw him there. When these have finished, a second choir succeeds, of swans [7] and swallows and nightingales; and when their turn is done, all the trees begin to pipe, conducted by the winds.

[1] Epic poetry was performed by a bard, like Demodocus in the *Odyssey*, accompanied by the lyre and

song. It appears that Lucian had a real respect for Homer, notwithstanding what he said about him in his preface. *Odyssey* 8.42-45: "And summon hither the divine minstrel, Demodocus; for to him above all others has the god granted skill in song, to give delight in whatever way his spirit prompts."[xix]

[2] Odysseus | A legendary Greek king of Ithaca and a hero of Homer's epic poem the *Odyssey*. Odysseus also plays a key role in Homer's *Iliad* and other works in that same Epic Cycle. Husband of Penelope, father of Telemachus, and son of Laërtes and Anticlea, Odysseus is renowned for his brilliance, guile, and versatility (*polytropos*), and is hence known by the epithet Odysseus the Cunning (*mētis*, or "cunning intelligence"). He is most famous for the ten eventful years he took to return home after the decade-long Trojan War and his famous Trojan Horse ploy to capture the city of Troy.

[3] Eunomus the Locrian | A famous musician. Clement of Alexandria gives us a full account of him. In a musical contest in summer time Eunomus broke a string of his lyre; whereupon a grasshopper that had been chirping near sprang upon the neck of the instrument and sang as upon a branch. The minstrel, adapting his strain to the grasshopper's song, made up for the want of the missing string. According to Strabo, a statue of Eunomus with the grasshopper and the lyre was erected at Locri.

[4] Arion of Lesbos | Arion, the celebrated lyric poet, harpist, and composer of the dithyramb. Dithyrambs were choral songs in honor of the god Dionysius.

[5] Anacreon | Anacreon, writer of lyric love poetry, died circa 530 BC. Later Greeks included him in the canonical list of nine lyric poets.

[6] Stesichorus | This poet, we are told, wrote some severe verses on Helen, for which he was punished by Castor and Pollux with a loss of sight. But on making his recantation in a palinodia, his eyes were graciously

restored to him. Lucian has disrespected Helen still more grossly, by making her run away with Cinyrus; but he, being not over superstition, defied the power of Castor and Pollux.

[7] Swans | Swans were a popular topic for encomium in antiquity.

SECTION 16

I have still to add the most important element in their good cheer: there are two springs hard by, called the Fountain of Laughter, and the Fountain of Delight [1]. They all take a draught of both these before the banquet begins, after which the time goes merrily and sweetly.

[1] Fountain of Laughter, and the Fountain of Delight | An allusion to writings of Theopompus of Chios via Aelian: "He added what is yet more wonderful, that there are men living amongst them called Meropes, who inhabit many great Cities; and that at the farthest end of their Country there is a place named Anostus, (from whence there is no return) which resembles a Gulf; it is neither very light nor very dark, the air being dusky intermingled with a kind of Red: That there are two Rivers in this place, one of Pleasure, the other of Grief; and that along each River grow Trees of the bigness of a Plane-tree. Those which grow up by the River of Grief bear fruit of this nature; if any one eats of them, he shall spend all the rest of his life in tears and grief, and so die. The other Trees which grow by the River of Pleasure produce fruit of a contrary nature, for who tastes thereof shall be eased from all his former desires: If he loved anything, he shall quite forget it; and in a short time shall become younger, and live over again his former years: he shall cast off old age, and return to the prime of his strength, becoming first a young man, then a child, lastly, an infant, and so die."[xx]

SECTION 17

I should now like to name the famous persons I saw. To begin with, all the demi-gods, and the besiegers of Troy, with the exception of Ajax the Locrian [1]; he, they said, was undergoing punishment in the place of the wicked. Of barbarians there were the two Cyruses [2], Anacharsis the Scythian [3], Zamolxis the Thracian [4], and the Latin Numa [5]; and then Lycurgus the Spartan [6], Phocion [7] and Tellus of Athens [8], and the Wise Men [9], but without Periander [10]. And I saw Socrates son of Sophroniscus [11] in converse with Nestor [12] and Palamedes [13]; clustered round him were Hyacinth the Spartan [14], Narcissus of Thespiae [15], Hylas [16], and many another comely boy [17]. With Hyacinth I suspected that he was in love; at least he was forever poking questions at him. I heard that Rhadamanthus was dissatisfied with Socrates, and had several times threatened him with expulsion, if he insisted on talking nonsense, and would not drop his irony and enjoy himself. Plato [18] was the only one I missed, but I was told that he was living in his own Utopia, working the constitution and laws which he had drawn up.

[1] Ajax the Locrian | Ravished Cassandra, the daughter of Priam, and priestess of Athena, who sent a tempest, dispersed the Hellenic army in their return home and sunk Ajax with a thunderbolt. Ajax, son of Oileus (to be distinguished from Ajax, son of Telemon), was shipwrecked on his return from Troy, but reached a rock in safety. As, however, he boasted that he would escape in defiance of the gods, Poseidon split the rock with his trident and drowned him.

[2] Two Cyruses | i.e. Cyrus the Elder, founder of the Persian Empire, and Cyrus the Younger, who was killed in 401 BC at the Battle of Cunaxa, when conspiring

against his brother Artaxerxes with the aid of the Greek Ten Thousand.

[3] Anacharsis the Scythian | A high born Scythian who travelled in search of knowledge and received instruction from Solon. His countrymen (some say his brother) killed him on his return for introducing new ceremonies and customs. Herodotus 4.76: "So when he came to Scythia he went down into the region called Hylaia (this is along by the side of the racecourse of Achilles and is quite full, as it happens, of trees of all kinds), — into this, I say, Anacharsis went down, and proceeded to perform all the ceremonies of the festival in honor of the goddess, with a kettle-drum and with images hung about himself. And one of the Scythians perceived him doing this and declared it to Saulios the king; and the king came himself also, and when he saw Anacharsis doing this, he shot him with an arrow and killed him. Accordingly at the present time if one asks about Anacharsis, the Scythians say that they do not know him, and for this reason, because he went out of his own country to Hellas and adopted foreign customs."[xxi]

[4] Zamolxis the Thracian | A scholar of Pythagoras who taught his master's philosophy to the Thracians who thereafter worshipped Zalmolxis as the Good Spirit to whom they expected to meet after death.

[5] Numa | Second king of Rome, and reputed author of much of Rome's primitive law and religion. Often paired with Lycurgus as is the case in Plutarch's *Parallel Lives*.

[6] Lycurgus the Spartan | Lycurgus was the legendary lawgiver of Sparta, who established the military-oriented reformation of Spartan society in accordance with the Oracle of Apollo at Delphi. All his reforms were directed towards the three Spartan virtues: equality (among citizens), military fitness, and austerity.

[7] Phocion | The leader of the peace party at Athens, and the chief opponent of Demosthenes on the war with

Philip. He was distinguished for the uprightness of his policies and became in high favor with Alexander. The Athenians accused him of treason, and put him to death, 317 BC.

[8] Tellus of Athens | Lived and died on behalf of his country. In the celebrated discourse with Croesus, Solon assigned him second place, according to Lucian, in respect to human happiness. Herodotus, 1.30, places him first. He died fighting bravely in a border war with the Eleusinians, and was honored with a public funeral. Herodotus 1.30: "'Now therefore a desire has come upon me to ask you whether you have seen any whom you deem to be of all men the most happy.' This Croesus asked supposing that he himself was the happiest of men; but Solon, using no flattery but the truth only, said: 'Yes, O king, Tellos the Athenian.' And Croesus, marveling at that which he said, asked him earnestly: 'In what respect do you judge Tellos to be the most happy?' And he said: 'Tellos, in the first place, living while his native State was prosperous, had sons fair and good and saw from all of them children begotten and living to grow up; and secondly he had what with us is accounted wealth, and after his life a most glorious end: for when a battle was fought by the Athenians at Eleusis against the neighboring people, he brought up supports and routed the foe and there died by a most fair death; and the Athenians buried him publicly where he fell, and honored him greatly.'"[xxii]

[9] Wisemen | The Seven Sages of Greece were Thales, Bias, Pittacus, Solon, Cleobulus, Chilon, Periander. The last named was tyrant of Corinth and forfeited his place in Elysium by the oppressive government of his later years.

[10] Periander | Considered one of the seven sages, Lucian excludes him because he was the king of Corinth and a tyrant. Controversial figure.

[11] Socrates son of Sophroniscus | Plato, *Apology* 40e-41b: "For if a man when he reaches the other world, after leaving behind these who claim to be judges, shall find those who are really judges who are said to sit in judgment there, Minos and Rhadamanthus, and Aeacus and Triptolemus, and all the other demigods who were just men in their lives, would the change of habitation be undesirable? Or again, what would any of you give to meet with Orpheus and Musaeus and Hesiod and Homer? I am willing to die many times over, if these things are true; for I personally should find the life there wonderful, when I met Palamedes or Ajax, the son of Telamon, or any other men of old who lost their lives through an unjust judgment, and compared my experience with theirs. I think that would not be unpleasant. And the greatest pleasure would be to pass my time in examining and investigating the people there, as I do those here, to find out who among them is wise and who thinks he is when he is not."[xxiii]

[12] Nestor | The son of Neleus and Chloris and the King of Pylos. One of the generals during the Trojan War. He became king after Heracles killed Neleus and all of Nestor's siblings. His wife was either Eurydice or Anaxibia; their children included Peisistratus, Thrasymedes, Pisidice, Polycaste, Stratichus, Aretus, Echephron, and Antilochus.

[13] Palamedes | One of the Greek heroes who fought against Troy, but was falsely accused of treachery and stoned to death.

[14] Hyacinth the Spartan | A beautiful youth of mythology who was killed accidentally by Apollo with a quoit.

[15] Narcissus of Thespiae | Hunter from the territory of Thespiae in Boeotia who was renowned for his beauty. He was the son of a river god named Cephissus and a nymph named Liriope. He was exceptionally proud, in

that he disdained those who loved him. Nemesis saw this and attracted Narcissus to a pool where he saw his own reflection in the water and fell in love with it, not realizing it was merely an image. Unable to leave the beauty of his reflection, Narcissus died.

[16] Hylas | Hylas was a youth who served as a companion of Heracles. His abduction by water nymphs was a theme of ancient art, and has been an enduring subject for Western art in the classical tradition.

[17] Comely boy | A malevolent sneer at Socrates, who had other pleasures in the company of beautiful young men besides that of instructing them. This is most probably a defamation of the character of that philosopher.

[18] Plato | His leaving and quitting Elysium to go live in his own republic is a stroke of true humor.

SECTION 18

For popularity, Aristippus and Epicurus [1] bore the palm, in virtue of their kindliness, sociability, and good-fellowship. Aesop the Phrygian [2] was there, and held the office of jester. Diogenes of Sinope [3] was much changed; he had married Lais the courtesan [4], and often in his cups would oblige the company with a dance, or other mad pranks. The Stoics were not represented at all; they were supposed to be still climbing the steep hill of Virtue [5]; and as to Chrysippus [6] himself, we were told that he was not to set foot on the island till he had taken a fourth course of hellebore. The Academics contemplated coming, but were taking time for consideration; they could not yet regard it as a certainty that any such island existed. There was probably the added difficulty that they were not comfortable about the judgment of Rhadamanthus, having themselves disputed the possibility of

judgment [7]. It was stated that many of them had started to follow persons travelling to the island, but, their energy failing, had abandoned the journey half-way and gone back.

[1] Aristippus and Epicurus | Aristippus and Epicurus were founders of two sensual schools of philosophy, the Epicurean and the Cyrenaic. Both deemed pleasure to be the end of living.

[2] Aesop the Phrygian | Aesop, the writer of fables, in distinction to Aesop the Roman actor. The slave Aesop is the author of fables in prose, which are no longer extant, with the so-called Aesopic prose fables being spurious. Many of Aesop's original fables were versified in Greek by Babrius and in Latin by Phaedrus.

[3] Diogenes of Sinope | Cynic philosopher whose habitation was a tub. In life, Diogenes went without marriage and family in the quest for self-sufficiency, or *autarkeia.*

[4] Lais the Courtesan | The celebrated courtesan of Corinth who had real life relations with Aristippus for whom Lucian substitutes Diogenes, the founder of the Cynic School which held opposing beliefs to Aristippus.

[5] Steep hill of Virtue | A reference to Hesiod *Works and Days* 286-292: "To you, foolish Perses, I will speak good sense. Badness can be got easily and in shoals; the road to her is smooth, and she lives very near us. But between us and Goodness [Virtue] the gods have placed the sweat of our brows; long and steep is the path that leads to her, and it is rough at the first; but when a man has reached the top, then is she easy to reach, though before that she was hard."[xxiv]

[6] Chrysippus | The greatest of the Stoics asserted that no man could be a philosopher who had not drunk thrice of hellebore, the antidote to madness.

[7] Disputed possibility of judgment | A central tenet of

Ancient Skepticism and the Middle Academy. These philosophers disbelieved in the judgment of the senses, and so, holding that was no criterion or standard of truth, kept their judgment in suspense, and could never reach a definite conclusion. It is obvious that this would be injurious to Rhadamanthus' profession and render his office entirely useless. He, therefore, could not be entirely indifferent to it.

SECTION 19

I have mentioned the most noteworthy of the company, and add that the most highly respected among them are, first Achilles, and second Theseus. With regard to love affairs, they think there is nothing indecent in doing what they please before everybody [1]. As to the boys, Socrates swore he meant no harm; and yet, if we credit Narcissus and Hyacinthus, he foreswore himself. The women are all common to all; their love is only Platonic. Boys are supply themselves to anyone at any time without contention.

[1] Before everybody | i.e. copulate openly. The Greeks held this practice to be associated with the norms of barbarians. Herodotus 3.101: "The sexual intercourse of all these Indians of whom I have spoken is open like that of cattle, and they have all one color of skin, resembling that of the Ethiopians".[xxv] Xenophon *Anabasis* 5.4.33-4: "Mossynoecians sought after the women in the Hellenic army, and would gladly have laid with them openly in broad daylight, for that was their custom. ".[xxvi]

SECTION 20

Before many days had passed, I accosted the poet Homer, when we were both disengaged, and asked him, among other things, where he came from; it was

still a burning question with us, I explained. He said he was aware that some brought him from Chios, others from Smyrna, and others again from Colophon; the fact was, he was a Babylonian [1], generally known not as Homer, but as Tigranes; but when later in life he was given as a *homer* or hostage to the Greeks, that name clung to him. Another of my questions was about the so-called spurious lines; had he written them, or not? He said they were all genuine; so I now knew what to think of the critics Zenodotus and Aristarchus [2], and all their laborious study. Having got a categorical answer on that point, I tried him next on his reason for starting the Iliad at the wrath of Achilles; he said he had no exquisite reason; it had just come into his head that way [3]. Another thing I wanted to know was whether he had composed the *Odyssey* before the *Iliad*, as generally believed. He said this was not so. As to his reported blindness [4], I did not need to ask; he had his sight, so there was an end of that. It became a habit of mine, whenever I saw him at leisure, to go up and ask him things, and he answered quite readily — especially after his acquittal; a libel suit had been brought against him by Thersites [5], on the ground of the ridicule to which he is subjected in the poem; Homer had briefed Odysseus [6], and been acquitted.

[1] Zenodorus and Aristarchus | Alexandrine editors of Homer, and in making recensions of the text rejected and omitted several passages as spurious. Lucian accuses them of bad taste in so doing.

[2] Babylonian | It is obvious that Lucian merely designs to banter the “micrologists”, who induce controversy, concerning the unknown birthplace of Homer, the subject of entire treatises. A certain Alexander of Paphos has even made him an Egyptian; Lucian pushes Homer still more distant from Greece and places as far off as

Babylon.

[3] That way | The *Iliad* begins with the lines, "Sing, goddess, of the wrath of Achilles", with the first Greek word being "Wrath", *Mênin*. Lucian laughs at a certain pedantic school of criticism that pretended to discover mysterious and hidden meanings in every word. The so-called "micrologists".

[4] The idea that Homer was blind derives from the *Homeric Hymn to Apollo* in which the bard says: "Remember me in after time whenever anyone of men on earth, a stranger who has seen and suffered much, comes here and asks of you: "Whom think ye, girls, is the sweetest singer that comes here, and in whom do you most delight?" Then answer, each and all, with one voice: "He is a blind man, and dwells in rocky Chios: his lays are evermore supreme.""""[xxvii]

[5] Thersites | This passage is from the *Iliad* episode where Thersites abuses Agamemnon, the king, but then is stopped by Odysseus with a golden scepter.

[6] Odysseus | In the *Iliad*, Odysseus is represented as wily and glib of tongue.

SECTION 21

It was during our sojourn that Pythagoras [1] arrived; he had undergone seven transmigrations, lived the lives of that number of animals, and completed his psychic travels. It was the entire right half of him that was gold. He was at once given the franchise, but the question was still pending whether he was to be known as Pythagoras or Euphorbus. Empedocles [2] also came, scorched all over and baked right through; but not all his entreaties could gain him admittance.

[1] Pythagoras | Believed in the theory of transmigration and asserted that his own soul had inhabited the bodies

of five men, of whom Euphorbus the Trojan was one. He was said to have had a golden thigh.

[2] Empedocles | A philosopher of Agrigentum (about 440 BC) who was probably refused admittance on account of his skeptical opinions, met with his death by falling into the crater of Etna. Favorite of Lucian's satire; *Dialogues of the Dead* 6:

"*Aeacus*. That is Empedocles. He was half-roasted when he got here from Etna.

Menippus. Tell me, my brazen-slippered friend, what induced you to jump into the crater?

Empedocles. I did it in a fit of melancholy."[xxviii]

Icaromenippus 13: "At this moment of depression — I was very near tears — who should come up behind me but Empedocles the physicist? His complexion was like charcoal variegated with ashes, as if he had been baked. I will not deny that I felt some tremors at the sight of him, taking him for some lunar spirit. But he said: 'Do not be afraid, Menippus; A mortal I, no God; how vain thy dreams. I am Empedocles the physicist. When I threw myself into the crater in such a hurry, the smoke of Etna whirled me off up here; and now I live in the Moon, doing a good deal of high thinking on a diet of dew. So I have come to help you out of your difficulty; you are distressed, I take it, at not being able to see everything on the Earth.' 'Thank you so much, you good Empedocles,' I said; 'as soon as my wings have brought me back to Greece, I will remember to pour libations to you up the chimney, and salute you on the first of every month with three moonward yawns.'"[xxix]

SECTION 22

The progress of time brought round the Games of the Dead [1]. The umpires were Achilles, holding that office for the fifth, and Theseus for the seventh time.

A full report would take too long; but I will summarize the events. The wrestling went to Carus the Heraclid [2], who won the garland from Odysseus. The boxing resulted in a tie; the pair being the Egyptian Areus [3], whose grave is in Corinth, and Epeus [4]. For mixed boxing and wrestling they have no prize. Who won the flat race, I have forgotten. In poetry, Homer really did much the best, but the award was for Hesiod [5]. All prizes were plaited wreaths of peacock feathers.

[1] Games of the Dead | Gr. *Thanatusia,* in imitation to games played at weddings or funerals. Modeled on the Olympic contests and the Funeral Games for Patroclus and athletic contents among the Phaeacians.

[2] Carus the Heraclid | Otherwise unknown; probably invented by Lucian.

[3] Areus | An Alexandrine philosopher, who with his two sons, Dionysius and Nicantor, instructed Augustus in philosophy. He was also a writer on rhetoric.

[4] Epeus | Winner of the boxing-match at the funeral games of Patroclus in the *Iliad.*

[5] The award was for Hesiod | Plutarch mentions a contest between Homer and Hesiod at Chalcis, in which the latter won unfairly.

SECTION 23

Just after the Games were over, news came that the Damned had broken their fetters, overpowered their guard, and were on the point of invading the island [1], the ringleaders being Phalaris of Agrigentum [2], Busiris the Egyptian [3], Diomedes the Thracian [4], Sciron [5], and Pityocamptes. Rhadamanthus at once drew up the Heroes on the beach, giving the command to Theseus, Achilles, and Ajax Telamonius, now in his right senses. The battle was fought, and

won by the Heroes, thanks especially to Achilles. Socrates, who was in the right wing, distinguished himself still more than in his lifetime at Delium [6], standing firm and showing no sign of trepidation as the enemy came on; he was afterwards given as a reward of valor a large and beautiful park in the outskirts, to which he invited his friends for conversation, naming it the Post-mortem Academy.

[1] Broken fetters, overpowered guard, invading island | Perhaps a satirical take on the Myth of Er: Plato *Republic* 615d-616a: "'For indeed this was one of the dreadful sights we beheld; when we were near the mouth and about to issue forth and all our other sufferings were ended, we suddenly caught sight of him and of others, the most of them, I may say, tyrants. But there were some of private station, of those who had committed great crimes. And when these supposed that at last they were about to go up and out, the mouth would not receive them, but it bellowed when anyone of the incurably wicked or of those who had not completed their punishment tried to come up. And thereupon,' he said, 'savage men of fiery aspect who stood by and took note of the voice laid hold on them3 and bore them away. ".[xxx]

[2] Phalaris of Agrigentum | The famous tyrant of Agrigentum, renowned for his ingenious contrivance of roasting his enemies in a brazen bull, and not less memorable for some spurious epistles. Some later traditions paint Phalaris as a mild and just ruler, forced into severe measures by occasional necessity, and especially as a patron of arts and literature. Lucian's own expositions *Phalaris I & II* are rhetorical exercises in support of the view of Phalaris in the later tradition of mildness and justice.

[3] Busiris the Egyptian | Sacrificed to Zeus all the strangers that came into his kingdom; also he was killed by Heracles.

[4] Diomedes the Thracian | A king of Thrace who fed his horses with human flesh. Also slain by Heracles.

[5] Scyron | Scyron and Pityocamptes were two famous robbers who used to seize on travelers and commit the most horrid cruelties on them.

[6] At Delium | Socrates fought at the Battle of Delium, 424 BC, and, when the Athenians were routed and fled in disorder, he retreated quietly and steadily, calmingly surveying friends and foes. On this occasion his superior courage was shown by not retreating at all. Plato *Symposium* 36: "And further let me tell you, gentlemen, what a notable figure he made when the army was retiring in flight from Delium: I happened to be there on horseback, while he marched under arms. The troops were in utter disorder, and he was retreating along with Laches, when I chanced to come up with them and, as soon as I saw them, passed them the word to have no fear, saying I would not abandon them. Here, indeed, I had an even finer view of Socrates than at Potidaea—for personally I had less reason for alarm, as I was mounted; and I noticed, first, how far he outdid Laches in collectedness, and next I felt—to use a phrase of yours, Aristophanes—how there he stepped along, as his wont is in our streets, 'strutting like a proud marsh-goose, with ever a side-long glance,' turning a calm sidelong look on friend and foe alike, and convincing anyone even from afar that whoever cares to touch this person will find he can put up a stout enough defense. The result was that both he and his comrade got away unscathed: for, as a rule, people will not lay a finger on those who show this disposition in war; it is men flying in headlong rout that they pursue."[xxxi]

SECTION 24

The defeated party were seized, re-fettered, and sent back for severer torments. Homer added to his

poems a description of this battle and at my departure handed me the manuscript to bring back to the living world; but it was unfortunately lost with our other property. It began with the line:

Tell now, my Muse, how fought the mighty Dead.

According to their custom after successful war, they boiled beans, held the feast of victory, and kept high holiday. From this Pythagoras alone held aloof, fasting and sitting far off, in sign of his abhorrence of bean-eating [1].

[1] Pythagoras ... abhorrence of bean-eating | Pythagoras, for an unknown reason (it is said because he believed the souls of the dead to inhabit beans) refused to eat this vegetable, though a vegetarian.

SECTION 25

We were in the middle of our seventh month, when an incident happened. Scintharus's son, Cinyras [1], a fine figure of a man, had fallen in love with Helen some time before, and it was obvious that she was very much taken with the young fellow; there used to be nods and becks and takings of wine between them at table, and they would go off by themselves for strolls in the wood. At last love and despair inspired Cinyras with the idea of an elopement. Helen consented [2], and they were to fly to one of the neighboring islands, Cork or Cheese Island. They had taken three of the boldest of my crew into their confidence; Cinyras said not a word to his father, knowing that he would put a stop to it. The plan was carried out; under cover of night, and in my absence — I had fallen asleep at table —, they got Helen away unobserved and rowed off as hard as they could.

[1] Cinyras (or Kinyras) | A Greek reader would notice that the word *kino*, which means "copulate", is an

insinuation that he will suffer frustration from pent up sexuality and lust.

[2] Helen consented | In some versions of the abduction of Helen by Paris, Helen is a willing participant. Herodotus 1.4: "Now they say that in their judgment, though it is an act of wrong to carry away women by force, it is a folly to set one's heart on taking vengeance for their rape, and the wise course is to pay no regard when they have been carried away; for it is evident that they would never be carried away if they were not themselves willing to go."

SECTION 26

About midnight Menelaus woke up, and finding his wife's place empty raised an alarm, and got his brother to go with him to King Rhadamanthus. Just before dawn the look-outs announced that they could make out the boat, far out at sea. So Rhadamanthus sent fifty of the Heroes on board a boat hollowed out of an asphodel trunk [1], with orders to give chase. Pulling their best, they overtook the fugitives at noon, as they were entering the milky sea near the Isle of Cheese; so nearly was the escape executed. The boat was towed back with a chain of roses. Helen shed tears, and so felt her situation as to draw a veil over her face. As to Cinyras and his associates, Rhadamanthus interrogated them to find whether they had more accomplices, and, being assured to the contrary, had them whipped with mallow twigs, bound, and dismissed to the place of the wicked.

[1] Asphodel trunk | The asphodel is mentioned by several poets in connection with the mythology of death, and by association, the afterlife - specifically the Isles of the Blessed and Elysium - part of the ancient Greek concept of the afterlife. Probably not hefty enough to make a boat of. Some examples from the *Odyssey* Books

11 and 24:

- (Book 11.1) "So I spoke, and the spirit of the son of Aeacus departed with long strides over the field of *asphodel*, joyful in that I said that his son was preeminent."
- (Book 11.2) "And after him I marked huge Orion driving together over the field of *asphodel* wild beasts which he himself had slain on the lonely hills, and in his hands he held a club all of bronze, ever unbroken."
- (Book 24) "Past the streams of Oceanus they went, past the rock Leucas, past the gates of the sun and the land of dreams, and quickly came to the mead of *asphodel*, where the spirits dwell, phantoms of men who have done with toils."[xxxii]

SECTION 27

It was further determined that we should be expelled prematurely from the island; we were allowed only one day's grace. This drew from me loud laments and tears for the bliss that I was now to exchange for renewed wanderings. They consoled me for their sentence, however, by telling me that it would not be many years before I should return to them, and assigning me my chair and my place at table — a distinguished one — in anticipation. I then went to Rhadamanthus, and was urgent with him to reveal the future to me, and give me directions for our voyage. He told me that I should come to my native land after many wanderings and perils, but as to the time of my return he would give me no certainty. He pointed, however, to the neighboring islands, of which five were visible, besides one more distant, and informed me that the wicked inhabited these, the near ones, that is, 'from which you see the great flames rising; the sixth yonder is the City of Dreams;

and beyond that again, but not visible at this distance, is Calypso's isle [1]. When you have passed these, you will come to the great continent which is opposite your own [2]; there you will have many adventures, traverse divers tribes, sojourn among inhospitable men, and at last reach your own continent.' That was all he would say.

[1] Calypso's isle | Calypso, a nymph who lived on the island of Ogygia, where Odysseus in his wanderings was shipwrecked. She fell in love with him and promised him immortality on condition that he would remain with her and not return to his wife Penelope. Odysseus refused, whereupon Calypso detained him in the island for seven years until compelled by the gods to release him.

[2] Great continent which is opposite your own | We never heard whether the narrator performed this voyage. The ancients had a vague notion of a large continent island far away to west, where America is. This was sometimes described as the island of Atlantis, very fruitful and populous, and larger than Asia and Africa combined. Aristotle *De Mundo* speaks of countries at a vast distance off and opposite to ours. In Aelian's *Varia Historia* 3.18, Silenus the Satyr is represented as holding a conversation with Midas. He tells him that Europe, Asia, and Africa are islands bounded by the Ocean stream and that the only existing continent is "outside of the world"; an immense tract of land with gigantic inhabitants, whose strange customs he proceeds to describe. It is to this similar belief that Lucian here alludes. Aelian *Varia Historia* 3.18: "Amongst other things, Silenus told Midas that Europe, Asia and Africa were Islands surrounded by the Ocean: That there was but one Continent only, which was beyond this world and that as to magnitude it was infinite."[xxxiii]

SECTION 28

But he pulled up a mallow root [1] and handed it to me, bidding me invoke it at times of greatest danger. When I arrived in this world, he charged me to abstain from stirring fire with a knife, from lupines, and from the society of boys over eighteen [2]; these things if I kept in mind, I might look for return to the island. That day I made ready for our voyage, and when the banquet hour came, I shared it. On the morrow I went to the poet Homer and besought him to write me a couplet for inscription; when he had done it, I carved it on a beryl pillar which I had set up close to the harbor; it ran thus:

This island, ere he took his homeward way, the blissful Gods gave Lucian to survey.

[1] The mallow plant is associated with the dead and was considered sacred by Pythagoreans. It is meant to have magical powers. It is analogous to the root "moly" from the *Odyssey*, which Hermes gave Odysseus. *Odyssey* 10.303-305: "So saying, Argeiphontes gave me the herb, drawing it from the ground, and showed me its nature. At the root it was black, but its flower was like milk. Moly the gods call it, and it is hard for mortal men to dig; but with the gods all things are possible."[xxxiv]

[2] Precepts | Only the first of the three is an actual Pythagorean precept. Lucian satirizes the Pythagorean symbols as collected by Iambilichus. Iambilichus lived a few generations after Lucian.

SECTION 29

I stayed out that day too, and next morning started, the Heroes attending to see me off. Odysseus took the opportunity to come unobserved by Penelope and give me a letter for Calypso in the isle Ogygia. Rhadamanthus sent on board with me the ferryman Nauplius, who, in case we were driven on to the islands, might secure us from seizure by guaranteeing

that our destination was different. As soon as our progress brought us out of the scented air, it was succeeded by a horrible smell as of bitumen, brimstone, and pitch all burning together; mingled with this were the disgusting and intolerable fumes of roasting human flesh; the air was dark and thick, distilling a pitchy dew upon us; we could also hear the crack of whips and the yelling of many voices.

SECTION 30

We only touched at one island, on which we also landed. It was completely surrounded by precipitous cliffs, arid, stony, rugged, treeless, and unwatered. We contrived to clamber up the rocks, and advanced along a track beset with thorns and snags — a hideous scene. When we reached the prison and the place of punishment, what first drew our wonder was the character of the whole. The very ground stood thick with a crop of knife-blades and pointed stakes; and it was ringed round with rivers [1], one of slime, a second of blood, and the innermost of flame. This last was very broad and quite impassable; the flame flowed like water, swelled like the sea, and teemed with fish, some resembling firebrands, and others, the small ones, live coals; these were called lamplets.

[1] Rivers | Lucian probably had in mind the description in Plato's *Phaedo* 60 of the Rivers of Hades: "Many streams of mud both thinner and thicker, like in Sicily the rivers of mud flowing before the lava and the lava itself; and so which fill each of the regions, as to each by chance the flowing around each time occurs. And all these move up and down like some oscillation within the earth; and so this oscillation through nature is some such thing."[xxxv]

SECTION 31

One narrow way led across all three; its gate was kept by Timon of Athens [1]. Nauplius secured us admission, however, and then we saw the chastisement of many kings, and many common men; some were known to us; indeed there hung Cinyras [2], swinging in eddies of smoke. Our guides described the life and guilt of each culprit; the severest torments were reserved for those who in life had been liars and written false history; the class was numerous, and included Ctesias of Cnidus, and Herodotus. The fact was an encouragement to me, knowing that I had never told a lie. [3]

[1] Timon of Athens | According to Lucian's dialogue *Timon the Misanthrope*, Timon was the wealthy son of Echecratides who lavished his money on flattering friends. When funds ran out, friends deserted and Timon was reduced to working in the fields. One day, he found a pot of gold and soon his fair-weather friends were back. This time, he drove them away with dirt clods.

[2] Cinyras | Who had just run off with Helen and was unfortunately caught in the act.

[3] Never told a lie | In fact, those are only outrageous lines, which are intended to be imposed on light readers to coax them into believing the truth of the story. There can clearly be no bigger liar than the author of the *True History*.

SECTION 32

I soon found the sight more than I could bear, and returning to the ship bade farewell to Nauplius and resumed the voyage. Very soon we seemed quite close to the Isle of Dreams [1], though there was a certain dimness and vagueness about its outline; but it had something dreamlike in its very nature; for as we approached it receded, and seemed to get further and further off. At last we reached it and sailed into

Slumber, the port, close to the ivory gates where stands the temple of the Rooster [2] It was evening when we landed, and upon proceeding to the city we saw many strange dreams. But I intend first to describe the city, as it has not been done before; Homer indeed mentions it, but gives no detailed description.

[1] Isle of Dreams | Gr. *Hypnos*, sleep. An improvement upon Homer's description of Dreamland with its two gates of horn and ivory, from where come true and false dreams respectively. *Odyssey* 19.562: "Stranger, dreams verily are baffling and unclear of meaning, and in no wise do they find fulfillment in all things for men. For two are the gates of shadowy dreams, and one is fashioned of horn and one of ivory. Those dreams that pass through the gate of sawn ivory deceive men, bringing words that find no fulfillment. But those that come forth through the gate of polished horn bring true issues to pass, when any mortal sees them."[xxxvi]

[2] Rooster | As herald of the morning.

SECTION 33

The whole place is embowered in wood, of which the trees are poppy and mandragora [1], all thronged with bats; this is the only winged thing that exists there. A river, called the Somnambule [2], flows close by, and there are two springs at the gates, one called Wakenot [3], and the other Nightlong [4]. The rampart is lofty and of many colors, in the rainbow style. The gates are not two, as Homer [5] says, but four, of which two look on to the plain Stupor; one of them is of iron, the other of pottery, and we were told that these are used by the grim, the murderous, and the cruel. The other pair faces the sea and port, and is of horn — it was by this that we had entered — and of ivory. On the right as you enter the city stands

the temple of Night, which deity divides with the Rooster their chief allegiance; the temple of the latter is close to the port. On the left is the palace of Sleep. He is the governor, with two lieutenants, Nightmare, son of Whimsy [6], and Flittergold, son of Fantasy [7]. A well in the middle of the market-place goes by the name of Heavyhead [8]; beside which are the temples of Deceit and Truth. In the market also is the shrine in which oracles are given, the priest and prophet, by special appointment from Sleep, being Antiphon the dream-interpreter. [9]

[1] Mandragora | A root which when ingested is supposed to promote sleep, very proper for the island of dreams. cf. Shakespeare *Othello* 3.3: "Not poppy nor mandragora ... shall ever medicine thee to that sweet sleep, which thou owedst yesterday".

[2] Somnambule | Gr. *Nyctiporus*, night-wanderers.

[3] Wakenot | Gr. *Negretus*, unwaked or wakeful.

[4] Nightlong | Gr. *Pannychia*, all night.

[5] Homer | Homer said there were two gates, one for truthful, the other for lying dreams. Virgil recognizes two gates – one of horn, for *verae umbrae* i.e. true spirits appearing in sleep, the other of ivory, for delusive dreams.

[6] Nightmare son of Whimsy | Gr. *Taraxion tou Mataogeous*, Fright, the son of vain-hope or Disappointment.

[7] Flittergold, son of Fantasy | Gr. *Plutoklea tou Phantasiosis*, the pride of riches; i.e. arising from riches, son of fantasy or deceit.

[8] Heavyhead | Gr. *Karkotis*, heavy-sleep.

[9] Antiphon the dream-interpreter | Perhaps this was leveled at a dream-interpreter of the time that is no longer known.

SECTION 34

The dreams themselves differed widely in character and appearance. Some were well-grown, smooth-skinned, shapely, handsome fellows, others rough, short, and ugly; some apparently made of gold, others of common cheap stuff. Among them some were found with wings, and other strange variations; others again were like the mummers in a pageant, tricked out as kings or Gods or what not [1]. Many of them we felt that we had seen in our world, and sure enough these came up and claimed us as old acquaintance; they took us under their charge, found us lodgings, entertained us with lavish kindness, and, not content with the magnificence of this present reception, promised us royalties and provinces. Some of them also took us to see our friends, doing the return trip all in the day.

[1] Tricked out as kings of Gods or what not | Lucian often uses dream sequences to show munificent, unrealistic, and unfulfillable promises. Even waking dreams are satirized as fantastical as seen in Lucian's dialogue *The Ship*.

SECTION 35

For thirty days and nights we abode there — a very feast of sleep. Then on a sudden came a mighty clap of thunder: we woke; jumped up; provisioned; put off. In three days we were at the Isle of Ogygia, where we landed. Before delivering the letter, I opened and read it; here are the contents: ***ODYSSEUS TO CALYPSO, GREETING. Know that in the faraway days when I built my raft and sailed away from you, I suffered shipwreck; I was hard put to it, but Leucothea brought me safe to the land of the Phaeacians; they gave me passage home, and there I found a great company suing for my wife's hand and***

***living riotously upon our goods. All them I slew, and in after years was slain by Telegonus [1], the son that Circe bare me. And now I am in the Island of the Blest, ruing the day when I left the life I had with you, and the everlasting life you proffered. I watch for opportunity, and meditate escape and return.* [2] Some words were added, commending us to her hospitality.**

[1] Telegonus | Telegonus was sent by Circe to seek for his father. Being shipwrecked on the island of Ithaca and pressed by hunger, he began to ravage the fields. Thereupon, Odysseus marched against him, and was killed by his son, neither knowing the other.

[2] ODYSSEUS ... |This letter gives an account of *Odyssey* 5-24 with the story from the Telegony, 6th Century BC written by Eugammon.

SECTION 36

A little way from the sea I found the cave just as it is in Homer and herself therein at her spinning [1]. She took and read the letter, wept for a space, and then offered us entertainment; royally she feasted us, putting questions the while about Odysseus and Penelope [2]; what were her looks? And was she as discreet as Odysseus had been used to vaunt her? To which we made such answers as we thought she would like.

[1] A little way from the sea I found the cave just as it is in Homer and herself therein at her spinning | *Odyssey* 5.57-62: "But when he had reached the island which lay afar, then forth from the violet sea he came to land, and went his way until he came to a great cave, wherein dwelt the fair-tressed nymph; and he found her within. A great fire was burning on the hearth, and from afar over the isle there was a fragrance of cleft cedar and juniper, as they burned; but she within was singing with a sweet voice as she went to and fro before the loom, weaving

with a golden shuttle."[xxxvii]

[2] Penelope | Passage implies that he denigrated Penelope's looks and chastity. *Odyssey* 5.215-5.217: "Mighty goddess, be not wroth with me for this. I know full well of myself that wise Penelope is meaner to look upon than thou in comeliness and in stature, for she is a mortal, while thou art immortal and ageless."[xxxviii]

SECTION 37

Leaving her, we went on board, and spent the night at anchor just off shore; in the morning we started with a stiff breeze, which grew to a gale lasting two days; on the third day we fell in with the Pumpkin-pirates [1]. These are savages of the neighboring islands who prey upon passing ships. They use large boats made of pumpkins ninety feet long. The pumpkin is dried and hollowed out by removal of the pulp, and the boat is completed by the addition of cane masts and pumpkin-leaf sails. Two boatfuls of them engaged us, and we had many casualties from their pumpkin-seed missiles. The fight was long and well matched; but about noon we saw a squadron of Nut-tars [2] coming up in rear of the enemy. It turned out that the two parties were at war; for as soon as our assailants observed the others, they left us alone and turned to engage them.

[1] Pumpkin-pirates | Gr. *Kolokyntho-peiratai.*

[2] Nut-tars Sailors | Gr. *Karyonautai.*

SECTION 38

Meanwhile we hoisted sail and made the best of our way off, leaving them to fight it out. It was clear that the Nut-tars must win, as they had both superior numbers — there were five sail of them — and

stronger vessels. These were made of nutshells, halved and emptied, measuring ninety feet from stem to stern. As soon as they were hull down, we attended to our wounded; and from that time we made a practice of keeping on our armor, to be in instant readiness for an attack — no vain precaution either.

SECTION 39

Before sunset, for instance, there assailed us from a bare island some twenty men mounted on large dolphins [1] — pirates again. Their dolphins carried them quite well, curveting and neighing. When they got near, they divided, and subjected us to a cross fire of dry cuttlefish and crabs' eyes. But our arrows and javelins were too much for them, and they fled back to the island, few of them unwounded.

[1] Dolphins | Follows tradition of men riding dolphins. Herodotus 1.24: "Then as the measure ended, Arion threw himself into the sea just as he was, in his full minstrel's garb; and they went on sailing away to Corinth, but him, they say, a dolphin supported on its back and brought him to shore at Tainaron: and when he had come to land he proceeded to Corinth with his minstrel's garb."[xxxix] Aulus Gellius *Attic Nights* 6.8: "I have appended the words of that learned man Apion, from the fifth book of his *Egyptian History*, in which he tells of an amorous dolphin and a boy who did not reject its advances, of their intimacy and play with each other, the dolphin carrying the boy and the boy bestriding the fish; and Apion declares that of all this he himself and many others were eye-witnesses."[xl]

SECTION 40

At midnight, in calm weather, we found ourselves colliding with an enormous halcyon's nest; it was full

seven miles round. The halcyon was brooding, not much smaller herself than the nest. She got up, and very nearly capsized us with the fanning of her wings; however, she went off with a melancholy cry. When it was getting light, we got on to the nest, and found on examination that it was composed like a vast raft of large trees. There were five hundred eggs, larger in girth than a tun of Chian [1]. We could make out the chicks inside and hear them croaking; we hewed open one egg with hatchets, and dug out an unfledged chick bulkier than twenty vultures. [2]

[1] Chian | The Chian wine-jar held about three or four quarts.

[2] Twenty vultures | Reminiscent of the Story of Roc and its egg from the *Second Voyage of Sinbad the Sailor*. The roc appears in Arabic geographies and natural history, popularized in Arabian fairy tales and sailors' folklore. Ibn Battuta (iv. 305ff) tells of a mountain hovering in air over the China Seas, which was the roc. Whether Lucian may have borrowed from the Arabian Nights (or rather from the common material out of which the tales were built) is unknown.

SECTION 41

Sailing on, we had left the nest some five and twenty miles behind, when a miracle happened. The wooden goose [1] of our stern-post suddenly clapped its wings and started cackling; Scintharus, who was bald, recovered his hair; most striking of all, the ship's mast came to life, putting forth branches sideways, and fruit at the top; this fruit was figs, and a bunch of black grapes, not yet ripe [2]. These sights naturally disturbed us, and we fell to praying the Gods to avert any disaster they might portend [3].

[1] Wooden goose | Meaning the carved head; goose heads were often used at the prow of ships.

[2] Grapes, not yet ripe | Attests to the force of Dionysius as seen in his Homeric Hymn when captured by Tyrrhenian pirates: "And all at once a vine spread out both ways along the top of the sail with many clusters hanging down from it, and a dark ivy-plant twined about the mast, blossoming with flowers, and with rich berries growing on it; and all the thole-pins were covered with garlands." Lucian and his comrades have the right to be worried by the omen.

[3] Praying to the gods | Lucian's satire is directed at the common superstition, which saw in every strange occurrence an omen of divine anger, requiring prayer or sacrifice to avert it.

SECTION 42

We had preceded something less than fifty miles when we saw a great forest, thick with pines and cypresses. This we took for the mainland; but it was in fact deep sea, set with trees; they had no roots, but yet remained in their places, floating upright, as it were. When we came near and realized the state of the case, we could not tell what to do; it was impossible to sail between the trees, which were so close as to touch one another, and we did not like the thought of turning back. I climbed the tallest tree to get a good view, and found that the wood was five or six miles across, and was succeeded by open water. So we determined to hoist the ship on to the top of the foliage, which was very dense, and get her across to the other sea, if possible. It proved to be so. We attached a strong cable, got up on the tree-tops, and hauled her after us with some difficulty; then we laid her on the branches, hoisted sail, and floating thus were propelled by the wind. A line of Antimachus came into my head:

***And as they voyaged thus the woodland through* — [1]**

[1] This passage refers to the Argonauts having to move their ship through the deserts of Libya to reach the other sea. Antimachus of Colophon wrote the *Thebiad*, several lines of which are cited by Athenaeus and in some elegiac poems. The emperor Hadrian is said to have preferred him to Homer.

SECTION 43

Well, we made our way over and reached the water, into which we let her down in the same way. We then sailed through clear transparent sea, till we found ourselves on the edge of a great gorge [1] which divided water from water, like the land fissures which are often produced by earthquakes. We got the sails down and brought her to just in time to escape making the plunge. We could bend over and see an awful mysterious gulf perhaps a hundred miles deep, the water standing wall against wall. Glances round showed us not far off to the right a water bridge which spanned the chasm, and gave a moving surface crossing from one sea to the other. We got out the sweeps, pulled her to the bridge, and with great exertions affected that astonishing passage.

[1] Great gorge | Reminds the reader of Herodotus 4.85: "These then were left, having been slain upon the spot where they were: and Dareios meanwhile set forth from Susa and arrived at the place on the Bosphorus where the bridge of ships had been made, in the territory of Chalcedon; and there he embarked in a ship and sailed to the so-called Kyanean rocks, which the Hellenes say formerly moved backwards and forwards; and taking his seat at the temple he gazed upon the Pontus, which is a sight well worth seeing. Of all seas indeed it is the most marvelous in its nature. The length of it is eleven thousand one hundred furlongs, and the breadth, where it is broadest, three thousand three hundred: and of this great Sea the mouth is but four furlongs broad, and the

length of the mouth, that is of the neck of water which is called Bosphorus, where, as I said, the bridge of ships had been made, is not less than a hundred and twenty furlongs. This Bosphorus extends to the Propontis; and the Propontis, being in breadth five hundred furlongs and in length one thousand four hundred, has its outlet into the Hellespont, which is but seven furlongs broad at the narrowest place, though it is four hundred furlongs in length: and the Hellespont runs out into that expanse of sea which is called the Aegean."[xli]

SECTION 44

There followed a sail through smooth water, and then a small island, easy of approach, and inhabited; its occupants were the Ox-heads, savage men with horns, after the fashion of our poets' Minotaur [1]. We landed and went in search of water and provisions, of which we were now in want. The water we found easily, but nothing else; we heard, however, not far off, a numerous lowing; supposing it to indicate a herd of cattle, we went a little way towards it, and came upon these men. They gave chase as soon as they saw us, and seized three of my comrades, the rest of us getting off to sea. We then armed — for we would not leave our friends unavenged — and in full force fell on the Ox-heads as they were dividing our slaughtered men's flesh. Our combined shout put them to flight, and in the pursuit we killed about fifty, took two alive, and returned with our captives. We had found nothing to eat; the general opinion was for slaughtering the prisoners; but I refused to accede to this [2], and kept them in bonds till an embassy came from the Ox-heads to ransom them; so we understood the motions they made, and their tearful supplicatory lowings. The ransom consisted of a quantity of cheese, dried fish, onions, and four deer; these were three-footed, the two forefeet being

joined into one. In exchange for all this we restored the prisoners, and after one day's further stay departed.

[1] Minotaur | The Minotaur was an ox-headed, man-eating monster, who lived in the Labyrinth in Crete. He was slain by Theseus with the help of Ariadne.

[2] I refused to accede to this | Lucian is trying not to have a repeat of the Island of the Sun episode from the *Odyssey* 12 where hunger and fatigued trumped logic. Tiresias and Circe both warn Odysseus to shun the Isle of Helios. When Eurylochus begs to be allowed to land to prepare supper, Odysseus grudgingly agrees, on condition that the crew swears that if they come upon a herd of cattle or a great flock of sheep, no one will kill any of them. They are held on the isle for a month by unfavorable winds, and when Odysseus goes up the island to pray to the gods and ask for help, Eurylochus convinces the crew to drive off the best of the cattle of Helios and sacrifice them to the gods: "if he be somewhat wroth for his cattle with straight horns, and is fain to wreck our ship, and the other gods follow his desire, rather with one gulp at the wave would I cast my life away, than be slowly straitened to death in a desert isle." Lampetie tells Helios that they have slain his cattle, and he in turn begs Zeus and the other gods to take vengeance on the company of Odysseus. He threatens that if they do not pay him full atonement for the cattle that he will go down to Hades and shine among the dead. Zeus promises to smite their ship with a lightning bolt, and cleave it in pieces in the midst of the ocean. When he returns to the ship, Odysseus rebukes his companions, but it is too late, the cattle are dead and gone. Soon the gods show signs and wonders to them. The skins begin creeping, and the flesh bellowing upon the spits, both the roast and raw, and there is a sound like the voice of cattle. For six days Odysseus's company feast on the cattle of Helios. On the seventh day, the

wind changes. After they set sail, Zeus keeps his word and the ship is destroyed by lightning. Odysseus escapes by swimming to Calypso's island. The next seven years he stays on her island and she treats him to all of her gifts.

SECTION 45

By this time we were beginning to observe fish, birds on the wing, and other signs of land not far off; and we shortly saw men, practicing a mode of navigation new to us; for they were boat and crew in one. The method was this: they float on their backs, erect a sail, and then, holding the sheets with their hands, catch the wind. These were succeeded by others who sat on corks, to which were harnessed pairs of dolphins, driven with reins. They neither attacked nor avoided us, but drove along in all confidence and peace, admiring the shape of our craft and examining it all round.

SECTION 46

That evening we touched at an island of no great size. It was occupied by what we took for women, talking Greek. They came and greeted us with kisses, were attired like courtesans, all young and fair, and with long robes sweeping the ground. Cabbalusa was the name of the island, and Hydramardia the city's [1]. These women paired off with us and led the way to their separate homes.

I myself tarried a little, under the influence of some presentiment, and looking more closely observed quantities of human bones and skulls lying about [2]. I did not care to raise an alarm, gather my men, and resort to arms; instead, I drew out my mallow [3], and prayed earnestly to it for escape from our

perilous position. Shortly after, as my hostess was serving me, I saw that in place of human feet she had ass's hoofs; whereupon I drew my sword, seized, bound, and closely questioned her. Reluctantly enough she had to confess; they were sea-women called Ass-shanks [4], and their food was travelers. 'When we have made them drunk,' she said, 'and gone to rest with them, we overpower them in their sleep.' After this confession I left her there bound, went up on to the roof, and shouted for my comrades. When they appeared, I repeated it all to them, showed them the bones, and brought them in to see my prisoner; she at once vanished, turning to water; however, I thrust my sword into this experimentally, upon which the water became blood.

[1] Cabbalusa ... Hydramardia | Much brainpower has been spent trying to figure out the import or even location of these Greek names. It has been suggested that they were distorted by a transcriber. No verdict has been made as to their meaning.

[2] Skulls lying about | Lucian, like Odysseus, can see the signs of embroilment. Passage has two parallels from the Odyssey. *Odyssey* 10.312: "So she spoke, but I, drawing my sharp sword from beside my thigh, rushed upon Circe, as though I would slay her."[xlii] *Odyssey* 12.42-46: "Whoso in ignorance draws near to them and hears the Sirens' voice, he nevermore returns, that his wife and little children may stand at his side rejoicing, but the Sirens beguile him with their clear-toned song, as they sit in a meadow, and about them is a great heap of bones of moldering men, and round the bones the skin is shriveling."[xliii]

[3] My mallow | Refers to the mallow given by way of charm earlier on his departure from the happy island.

[4] Ass-shanks | Gr. *Onoscileas*, aft-legged.

SECTION 47

Then we marched hurriedly down to our ship and sailed away. With the first glimmering of dawn we made out a mainland [1], which we took for the continent that faces our own. We reverently saluted it, made prayer, and held counsel upon our best course. Some were for merely landing and turning back at once, others for leaving the ship, and going into the interior to make trial of the inhabitants. But while we were deliberating, a great storm arose, which dashed us, a complete wreck, on the shore. We managed to swim to land, each snatching up his arms and anything else he could.

Such are the adventures that befell me up to our arrival at that other continent: our sea-voyage; our cruise among the islands and in the air; then our experiences in and after the whale; with the Heroes; with the dreams; and finally with the Ox-heads and the Ass-shanks. Our fortunes on the continent will be the subject of the following books [2].

[1] Mainland | There may be two parallels to this passage in ancient texts: Plato *Timaeus* 24e: "For it is related in our records how once upon a time your State stayed the course of a mighty host, which, starting from a distant point in the Atlantic ocean, was insolently advancing to attack the whole of Europe, and Asia to boot. For the ocean there was at that time navigable; for in front of the mouth which you Greeks call, as you say, 'the pillars of Heracles,' there lay an island which was larger than Libya and Asia together; and it was possible for the travelers of that time to cross from it to the other islands, and from the islands to the whole of the continent".[xliv] Aelian *Various History* 3.18: "Amongst other things, Silenus told Midas that Europe, Asia and Africa were Islands surrounded by the Ocean: That there was but one Continent only, which was beyond this

world and that as to magnitude it was infinite”.[xlv]

[2] Following books | The following books never appeared. It is highly proper that a history made entirely up of lies should conclude with a promise which the author never intends to keep.

APPENDIX

INTRODUCTION

Found in this Appendix are writings that bear a strong similarity to Lucian's *True History* in scope and content. The difference is that they were not satirical works, but actual works of ethnography, geography, history, and poetry. When read with the *True History*, it puts Lucian's work in perspective as the reader can understand the sort of literature that was available for Lucian to parody. Ancient Greek literature, from the time of Homer until the end of antiquity, always had a running thread for trying to understand diverse landscapes and attempting to coherently understand things that are not fully known. Please enjoy these tracts for themselves, but also see them through the eyes of Lucian, always the skeptic, and see why the *True History* was written and whom it was addressing.

FR

INDICA BY CTESIAS; SUMMARIZED BY PHOTIUS IN BIBLIOTHECA

Photius, ; Freese, John H. *The Library of Photius. [translated] by J. H. Freese. Vol. 1*. London: S.P.C.K, 1920. Print.

Also read the same author's *History of India*, in one book, in which he employs the Ionic dialect more frequently. In regard to the river Indus, he says that, where it is narrowest, it is forty, where it is widest, two hundred stades broad. He declares that the population of India is almost greater than that of the whole world. He also mentions a worm found in this river, the only living creature which breeds there. Beyond India there are no countries inhabited by men. It never rains there, the country being watered by the river. He says of the pantarba, a kind of seal-stone, that 477 seal-stones and other precious stones, belonging to a Bactrian merchant, which had been thrown into the river, were drawn up from the bottom, all clinging together, by this stone.

He also speaks of elephants which knock down walls, of little apes with tails four cubits long, and of cocks of very large size; of the parrot about as large as a hawk, which has a human tongue and voice, a dark-red beak, a black, beard, and blue feathers up to the neck, which is red like cinnabar. It speaks Indian like a native, and if taught Greek, speaks Greek.

He next mentions a fountain which is filled every year with liquid gold, from which a hundred pitcherfuls are drawn. These pitchers have to be made of earth, since the gold when drawn off becomes solid, and it is necessary to break the vessel in order to get it out. The fountain is square, sixteen cubits in circumference, and a fathom deep. The gold in each pitcher weighs a talent. At the bottom of the fountain there is iron, and the author says that he possessed two swords made from it, one given him by the king, the other by his mother, Parysatis. If this iron be fixed in the ground, it keeps off clouds and hail and hurricanes Ctesias declares that the king twice proved its efficacy and that he himself was a witness to it.

The Indian dogs are very large and even attack lions. There are great mountains, from which are dug sardonyx, onyx, and other seal-stones. It is intensely hot and the sun appears ten times larger than in other countries; large numbers of people are suffocated by the heat. The sea is as large as that of Greece; it is so hot on the surface and to a depth of four fingers that fish cannot live near it, but keep on the bottom.

The river Indus flows across plains and between mountains, where the so-called Indian reed grows. It is so thick that two men can hardly get their arms round it, and as tall as the mast of a merchant-ship of largest tonnage. Some are larger, some smaller, as is natural considering the size of the mountain. Of these reeds some are male, others female. The male has no pith and is very strong, but the female has.

The martikhora is an animal found in this country. It has a face like a man's, a skin red as cinnabar, and is as large as a lion. It has three rows of teeth, ears and light-blue eyes like those of a man; its tail is like that of a land scorpion, containing a sting more than a cubit long at the end. It has other stings on each side of its tail and one on the top of its head, like the scorpion, with which it inflicts a wound that is always fatal. If it is attacked from a distance, it sets up its tail in front and discharges its stings as if from a bow; if attacked from behind, it straightens it out and launches its stings in a direct line to the distance of a hundred feet. The wound inflicted is fatal to all animals except the elephant. The stings are about a foot long and about as thick as a small rush. The martikhora is called in Greek anthropophagos (man-eater), because, although it preys upon other animals, it kills and devours a greater number of human beings. It fights with both its claws and stings, which, according to Ctesias, grow again after they have been discharged. There are a great number of these animals in India, which are hunted and killed with spears or arrows by natives mounted on elephants.

Observing that the Indians are extremely just, Ctesias goes on to describe their manners and customs. He mentions a sacred spot in an uninhabited district, which they honor under the name of the Sun and the Moon. It is a fifteen days' journey from mount Sardo. Here the Sun is always cool for thirty-five days in the year, so that his votaries may attend his feast and after its celebration may return home without being scorched. In India there is neither thunder, lightning, nor rain, but winds and hurricanes, which carry along everything that comes in their way, are frequent. The sun, after rising, is cool for half the day, but for the remainder is excessively hot in most parts of the country. It is not the heat of the sun that makes the Indians swarthy; they are so naturally. Some of them, both men and women, are very fair, though they are fewer in number. Ctesias says that he himself saw five white men and two white women. In support of his statement that the sun cools the air for thirty-five days, he mentions that the fire which streams from Aetna does no damage to the middle of the country through which it passes, because it is the abode of just men, but destroys the rest. In the island of Zacynthus there are fountains full of fish, out of which pitch is taken. In the island of Naxos there is a fountain from which sometimes flows a wine of very agreeable flavor. The water of the river Phasis, if allowed to stand a day and a night in a vessel, becomes a most delicious wine. Near Phaselis in Lycia there is a fire which never goes out, but burns on a rock both night and day. It cannot be extinguished by water, which rather increases the flame, but only by throwing earth upon it.

In the middle of India there are black men, called Pygmies, who speak the same language as the other inhabitants of the country. They are very short, the tallest being only two cubits in height, most of them only one and a half. Their hair is very long, going down to the knees and even lower, and their beards are larger than those of any other men. When their beards are full grown they leave off wearing clothes and let the hair of their head fall down behind far below the knees, while their beard trails down to the feet in front. When their body is thus entirely covered with hair they fasten it round them with a girdle, so that it serves them for clothes. They are snub-nosed and ugly. Their sheep are no bigger than lambs, their oxen, asses, horses, mules, and other beasts of burden about the size of rams. Being very skillful archers, 3000 of them attend on the king of India. They are very just and have the same laws as the Indians. They hunt the hare and the fox, not with dogs, but with ravens, kites, crows, and eagles.

There is a lake 800 stades in circumference, the surface of which, when riot ruffled by the wind, is covered with floating oil. Sailing over it in little boats, they ladle out the oil with little vessels and keep it for use. They also use oil of sesamum and nut-oil, but the oil from the lake is best. The lake also abounds in fish.

The country produces much silver and there are numerous silver mines, not very deep, but those of Bactria are said to be deeper. There is also gold, not found in rivers and washed, as in the river Pactolus, but in many large mountains which are inhabited by griffins. These are four-footed birds as large as a wolf, their legs and claws resembling those of a lion; their breast feathers are red, those of the rest of the body black. Although there is abundance of gold in the mountains, it is difficult to get it because of these birds.

The Indian sheep and goats are larger than asses, and as a rule have four young ones, sometimes six, at a time. There are neither tame nor wild pigs. The palm trees and dates are three times as large as those of Babylon. There is a river of honey that flows from a rock.

The author speaks at length of the Indians' love of justice, their loyalty to their kings and their contempt of death. He also mentions a fountain, the water from which, when drawn off, thickens like cheese. If three obols' weight of this thick mass be crushed, mixed with water, and given to anyone to drink, he reveals everything that he has ever done, being in a state of frenzy and delirium the whole day. The king makes use of this test when he desires to discover the truth about an accused person. If he confesses, he is ordered to starve himself to death; if he reveals nothing, he is acquitted.

The Indians are not subject to headache, ophthalmia, or even toothache; to ulcers on the mouth, or sores in any other part of the body. They live 120, 130, 150, and some even 200 years.

There is a serpent a span in length, of a most beautiful purple color, with a very white head, and without teeth. It is caught on the burning mountains, from which the sardonyx is dug. It does not sting, but its vomit rots the place where it falls. If it is hung up by the tail it discharges two kinds of poison, one yellow like amber, when it is alive, the other black, when it is dead. If one drinks only as much of the former as a grain of sesamum dissolved in water, his brain runs out through his nose and he dies immediately; if the other poison is administered, it brings on consumption, which does not prove fatal for at least a year.

There is a bird called dikaerum (meaning in Greek "just"), the size of a partridge's egg. It buries its excrement in the ground in order to hide it. If any one finds it and takes only a morsel of it about the size of a grain of sesamum in the morning, he is overcome by sleep, loses consciousness, and dies at sunset.

There is also a tree called parebum, about the size of an olive, which is only found in the royal gardens. It bears neither flowers nor fruit, and has only fifteen very stout roots, the smallest of which is as thick as a man's arm. If a piece of this root, about a span in length, be put near anybody of matter, gold, silver, brass, stones, in fact, everything except amber, it attracts it; if a cubit's length of it be used, it attracts lambs and birds, the latter being generally caught in this way. If you wish to solidify a gallon of water, you need only throw in a piece of the root the weight of an obol; the same with wine, which can be handled like wax, although on the next day it becomes liquid again. The root is also used as a remedy for those suffering from bowel complaints.

There is a river that flows through India, not large, but about two stades broad. It is called Hyparchus in Indian, meaning in Greek "bestowing all blessings." During thirty days in the year it brings down amber. It is said that in the mountains there are trees on the banks of the river where it passes through, which at a certain season of the year shed tears like the almond, fir, or any other tree, especially during these thirty days. These tears drop into the river and become hard. This tree is called in Indian Siptakhora, meaning in Greek "sweet," and from it the inhabitants gather amber. It also bears fruit in clusters like grapes, the stones of which are as large as the nuts of Pontus.

On these mountains there live men with the head of a dog, whose clothing is the skin of wild beasts. They speak no language, but bark like dogs, and in this manner make themselves understood by each other. Their teeth are larger than those of dogs, their nails like those of these animals, but longer and rounder. They inhabit the mountains as far as the river Indus. Their complexion is swarthy. They are extremely just, like the rest of the Indians with whom they associate. They understand the Indian language but are unable to converse, only barking or making signs with their hands and fingers by way of reply, like the deaf and dumb. They are called by the Indians Calystrii, in Greek Cynocephali ("dog-headed"). [They live on raw meat.] They number about 120,000.

Near the sources of this river grows a purple flower, from which is obtained a purple dye, as good in quality as the Greek and of an even more brilliant hue. In the same district there is an animal about the size of a beetle, red as cinnabar, with very long feet, and a body as soft as that of a worm. It breeds on the trees which produce amber, eats their fruit and kills them, as the woodlouse destroys the vines in Greece. The Indians crush these insects and use them for dyeing their robes and tunics and anything else they wish. The dye is superior to the Persian.

The Cynocephali living on the mountains do not practice any trade but live by hunting. When they have killed an animal they roast it in the sun. They also rear numbers of sheep, goats, and asses, drinking the milk of the sheep and whey made from it. They eat the fruit of the Siptakhora, whence amber is procured, since it is sweet. They also dry it and keep it in baskets, as the Greeks keep their dried grapes. They make rafts which they load with this fruit together with well-cleaned purple flowers and 260 talents of amber, with the same quantity of the purple dye, and 1000 additional talents of amber, which they send annually to the king of India. They exchange the rest for bread, flour, and cotton stuffs with the Indians, from whom they also buy swords for hunting wild beasts, bows, and arrows, being very skillful in drawing the bow and hurling the spear. They cannot be defeated in war, since they inhabit lofty and inaccessible mountains. Every five years the king sends them a present of 300,000 bows, as many spears, 120,000 shields, and 50,000 swords.

They do not live in houses, but in caves. They set out for the chase with bows and spears, and as they are very swift of foot, they pursue and soon overtake their quarry. The women have a bath once a month, the men do not have a bath at all, but only wash their hands. They anoint themselves three times a month with oil made from milk and wipe themselves with skins. The clothes of men and women alike are not skins with the hair on, but skins tanned and very fine. The richest wear linen clothes, but they are few in number. They have no beds, but sleep on leaves or grass. He who possesses the greatest number of sheep is considered the richest, and so in regard to their other possessions. All, both men and women, have tails above their hips, like dogs, but longer and more hairy. They are just, and live longer than any other men, 170, sometimes 200 years.

It is said that beyond their country, above the sources of the river, there are other men, black like the rest of the Indians. They do no work, do not eat grain nor drink water, but rear large numbers of cattle, cattle, goats, and sheep, whose milk is their only food. When they drink milk in the morning and then again at mid-day, they eat a sweet root which prevents the milk from curdling in the stomach, and at night makes them vomit all they have taken without any difficulty.

In India there are wild asses as large as horses, or even larger. Their body is white, their head dark red, their eyes bluish, and they have a horn in their forehead about a cubit in length. The lower part of the horn, for about two palms distance from the forehead, is quite white, the middle is black, the upper part, which terminates in a point, is a very flaming red. Those who drink out of cups made from it are proof against convulsions, epilepsy, and even poison, provided that before or after having taken it they drink some wine or water or other liquid out of these cups. The domestic and wild asses of other countries and all other solid-hoofed animals have neither huckle-bones nor gall-bladder, whereas the Indian asses have both. Their huckle-bone is the most beautiful that I have seen, like that of the ox in size and appearance; it is as heavy as lead and of the color of cinnabar all through. These animals are very strong and swift; neither the horse nor any other animal can overtake them. At first they run slowly, but the longer they run their pace increases wonderfully, and becomes faster and faster. There is only one way of catching them. When they take their young to feed, if they are surrounded by a large number of horsemen, being unwilling to abandon their foals, they show fight, butt with their horns, kick, bite, and kill many men and horses. They are at last taken, after they have been pierced with arrows and spears; for it is impossible to capture them alive. Their flesh is too bitter to eat, and they are only hunted for the sake of the horns and huckle-bones.

In the river Indus a worm is found resembling those which are usually found on fig-trees. Its average length is seven cubits, though some are longer, others shorter. It is so thick that a child ten years old could hardly put his arms round it. It has two teeth, one in the upper and one in the lower jaw. Everything it seizes with these teeth it devours. By day it remains in the mud of the river, but at night it comes out, seizes whatever it comes across, whether ox or camel, drags it into the river, and devours it all except the intestines. It is caught with a large hook baited with a lamb or kid attached by iron chains. After it has been caught, it is hung up for thirty days with vessels placed underneath, into which as much oil from the body drips as would fill ten Attic kotylae. At the end of the thirty days, the worm is thrown away, the vessels of oil are sealed arid taken as a present to the king of India, who alone is allowed to use it. This oil sets everything alight----wood or animals----over which it is poured, and the flame can only be extinguished by throwing a quantity of thick mud on it.

There are trees in India as high as cedars or cypresses, with leaves like those of the palm-tree, except that they are a little broader and have no shoots. They flower like the male laurel, but have no fruit. The tree is called by the Indians karpion, by the Greeks myrorodon (unguent-rose); it is not common. Drops of oil ooze out of it, which are wiped off with wool and then squeezed into stone alabaster boxes. The oil is reddish, rather thick, and so fragrant that it scents the air to a distance of five stades. Only the king and his family are allowed to use it. The king of India sent some to the king of Persia, and Ctesias, who saw it, says that he cannot compare the perfume with any other.

The Indians also have very excellent cheese and sweet wine, both of which Ctesias tested himself.

There is a square fountain in India, about five ells in circumference. The water is in a rock, about three cubits' depth down, and the water itself three fathoms. The Indians of highest rank----men, women, and children----bathe in it [not only for cleanliness, but as a preventive of disease]. They plunge feet foremost into the water, and when they jump into it, it throws them out again on to dry land, not only human beings, but every animal, living or dead, in fact, everything that is thrown into it except iron, silver, gold, and copper, which sink to the bottom. The water is very cold, and agreeable to drink; it makes a loud noise like that of water boiling in a caldron. It cures leprosy and scab. In Indian it is called ballade, and in Greek ophelime (useful).

In the mountains where the Indian reed grows there dwell a people about 30,000 in number. Their women only have children once in their life, which are born with beautiful teeth in the upper and lower jaw. Both male and female children have white hair ,on the head and eyebrows. Up to the age of thirty the men have white hair all over the body; it then begins to turn black, and at the age of sixty it is quite black. Both men and women have eight fingers and eight toes. They are very warlike, and 5000 of them----bowmen and spearmen----accompany the king of India on his military expeditions. Their ears are so long that their arms are covered with them as far as the elbow, and also their backs, and one ear touches the other.

[In Ethiopia there is an animal called crocottas, vulgarly kynolykos (dog-wolf), of amazing strength. It is said to imitate the human voice, to call men by name at night, and to devour those who approach it. It is as brave as a lion, as swift as a horse, and as strong as a bull. It cannot be overcome by any weapon of steel. In Chalcis in Euboea there are sheep which have no gall-bladder, and their flesh is so bitter that even the dogs refuse to eat it. They also say that beyond the gates of

Mauretania the rain is abundant in summer, arid that it is scorching hot in winter. Among the Cyonians there is a fountain which gives out oil instead of water, which the people use in all their food. In Metadrida there is another fountain, some little distance from the sea, the flow of which is so violent at midnight that it casts up on land fishes in such numbers that the inhabitants, unable to pick them up, leave most of them to rot on the ground.]

Ctesias relates these fables as perfect truth, adding that he himself had seen with his own eyes some of the things he describes, and had been informed of the rest by eye-witnesses. He says that he has omitted many far more marvelous things, for fear that those who had not seen them might think that his account was utterly untrustworthy.

ISLAND OF THE SUN BY IAMBULUS; SUMMARIZED BY DIODORUS SICULUS

Diodorus, , Charles H. Oldfather, Charles L. Sherman, Russel M. Geer, Francis R. Walton, and C B. Welles. *Library of History*. London: W. Heinemann, 1933. Print.

55 1 But with regard to the island which has been discovered in the ocean to the south and the marvelous tales told concerning it, we shall now endeavor to give a brief account, after we have first set forth accurately the causes which led to its discovery. There was a certain Iambulus who from his boyhood up had been devoted to the pursuit of education, and after the death of his father, who had been a merchant, he also gave himself to that calling; and while journeying inland to the spice-bearing region of Arabia he and his companions on the trip were taken captive by some robbers. Now at first he and one of his fellow-captives were appointed to be herdsmen, but later he and his companion were made captive by certain Ethiopians and led off to the coast of Ethiopia. They were kidnapped in order that, being of an alien people, they might affect the purification of the land. For among the Ethiopians who lived in that place there was a custom, which had been handed down from ancient times, and had been ratified by oracles of the gods, over a period of twenty generations or six hundred years, the generation being reckoned at thirty years; and at the time when the purification by means of the two men was to take place, a boat had been built for them sufficient in size and strong enough to withstand the storms at sea, one which could easily be manned by two men; and then loading it with food enough to maintain two men for six months and putting them on board they commanded them to set out to sea as the oracle had ordered. Furthermore, they commanded them to steer towards the south; for, they were told, they would come to a happy island and to men of honorable character, and

among them they would lead a blessed existence. And in like manner, they stated, their own people, in case the men whom they sent forth should arrive safely at the island, would enjoy peace and a happy life in every respect throughout six hundred years; but if, dismayed at the extent of the sea, they should turn back on their course they would, as impious men and destroyers of the entire nation, suffer the severest penalties. Accordingly, the Ethiopians, they say, held a great festal assembly by the sea, and after offering costly sacrifices they crowned with flowers the men who were to seek out the island and effect the purification of the nation and then sent them forth. And these men, after having sailed over a vast sea and been tossed about four months by storms, were carried to the island about which they had been informed beforehand; it was round in shape and had a circumference of about five thousand stades.

56 1 But when they were now drawing near to the island, the account proceeds, some of the natives met them and drew their boat to land; and the inhabitants of the island, thronging together, were astonished at the arrival of the strangers, but they treated them honorably and shared with them the necessities of life which their country afforded. The dwellers upon this island differ greatly both in the characteristics of their bodies and in their manners from the men in our part of the inhabited world; for they are all nearly alike in the shape of their bodies and are over four cubits in height, but the bones of the body have the ability to bend to a certain extent and then straighten out again, like the sinewy parts. They are also exceedingly tender in respect to their bodies and yet more vigorous than is the case among us; for when they have seized any object in their hands no man can extract it from the grasp of their fingers. There is absolutely no hair on any part of their bodies except on the head, eyebrows and eyelids, and on the chin, but the other parts of the body are so smooth that not even the least down can be seen on them. They are also remarkably beautiful and well-proportioned in the outline of the body. The openings of their ears are much more spacious

than ours and growths have developed that serve as valves, so to speak, to close them. And they have a peculiarity in regard to the tongue, partly the work of nature and congenital with them and partly intentionally brought about by artifice; among them, namely, the tongue is double for a certain distance, but they divide the inner portions still further, with the result that it becomes a double tongue as far as the base. Consequently they are very versatile as to the sounds they can utter, since they imitate not only every articulate language used by man but also the varied chatterings of the birds, and, in general, they reproduce any peculiarity of sounds. And the most remarkable thing of all is that at one and the same time they can converse perfectly with two persons who fall in with them, both answering questions and discoursing pertinently on the circumstances of the moment; for with one division of the tongue they can converse with the one person, and likewise with the other talk with the second.

Their climate is most temperate, we are told, considering that they live at the equator, and they suffer neither from heat nor from cold. Moreover, the fruits in their island ripen throughout the entire year, even as the poet writes,

Here pear on pear grows old, and apple close
On apple, yea, and clustered grapes on grapes,
And fig on fig.

And with them the day is always the same length as the night, and at midday no shadow is cast of any object because the sun is in the zenith.

57 These islanders, they go on to say, live in groups which are based on kinship and on political organizations, no more than four hundred kinsmen being gathered together in this way; and the members spend their time in the meadows, the land supplying them with many things for sustenance; for by reason of the fertility of the island and the mildness of the climate, food-stuffs are produced of themselves in greater quantity than

is sufficient for their needs. For instance, a reed grows there in abundance, and bears a fruit in great plenty that is very similar to the white vetch. Now when they have gathered this they steep it in warm water until it has become the size of a pigeon's egg; then after they have crushed it and rubbed it skillfully with their hands, they mold it into loaves, which are baked and eaten, and they are of surprising sweetness. There are also in the island, they say, abundant springs of water, the warm springs serving well for bathing and the relief of fatigue, the cold excelling in sweetness and possessing the power to contribute to good health. Moreover, the inhabitants give attention to every branch of learning and especially to astrology; and they use letters which, according to the value of the sounds they represent, are twenty-eight in number, but the characters are only seven, each one of which can be formed in four different ways. Nor do they write their lines horizontally, as we do, but from the top to the bottom perpendicularly. And the inhabitants, they tell us, are extremely long-lived, living even to the age of one hundred and fifty years, and experiencing for the most part no illness. Anyone also among them who has become crippled or suffers, in general, from any physical infirmity is forced by them, in accordance with an inexorable law, to remove himself from life. And there is also a law among them that they should live only for a stipulated number of years, and that at the completion of this period they should make away with themselves of their own accord, by a strange manner of death; for there grows among them a plant of a peculiar nature, and whenever a man lies down upon it, imperceptibly and gently he falls asleep and dies.

58 They do not marry, we are told, but possess their children in common, and maintaining the children who are born as if they belonged to all, they love them equally; and while the children are infants those who suckle the babes often change them around in order that not even the mothers may know their own offspring. Consequently, since there is no rivalry among them, they never experience civil disorders and they never cease placing the highest value upon internal harmony.

There are also animals among them, we are told, which are small in size but the object of wonder by reason of the nature of their bodies and the potency of their blood; for they are round in form and very similar to tortoises, but they are marked on the surface by two diagonal yellow stripes, at each end of which they have an eye and a mouth; consequently, though seeing with four eyes and using as many mouths, yet it gathers its food into one gullet, and down this its nourishment is swallowed and all flows together into one stomach; and in like manner its other organs and all its inner parts are single. It also has beneath it all around its body many feet, by means of which it can move in whatever direction it pleases. And the blood of this animal, they say, has a marvelous potency; for it immediately glues on to its place any living member that has been severed; even if a hand or the like should happen to have been cut off, by the use of this blood it is glued on again, provided that the cut is fresh, and the same thing is true of such other parts of the body as are not connected with the regions which are vital and sustain the person's life. Each group of the inhabitants also keeps a bird of great size and of a nature peculiar to itself, by means of which a test is made of the infant children to learn what their spiritual disposition is; for they place them upon the birds, and such of them as are able to endure the flight through the air as the birds take wing they rear, but such as become nauseated and filled with consternation they cast out, as not likely either to live many years and being, besides, of no account because of their dispositions.

In each group the oldest man regularly exercises the leadership, just as if he were a kind of king, and is obeyed by all the members; and when the first such ruler makes an end of his life in accordance with the law upon the completion of his one hundred and fiftieth year, the next oldest succeeds to the leadership. The sea about the island has strong currents and is subject to great flooding and ebbing of the tides and is sweet in taste. And as for the stars of our heavens, the Bears and many more, we are informed, are not visible at all. The number of these islands was seven, and they are very much the same in size and at about equal distances from one another, and all follow the same customs and laws.

59 Although all the inhabitants enjoy an abundant provision of everything from what grows of itself in these islands, yet they do not indulge in the enjoyment of this abundance without restraint, but they practice simplicity and take for their food only what suffices for their needs. Meat and whatever else is roasted or boiled in water are prepared by them, but all the other dishes ingeniously concocted by professional cooks, such as sauces and the various kinds of seasonings, they have no notion whatsoever. And they worship as gods that which encompasses all things and the sun, and, in general, all the heavenly bodies. Fishes of every kind in great numbers are caught by them by sundry devices and not a few birds. There is also found among them an abundance of fruit trees growing wild, and olive trees and vines grow there, from which they make both olive oil and wine in abundance. Snakes also, we are told, which are of immense size and yet do no harm to the inhabitants, have a meat which is edible and exceedingly sweet. And their clothing they make themselves from a certain reed which contains in the center a downy substance that is bright to the eye and soft, which they gather and mingle with crushed sea-shells and thus make remarkable garments of a purple hue. As for the animals of the islands, their natures are peculiar and so amazing as to defy credence.

All the details of their diet, we are told, follow a prescribed arrangement, since they do not all take their food at the same time nor is it always the same; but it has been ordained that on certain fixed days they shall eat at one time fish, at another time fowl, sometimes the flesh of land animals, and sometimes olives and the most simple side-dishes. They also take turns in ministering to the needs of one another, some of them fishing, others working at the crafts, others occupying themselves in other useful tasks, and still others, with the exception of those who have come to old age, performing the services of the group in a definite cycle. And at the festivals and feasts which are held among them, there are both pronounced and sung in honor of the gods' hymns and spoken laudations, and especially in honor of the sun, after whom they name both the islands and themselves.

They inter their dead at the time when the tide is at the ebb, burying them in the sand along the beach, the result being that at flood-tide the place has fresh sand heaped upon it. The reeds, they say, from which the fruit for their nourishment is derived, being a span in thickness increase at the times of full-moon and again decrease proportionately as it wanes. And the water of the warm springs, being sweet and health-giving, maintains its heat and never becomes cold, save when it is mixed with cold water or wine.

60 After remaining among this people for seven years, the account continues, Iambulus and his companion were ejected against their will, as being malefactors and as having been educated to evil habits. Consequently, after they had again fitted out their little boat they were compelled to take their leave, and when they had stored up provisions in it they continued their voyage for more than four months. Then they were shipwrecked upon a sandy and marshy region of India; and his companion lost his life in the surf, but Iambulus, having found his way to a certain village, was then brought by the natives into the presence of the king at Palibothra, a city which was distant a journey of many days from the sea. And since the king was friendly to the Greeks and devoted to learning he considered Iambulus worthy of cordial welcome; and at length, upon receiving a permission of safe-conduct, he passed over first of all into Persia and later arrived safe in Greece.

Now Iambulus felt that these matters deserved to be written down, and he added to his account not a few facts about India, facts of which all other men were ignorant at that time. But for our part, since we have fulfilled the promise made at the beginning of this Book, we shall bring it to a conclusion at this point.

ODYSSEY BY HOMER, BOOKS 9 – 12

Homer, , George E. Dimock, and A T. Murray. *Odyssey*. Cambridge, MA: Harvard University Press, 1919. Print.

BOOK 9 OF THE *ODYSSEY*

[1] Then Odysseus, of many wiles, answered him, and said: "Lord Alcinous, renowned above all men, verily this is a good thing, to listen to a minstrel such as this man is, like unto the gods in voice. For myself I declare that there is no greater fulfillment of delight than when joy possesses a whole people, and banqueters in the halls listen to a minstrel as they sit in order due, and by them tables are laden with bread and meat, and the cup-bearer draws wine from the bowl and bears it round and pours it into the cups. This seems to my mind the fairest thing there is. But thy heart is turned to ask of my grievous woes, that I may weep and groan the more. What, then, shall I tell thee first, what last? For woes full many have the heavenly gods given me. First now will I tell my name, that ye, too, may know it, and that I hereafter, when I have escaped from the pitiless day of doom, may be your host, though I dwell in a home that is afar.

[19] "I am Odysseus, son of Laertes, who is known among men for all manner of wiles, and my fame reaches unto heaven. But I dwell in clear-seen Ithaca, wherein is a mountain, Neriton, covered with waving forests, conspicuous from afar; and round it lie many isles hard by one another, Dulichium, and Same, and wooded Zacynthus. Ithaca itself lies close in to the mainland the furthest toward the gloom, but the others lie apart toward the Dawn and the sun—a rugged isle, but a good nurse of young men; and for myself no other thing can I see sweeter than one's own land. Of a truth Calypso, the beautiful goddess, sought to keep me by her in

her hollow caves, yearning that I should be her husband; and in like manner Circe would fain have held me back in her halls, the guileful lady of Aeaea, yearning that I should be her husband; but they could never persuade the heart within my breast. So true is it that naught is sweeter than a man's own land and his parents, even though it be in a rich house that he dwells afar in a foreign land away from his parents.

[36] "But come, let me tell thee also of my woeful home-coming, which Zeus laid upon me as I came from Troy. From Ilios the wind bore me and brought me to the Cicones, to Ismarus. There I sacked the city and slew the men; and from the city we took their wives and great store of treasure, and divided them among us, that so far as lay in me no man might go defrauded of an equal share. Then verily I gave command that we should flee with swift foot, but the others in their great folly did not hearken. But there much wine was drunk, and many sheep they slew by the shore, and sleek cattle of shambling gait.

[47] "Meanwhile the Cicones went and called to other Cicones who were their neighbors, at once more numerous and braver than they—men that dwelt inland and were skilled at fighting with their foes from chariots, and, if need were, on foot. So they came in the morning, as thick as leaves or flowers spring up in their season; and then it was that an evil fate from Zeus beset us luckless men, that we might suffer woes full many. They set their battle in array and fought by the swift ships, and each side hurled at the other with bronze-tipped spears. Now as long as it was morn and the sacred day was waxing, so long we held our ground and beat them off, though they were more than we. But when the sun turned to the time for the unyoking of oxen, then the Cicones prevailed and routed the Achaeans, and six of my well-greaved comrades perished from each ship; but the rest of us escaped death and fate. "Thence we sailed on, grieved at heart, glad to have escaped from death, though we had lost our dear comrades; nor did I let my curved ships pass on till we had called thrice on each of those hapless

comrades of ours who died on the plain, cut down by the Cicones.

[67] But against our ships Zeus, the cloud-gatherer, roused the North Wind with a wondrous tempest, and hid with clouds the land and the sea alike, and night rushed down from heaven. Then the ships were driven headlong, and their sails were torn to shreds by the violence of the wind. So we lowered the sails and stowed them aboard, in fear of death, and rowed the ships hurriedly toward the land. There for two nights and two days continuously we lay, eating our hearts for weariness and sorrow. But when now fair-tressed Dawn brought to its birth the third day, we set up the masts and hoisted the white sails, and took our seats, and the wind and the helmsmen steered the ships. And now all unscathed should I have reached my native land, but the wave and the current and the North Wind beat me back as I was rounding Malea, and drove me from my course past Cythera.

[82] "Thence for nine days' space I was borne by direful winds over the teeming deep; but on the tenth we set foot on the land of the Lotus-eaters, who eat a flowery food. There we went on shore and drew water, and straightway my comrades took their meal by the swift ships. But when we had tasted food and drink, I sent forth some of my comrades to go and learn who the men were, who here ate bread upon the earth; two men I chose, sending with them a third as a herald. So they went straightway and mingled with the Lotus-eaters, and the Lotus-eaters did not plan death for my comrades, but gave them of the lotus to taste. And whosoever of them ate of the honey-sweet fruit of the lotus, had no longer any wish to bring back word or to return, but there they were fain to abide among the Lotus-eaters, feeding on the lotus, and forgetful of their homeward way. These men, therefore, I brought back perforce to the ships, weeping, and dragged them beneath the benches and bound them fast in the hollow ships; and I bade the rest of my trusty comrades to embark with speed on the swift ships, lest perchance anyone should eat of the lotus and forget his

homeward way. So they went on board straightway and sat down upon the benches, and sitting well in order smote the grey sea with their oars.

[105] "Thence we sailed on, grieved at heart, and we came to the land of the Cyclopes, an overweening and lawless folk, who, trusting in the immortal gods, plant nothing with their hands nor plough; but all these things spring up for them without sowing or ploughing, wheat, and barley, and vines, which bear the rich clusters of wine, and the rain of Zeus gives them increase. Neither assemblies for council have they, nor appointed laws, but they dwell on the peaks of lofty mountains in hollow caves, and each one is lawgiver to his children and his wives, and they reck nothing one of another.

[116] "Now there is a level isle that stretches aslant outside the harbor, neither close to the shore of the land of the Cyclopes, nor yet far off, a wooded isle. Therein live wild goats innumerable, for the tread of men scares them not away, nor are hunters wont to come thither, men who endure toils in the woodland as they course over the peaks of the mountains. Neither with flocks is it held, nor with ploughed lands, but unsown and untilled all the days it knows naught of men, but feeds the bleating goats. For the Cyclopes have at hand no ships with vermilion cheeks, nor are there ship-wrights in their land who might build them well-benched ships, which should perform all their wants, passing to the cities of other folk, as men often cross the sea in ships to visit one another—craftsmen, who would have made of this isle also a fair settlement. For the isle is nowise poor, but would bear all things in season. In it are meadows by the shores of the grey sea, well-watered meadows and soft, where vines would never fail, and in it level ploughland, whence they might reap from season to season harvests exceeding deep, so rich is the soil beneath; and in it, too, is a harbor giving safe anchorage, where there is no need of moorings, either to throw out anchor-stones or to make fast stern cables, but one may beach

one's ship and wait until the sailors' minds bid them put out, and the breezes blow fair.

[140] "Now at the head of the harbor a spring of bright water flows forth from beneath a cave, and round about it poplars grow. Thither we sailed in, and some god guided us through the murky night; for there was no light to see, but a mist lay deep about the ships and the moon showed no light from heaven, but was shut in by clouds. Then no man's eyes beheld that island, nor did we see the long waves rolling on the beach, until we ran our well-benched ships on shore. And when we had beached the ships we lowered all the sails and ourselves went forth on the shore of the sea, and there we fell asleep and waited for the bright Dawn.

[152] "As soon as early Dawn appeared, the rosy-fingered, we roamed throughout the isle marveling at it; and the nymphs, the daughters of Zeus who bears the aegis, roused the mountain goats, that my comrades might have whereof to make their meal. Straightway we took from the ships our curved bows and long javelins, and arrayed in three bands we fell to smiting; and the god soon gave us game to satisfy our hearts. The ships that followed me were twelve, and to each nine goats fell by lot, but for me alone they chose out ten.

[161] "So then all day long till set of sun we sat feasting on abundant flesh and sweet wine. For not yet was the red wine spent from out our ships, but some was still left; for abundant store had we drawn in jars for each crew when we took the sacred citadel of the Cicones. And we looked across to the land of the Cyclopes, who dwelt close at hand, and marked the smoke, and the voice of men, and of the sheep, and of the goats. But when the sun set and darkness came on, then we lay down to rest on the shore of the sea. And as soon as early Dawn appeared, the rosy-fingered, I called my men together and spoke among them all: `Remain here now, all the rest of you, my trusty comrades, but I with my own ship and my own company will go and make trial of yonder men, to learn who

they are, whether they are cruel, and wild, and unjust, or whether they love strangers and fear the gods in their thoughts.'

[177] "So saying, I went on board the ship and bade my comrades themselves to embark, and to loose the stern cables. So they went on board straightway and sat down upon the benches, and sitting well in order smote the grey sea with their oars. But when we had reached the place, which lay close at hand, there on the land's edge hard by the sea we saw a high cave, roofed over with laurels, and there many flocks, sheep and goats alike, were wont to sleep. Round about it a high court was built with stones set deep in the earth, and with tall pines and high-crested oaks. There a monstrous man was wont to sleep, who shepherded his flocks alone and afar, and mingled not with others, but lived apart, with his heart set on lawlessness. For he was fashioned a wondrous monster, and was not like a man that lives by bread, but like a wooded peak of lofty mountains, which stands out to view alone, apart from the rest.

[193] "Then I bade the rest of my trusty comrades to remain there by the ship and to guard the ship, but I chose twelve of the best of my comrades and went my way. With me I had a goat-skin of the dark, sweet wine, which Maro, son of Euanthes, had given me, the priest of Apollo, the god who used to watch over Ismarus. And he had given it me because we had protected him with his child and wife out of reverence; for he dwelt in a wooded grove of Phoebus Apollo. And he gave me splendid gifts: of well-wrought gold he gave me seven talents, and he gave me a mixing-bowl all of silver; and besides these, wine, wherewith he filled twelve jars in all, wine sweet and unmixed, a drink divine. Not one of his slaves nor of the maids in his halls knew thereof, but himself and his dear wife, and one house-dame only. And as often as they drank that honey-sweet red wine he would fill one cup and pour it into twenty measures of water, and a smell would rise from the mixing-bowl marvelously sweet; then verily would

one not choose to hold back. With this wine I filled and took with me a great skin, and also provision in a scrip; for my proud spirit had a foreboding that presently a man would come to me clothed in great might, a savage man that knew naught of justice or of law.

[216] "Speedily we came to the cave, nor did we find him within, but he was pasturing his fat flocks in the fields. So we entered the cave and gazed in wonder at all things there. The crates were laden with cheeses, and the pens were crowded with lambs and kids. Each kind was penned separately: by themselves the firstlings, by themselves the later lambs, and by themselves again the newly weaned. And with whey were swimming all the well-wrought vessels, the milk-pails and the bowls into which he milked. Then my comrades spoke and besought me first of all to take of the cheeses and depart, and thereafter speedily to drive to the swift ship the kids and lambs from out the pens, and to sail over the salt water. But I did not listen to them—verily it would have been better far—to the end that I might see the man himself, and whether he would give me gifts of entertainment. Yet, as it fell, his appearing was not to prove a joy to my comrades.

[231] "Then we kindled a fire and offered sacrifice, and ourselves, too, took of the cheeses and ate, and thus we sat in the cave and waited for him until he came back, herding his flocks. He bore a mighty weight of dry wood to serve him at supper time, and flung it down with a crash inside the cave, but we, seized with terror, shrank back into a recess of the cave. But he drove his fat flocks into the wide cavern—all those that he milked; but the males—the rams and the goats—he left without in the deep court. Then he lifted on high and set in place the great door-stone, a mighty rock; two and twenty stout four-wheeled wagons could not lift it from the ground, such a towering mass of rock he set in the doorway. Thereafter he sat down and milked the ewes and bleating goats all in turn, and beneath each dam he placed her young. Then presently he curdled half the white milk, and gathered it in

wicker baskets and laid it away, and the other half he set in vessels that he might have it to take and drink, and that it might serve him for supper.

[250] But when he had busily performed his tasks, then he rekindled the fire, and caught sight of us, and asked: `Strangers, who are ye? Whence do ye sail over the watery ways? Is it on some business, or do ye wander at random over the sea, even as pirates, who wander, hazarding their lives and bringing evil to men of other lands?'

[256] "So he spoke, and in our breasts our spirit was broken for terror of his deep voice and monstrous self; yet even so I made answer and spoke to him, saying: `We, thou must know, are from Troy, Achaeans, driven wandering by all manner of winds over the great gulf of the sea. Seeking our home, we have come by another way, by other paths; so, I ween, Zeus was pleased to devise. And we declare that we are the men of Agamemnon, son of Atreus, whose fame is now mightiest under heaven, so great a city did he sack, and slew many people; but we on our part, thus visiting thee, have come as suppliants to thy knees, in the hope that thou wilt give us entertainment, or in other wise make some present, as is the due of strangers. Nay, mightiest one, reverence the gods; we are thy suppliants; and Zeus is the avenger of suppliants and strangers—Zeus, the strangers' god—who ever attends upon reverend strangers.'

[272] "So I spoke, and he straightway made answer with pitiless heart: `A fool art thou, stranger, or art come from afar, seeing that thou biddest me either to fear or to shun the gods. For the Cyclopes reck not of Zeus, who bears the aegis, nor of the blessed gods, since verily we are better far than they. Nor would I, to shun the wrath of Zeus, spare either thee or thy comrades, unless my own heart should bid me. But tell me where thou didst moor thy well-wrought ship on thy coming. Was it haply at a remote part of the land, or close by? I fain would know.'

[281] "So he spoke, tempting me, but he trapped me not because of my great cunning; and I made answer again in crafty words: `My ship Poseidon, the earth-shaker, dashed to pieces, casting her upon the rocks at the border of your land; for he brought her close to the headland, and the wind drove her in from the sea. But I, with these men here, escaped utter destruction.'

[287] "So I spoke, but from his pitiless heart he made no answer, but sprang up and put forth his hands upon my comrades. Two of them at once he seized and dashed to the earth like puppies, and the brain flowed forth upon the ground and wetted the earth. Then he cut them limb from limb and made ready his supper, and ate them as a mountain-nurtured lion, leaving naught—ate the entrails, and the flesh, and the marrowy bones. And we with wailing held up our hands to Zeus, beholding his cruel deeds; and helplessness possessed our souls. But when the Cyclops had filled his huge maw by eating human flesh and thereafter drinking pure milk, he lay down within the cave, stretched out among the sheep. And I formed a plan in my great heart to steal near him, and draw my sharp sword from beside my thigh and smite him in the breast, where the midriff holds the liver, feeling for the place with my hand. But a second thought checked me, for right there should we, too, have perished in utter ruin. For we should not have been able to thrust back with our hands from the high door the mighty stone which he had set there. So then, with wailing, we waited for the bright Dawn.

[308] "As soon as early Dawn appeared, the rosy-fingered, he rekindled the fire and milked his goodly flocks all in turn, and beneath each dam placed her young. Then, when he had busily performed his tasks, again he seized two men at once and made ready his meal. And when he had made his meal he drove his fat flocks forth from the cave, easily moving away the great door-stone; and then he put it in place again, as one might set the lid upon a quiver. Then with loud whistling the

Cyclops turned his fat flocks toward the mountain, and I was left there, devising evil in the deep of my heart, if in any way I might take vengeance on him, and Athena grant me glory.

[318] "Now this seemed to my mind the best plan. There lay beside a sheep-pen a great club of the Cyclops, a staff of green olive-wood, which he had cut to carry with him when dry; and as we looked at it we thought it as large as is the mast of a black ship of twenty oars, a merchantman, broad of beam, which crosses over the great gulf; so huge it was in length and in breadth to look upon. To this I came, and cut off therefrom about a fathom's length and handed it to my comrades, bidding them dress it down; and they made it smooth, and I, standing by, sharpened it at the point, and then straightway took it and hardened it in the blazing fire. Then I laid it carefully away, hiding it beneath the dung, which lay in great heaps throughout the cave. And I bade my comrades cast lots among them, which of them should have the hardihood with me to lift the stake and grind it into his eye when sweet sleep should come upon him. And the lot fell upon those whom I myself would fain have chosen; four they were, and I was numbered with them as the fifth. At even then he came, herding his flocks of goodly fleece, and straightway drove into the wide cave his fat flocks one and all, and left not one without in the deep court, either from some foreboding or because a god so bade him. Then he lifted on high and set in place the great door-stone, and sitting down he milked the ewes and bleating goats all in turn, and beneath each dam he placed her young. But when he had busily performed his tasks, again he seized two men at once and made ready his supper.

[345] "Then I drew near and spoke to the Cyclops, holding in my hands an ivy bowl of the dark wine: `Cyclops, take and drink wine after thy meal of human flesh, that thou mayest know what manner of drink this is which our ship contained. It was to thee that I was bringing it as a drink offering, in the hope that, touched with pity, thou mightest send me on my way home; but thou ragest in a way that is past all bearing.

Cruel man, how shall any one of all the multitudes of men ever come to thee again hereafter, seeing that thou hast wrought lawlessness?'

[354] "So I spoke, and he took the cup and drained it, and was wondrously pleased as he drank the sweet draught, and asked me for it again a second time: 'Give it me again with a ready heart, and tell me thy name straightway, that I may give thee a stranger's gift whereat thou mayest be glad. For among the Cyclopes the earth, the giver of grain, bears the rich clusters of wine, and the rain of Zeus gives them increase; but this is a streamlet of ambrosia and nectar.'

[360] "So he spoke, and again I handed him the flaming wine. Thrice I brought and gave it him, and thrice he drained it in his folly. But when the wine had stolen about the wits of the Cyclops, then I spoke to him with gentle words: `Cyclops, thou askest me of my glorious name, and I will tell it thee; and do thou give me a stranger's gift, even as thou didst promise. Noman is my name, Noman do they call me—my mother and my father, and all my comrades as well.' "

[368] So I spoke, and he straightway answered me with pitiless heart: `Noman will I eat last among his comrades, and the others before him; this shall be thy gift.'

[371] "He spoke, and reeling fell upon his back, and lay there with his thick neck bent aslant, and sleep, that conquers all, laid hold on him. And from his gullet came forth wine and bits of human flesh, and he vomited in his drunken sleep. Then verily I thrust in the stake under the deep ashes until it should grow hot, and heartened all my comrades with cheering words, that I might see no man flinch through fear. But when presently that stake of olive-wood was about to catch fire, green though it was, and began to glow terribly, then verily I drew nigh, bringing the stake from the fire, and my comrades stood round me and a god breathed into us great courage. They took the stake of olive-wood, sharp at the point, and

thrust it into his eye, while I, throwing my weight upon it from above, whirled it round, as when a man bores a ship's timber with a drill, while those below keep it spinning with the thong, which they lay hold of by either end, and the drill runs around unceasingly. Even so we took the fiery-pointed stake and whirled it around in his eye, and the blood flowed around the heated thing. And his eyelids wholly and his brows roundabout did the flame singe as the eyeball burned, and its roots crackled in the fire. And as when a smith dips a great axe or an adze in cold water amid loud hissing to temper it—for therefrom comes the strength of iron—even so did his eye hiss round the stake of olive-wood.

[395] "Terribly then did he cry aloud, and the rock rang around; and we, seized with terror, shrank back, while he wrenched from his eye the stake, all befouled with blood, and flung it from him, wildly waving his arms. Then he called aloud to the Cyclopes, who dwelt round about him in caves among the windy heights, and they heard his cry and came thronging from every side, and standing around the cave asked him what ailed him: `What so sore distress is thine, Polyphemus, that thou criest out thus through the immortal night, and makest us sleepless? Can it be that some mortal man is driving off thy flocks against thy will, or slaying thee thyself by guile or by might?'

[408] "Then from out the cave the mighty Polyphemus answered them: `My friends, it is Noman that is slaying me by guile and not by force.'

[409] "And they made answer and addressed him with winged words: `If, then, no man does violence to thee in thy loneliness, sickness which comes from great Zeus thou mayest in no wise escape. Nay, do thou pray to our father, the lord Poseidon.'

[413] "So they spoke and went their way; and my heart laughed within me that my name and cunning device had so

beguiled. But the Cyclops, groaning and travailing in anguish, groped with his hands and took away the stone from the door, and himself sat in the doorway with arms outstretched in the hope of catching anyone who sought to go forth with the sheep—so witless, forsooth, he thought in his heart to find me. But I took counsel how all might be the very best, if I might haply find some way of escape from death for my comrades and for myself. And I wove all manner of wiles and counsel, as a man will in a matter of life and death; for great was the evil that was nigh us. And this seemed to my mind the best plan. Rams there were, well-fed and thick of fleece, fine beasts and large, with wool dark as the violet. These I silently bound together with twisted withes on which the Cyclops, that monster with his heart set on lawlessness, was wont to sleep. Three at a time I took. The one in the middle in each case bore a man, and the other two went, one on either side, saving my comrades. Thus every three sheep bore a man. But as for me—there was a ram, far the best of all the flock; him I grasped by the back, and curled beneath his shaggy belly, lay there face upwards with steadfast heart, clinging fast with my hands to his wondrous fleece. So then, with wailing, we waited for the bright dawn.

[437] "As soon as early Dawn appeared, the rosy-fingered, then the males of the flock hastened forth to pasture and the females bleated unmilked about the pens, for their udders were bursting. And their master, distressed with grievous pains, felt along the backs of all the sheep as they stood up before him, but in his folly he marked not this, that my men were bound beneath the breasts of his fleecy sheep. Last of all the flock the ram went forth, burdened with the weight of his fleece and my cunning self. And mighty Polyphemus, as he felt along his back, spoke to him, saying: `Good ram, why pray is it that thou goest forth thus through the cave the last of the flock? Thou hast not heretofore been wont to lag behind the sheep, but wast ever far the first to feed on the tender bloom of the grass, moving with long strides, and ever the first didst reach the streams of the river, and the first didst long to return to the

fold at evening. But now thou art last of all. Surely thou art sorrowing for the eye of thy master, which an evil man blinded along with his miserable fellows, when he had overpowered my wits with wine, even Noman, who, I tell thee, has not yet escaped destruction. If only thou couldst feel as I do, and couldst get thee power of speech to tell me where he skulks away from my wrath, then should his brains be dashed on the ground here and there throughout the cave, when I had smitten him, and my heart should be lightened of the woes which good-for-naught Noman has brought me.'

[461] "So saying, he sent the ram forth from him. And when we had gone a little way from the cave and the court, I first loosed myself from under the ram and set my comrades free. Speedily then we drove off those long-shanked sheep, rich with fat, turning full often to look about until we came to the ship. And welcome to our dear comrades was the sight of us who had escaped death, but for the others they wept and wailed; yet I would not suffer them to weep, but with a frown forbade each man. Rather I bade them to fling on board with speed the many sheep of goodly fleece, and sail over the salt water. So they went on board straightway and sat down upon the benches, and sitting well in order smote the grey sea with their oars. But when I was as far away as a man's voice carries when he shouts, then I spoke to the Cyclops with mocking words: `Cyclops, that man, it seems, was no weakling, whose comrades thou wast minded to devour by brutal strength in thy hollow cave. Full surely were thy evil deeds to fall on thine own head, thou cruel wretch, who didst not shrink from eating thy guests in thine own house. Therefore has Zeus taken vengeance on thee, and the other gods.'

[480] "So I spoke, and he waxed the more wroth at heart, and broke off the peak of a high mountain and hurled it at us, and cast it in front of the dark-prowed ship. And the sea surged beneath the stone as it fell, and the backward flow, like a flood from the deep, bore the ship swiftly landwards and drove it upon the shore. But I seized a long pole in my hands and

shoved the ship off and along the shore, and with a nod of my head I roused my comrades, and bade them fall to their oars that we might escape out of our evil plight. And they bent to their oars and rowed. But when, as we fared over the sea, we were twice as far distant, then was I fain to call to the Cyclops, though round about me my comrades, one after another, sought to check me with gentle words: 'Reckless one, why wilt thou provoke to wrath a savage man, who but now hurled his missile into the deep and drove our ship back to the land, and verily we thought that we had perished there? And had he heard one of us uttering a sound or speaking, he would have hurled a jagged rock and crushed our heads and the timbers of our ship, so mightily does he throw.'

[500] "So they spoke, but they could not persuade my great-hearted spirit; and I answered him again with angry heart: `Cyclops, if any one of mortal men shall ask thee about the shameful blinding of thine eye, say that Odysseus, the sacker of cities, blinded it, even the son of Laertes, whose home is in Ithaca.'

[506] "So I spoke, and he groaned and said in answer: `Lo now, verily a prophecy uttered long ago is come upon me. There lived here a soothsayer, a good man and tall, Telemus, son of Eurymus, who excelled all men in soothsaying, and grew old as a seer among the Cyclopes. He told me that all these things should be brought to pass in days to come, that by the hands of Odysseus I should lose my sight. But I ever looked for some tall and comely man to come hither, clothed in great might, but now one that is puny, a man of naught and a weakling, has blinded me of my eye when he had overpowered me with wine. Yet come hither, Odysseus that I may set before thee gifts of entertainment, and may speed thy sending hence, that the glorious Earth-shaker may grant it thee. For I am his son, and he declares himself my father; and he himself will heal me, if it be his good pleasure, but none other either of the blessed gods or of mortal men.'

[523] "So he spoke, and I answered him and said: `Would that I were able to rob thee of soul and life, and to send thee to the house of Hades, as surely as not even the Earth-shaker shall heal thine eye.'

[526] "So I spoke, and he then prayed to the lord Poseidon, stretching out both his hands to the starry heaven: `Hear me, Poseidon, earth-enfolder, thou dark-haired god, if indeed I am thy son and thou declarest thyself my father; grant that Odysseus, the sacker of cities, may never reach his home, even the son of Laertes, whose home is in Ithaca; but if it is his fate to see his friends and to reach his well-built house and his native land, late may he come and in evil case, after losing all his comrades, in a ship that is another's; and may he find woes in his house.'

[536] "So he spoke in prayer, and the dark-haired god heard him. But the Cyclops lifted on high again a far greater stone, and swung and hurled it, putting into the throw measureless strength. He cast it a little behind the dark-prowed ship, and barely missed the end of the steering-oar. And the sea surged beneath the stone as it fell, and the wave bore the ship onward and drove it to the shore.

[543] "Now when we had come to the island, where our other well-benched ships lay all together, and round about them our comrades, ever expecting us, sat weeping, then, on coming thither, we beached our ship on the sands, and ourselves went forth upon the shore of the sea. Then we took from out the hollow ship the flocks of the Cyclops, and divided them, that so far as in me lay no man might go defrauded of an equal share. But the ram my well-greaved comrades gave to me alone, when the flocks were divided, as a gift apart; and on the shore I sacrificed him to Zeus, son of Cronus, god of the dark clouds, who is lord of all, and burned the thigh-pieces. Howbeit he heeded not my sacrifice, but was planning how all my well-benched ships might perish and my trusty comrades.

[556] "So, then, all day long till set of sun we sat feasting on abundant flesh and sweet wine; but when the sun set and darkness came on, then we lay down to rest on the shore of the sea. And as soon as early Dawn appeared, the rosy-fingered, I roused my comrades, and bade them themselves to embark and to loose the stern cables. So they went on board straightway and sat down upon the benches, and sitting well in order smote the grey sea with their oars. Thence we sailed on, grieved at heart, glad to have escaped death, though we had lost our dear comrades.

BOOK 10 OF THE *ODYSSEY*

[1] "Then to the Aeolian isle we came, where dwelt Aeolus, son of Hippotas, dear to the immortal gods, in a floating island, and all around it is a wall of unbreakable bronze, and the cliff runs up sheer. Twelve children of his, too, there are in the halls, six daughters and six sturdy sons, and he gave his daughters to his sons to wife. These, then, feast continually by their dear father and good mother, and before them lies boundless good cheer. And the house, filled with the savor of feasting, resounds all about even in the outer court by day, and by night again they sleep beside their chaste wives on blankets and on corded bedsteads.

[13] "To their city, then, and fair palace did we come, and for a full month he made me welcome and questioned me about each thing, about Ilios, and the ships of the Argives, and the return of the Achaeans. And I told him the entire tale in due order. But when I, on my part, asked him that I might depart and bade him send me on my way, he, too, denied me nothing, but furthered my sending. He gave me a wallet, made of the hide of an ox nine years old, which he flayed, and therein he bound the paths of the blustering winds; for the son of Cronus had made him keeper of the winds, both to still and to rouse whatever one he will. And in my hollow ship he bound it fast with a bright cord of silver that not a breath might escape,

were it never so slight. But for my furtherance he sent forth the breath of the West Wind to blow, that it might bear on their way both ships and men. Yet this he was not to bring to pass, for we were lost through our own folly.

[28] "For nine days we sailed, night and day alike, and now on the tenth our native land came in sight, and lo, we were so near that we saw men tending the beacon fires. Then upon me came sweet sleep in my weariness, for I had ever kept in hand the sheet of the ship, and had yielded it to none other of my comrades, that we might the sooner come to our native land. But my comrades meanwhile began to speak one to another, and said that I was bringing home for myself gold and silver as gifts from Aeolus, the great-hearted son of Hippotas. And thus would one speak, with a glance at his neighbor: `Out on it, how beloved and honored this man is by all men, to whose city and land soever he comes! Much goodly treasure is he carrying with him from the land of Troy from out the spoil, while we, who have accomplished the same journey as he, are returning, bearing with us empty hands. And now Aeolus has given him these gifts, granting them freely of his love. Nay, come, let us quickly see what is here, what store of gold and silver is in the wallet.'

[46] "So they spoke, and the evil counsel of my comrades prevailed. They loosed the wallet, and all the winds leapt forth, and swiftly the storm-wind seized them and bore them weeping out to sea away from their native land; but as for me, I awoke, and pondered in my goodly heart whether I should fling myself from the ship and perish in the sea, or endure in silence and still remain among the living. However, I endured and abode, and covering my head lay down in the ship. But the ships were borne by an evil blast of wind back to the Aeolian isle; and my comrades groaned.

[56] "There we went ashore and drew water, and straightway my comrades took their meal by the swift ships. But when we had tasted of food and drink, I took with me a herald and one

companion and went to the glorious palace of Aeolus, and I found him feasting beside his wife and his children. So we entered the house and sat down by the doorposts on the threshold, and they were amazed at heart, and questioned us: `How hast thou come hither, Odysseus? What cruel god assailed thee? Surely we sent thee forth with kindly care, that thou mightest reach thy native land and thy home, and whatever place thou wouldest.'

[66] "So said they, but I with a sorrowing heart spoke among them and said: `Bane did my evil comrades work me, and therewith sleep accursed; but bring ye healing, my friends, for with you is the power.'

[70] "So I spoke and addressed them with gentle words, but they were silent. Then their father answered and said: `Begone from our island with speed, thou vilest of all that live. In no wise may I help or send upon his way that man who is hated of the blessed gods. Begone, for thou comest hither as one hated of the immortals.'

[76] "So saying, he sent me forth from the house, groaning heavily. Thence we sailed on, grieved at heart. And worn was the spirit of the men by the grievous rowing, because of our own folly, for no longer appeared any breeze to bear us on our way. So for six days we sailed, night and day alike, and on the seventh we came to the lofty citadel of Lamus, even to Telepylus of the Laestrygonians, where herdsman calls to herdsman as he drives in his flock, and the other answers as he drives his forth. There a man who never slept could have earned a double wage, one by herding cattle, and one by pasturing white sheep; for the out goings of the night and of the day are close together.

[87] "When we had come thither into the goodly harbor, about which on both sides a sheer cliff runs continuously, and projecting headlands opposite to one another stretch out at the mouth, and the entrance is narrow, then all the rest steered

their curved ships in, and the ships were moored within the hollow harbor close together; for therein no wave ever swelled, great or small, but all about was a bright calm. But I alone moored my black ship outside, there on the border of the land, making the cables fast to the rock. Then I climbed to a rugged height, a point of outlook, and there took my stand; from thence no works of oxen or of men appeared; smoke alone we saw springing up from the land. So then I sent forth some of my comrades to go and learn who the men were, who here ate bread upon the earth—two men I chose, and sent with them a third as a herald. Now when they had gone ashore, they went along a smooth road by which wagons were wont to bring wood down to the city from the high mountains.

[105] "And before the city they met a maiden drawing water, the goodly daughter of Laestrygonian Antiphates, who had come down to the fair-flowing spring Artacia, from whence they were wont to bear water to the town. So they came up to her and spoke to her, and asked her who was king of this folk, and who they were of whom he was lord. And she showed them forth with the high-roofed house of her father. Now when they had entered the glorious house, they found there his wife, huge as the peak of a mountain, and they were aghast at her. At once she called from the place of assembly the glorious Antiphates, her husband, and he devised for them woeful destruction. Straightway he seized one of my comrades and made ready his meal, but the other two sprang up and came in flight to the ships.

[118] Then he raised a cry throughout the city, and as they heard it the mighty Laestrygonians came thronging from all sides, a host past counting, not like men but like the Giants. They hurled at us from the cliffs with rocks huge as a man could lift, and at once there rose throughout the ships a dreadful din, alike from men that were dying and from ships that were being crushed. And spearing them like fishes they bore them home, a loathly meal. Now while they were slaying those within the deep harbor, I meanwhile drew my sharp

sword from beside my thigh, and cut therewith the cables of my dark-prowed ship; and quickly calling to my comrades bade them fall to their oars, that we might escape from out our evil plight. And they all tossed the sea with their oar-blades in fear of death, and joyfully seaward, away from the beetling cliffs, my ship sped on; but all those other ships were lost together there.

[133] "Thence we sailed on, grieved at heart, glad to have escaped death, though we had lost our dear comrades; and we came to the isle of Aeaea, where dwelt fair-tressed Circe, a dread goddess of human speech, own sister to Aeetes of baneful mind; and both are sprung from Helius, who gives light to mortals, and from Perse, their mother, whom Oceanus begot. Here we put in to shore with our ship in silence, into a harbor where ships may lie, and some god guided us. Then we disembarked, and lay there for two days and two nights, eating our hearts for weariness and sorrow.

[144] "But when fair-tressed Dawn brought to its birth the third day, then I took my spear and my sharp sword, and quickly went up from the ship to a place of wide prospect, in the hope that I might see the works of men, and hear their voice. So I climbed to a rugged height, a place of outlook, and there took my stand, and I saw smoke rising from the broad-wayed earth in the halls of Circe, through the thick brush and the wood. And I debated in mind and heart, whether I should go and make search, when I had seen the flaming smoke. And as I pondered, this seemed to me to be the better way, to go first to the swift ship and the shore of the sea, and give my comrades their meal, and send them forth to make search.

[156] "But when, as I went, I was near to the curved ship, then some god took pity on me in my loneliness, and sent a great, high-horned stag into my very path. He was coming down to the river from his pasture in the wood to drink, for the might of the sun oppressed him; and as he came out I struck him on the spine in the middle of the back, and the bronze spear

passed right through him, and down he fell in the dust with a moan, and his spirit flew from him. Then I planted my foot upon him, and drew the bronze spear forth from the wound, and left it there to lie on the ground. But for myself, I plucked twigs and osiers, and weaving a rope as it were a fathom in length, well twisted from end to end, I bound together the feet of the monstrous beast, and went my way to the black ship, bearing him across my back and leaning on my spear, since in no wise could I hold him on my shoulder with one hand, for he was a very mighty beast. Down I flung him before the ship, and heartened my comrades with gentle words, coming up to each man in turn: `Friends, not yet shall we go down to the house of Hades, despite our sorrows, before the day of fate comes upon us. Nay, come, while there is yet food and drink in our swift ship, let us bethink us of food that we pine not with hunger.'

[178] "So I spoke, and they quickly hearkened to my words. From their faces they drew their cloaks, and marveled at the stag on the shore of the unresting sea, for he was a very mighty beast. But when they had satisfied their eyes with gazing, they washed their hands, and made ready a glorious feast. So then all day long till set of sun we sat feasting on abundant flesh and sweet wine. But when the sun set and darkness came on, then we lay down to rest on the shore of the sea. And as soon as early Dawn appeared, the rosy-fingered, I called my men together, and spoke among them all: `Hearken to my words, comrades, for all your evil plight. My friends, we know not where the darkness is or where the dawn, neither where the sun, who give light to mortals, goes beneath the earth, nor where he rises; but let us straightway take thought if any device be still left us. As for me I think not that there is. For I climbed to a rugged point of outlook, and beheld the island, about which is set as a crown the boundless deep. The isle itself lies low, and in the midst of it my eyes saw smoke through the thick brush and the wood.'

[198] “So I spoke, and their spirit was broken within them, as they remembered the deeds of the Laestrygonian, Antiphates, and the violence of the great-hearted Cyclops, the man-eater. And they wailed aloud, and shed big tears. But no good came of their mourning. Then I told off in two bands all my well-greaved comrades, and appointed a leader for each band. Of the one I took command, and of the other godlike Eurylochus. Quickly then we shook lots in a brazen helmet, and out leapt the lot of great-hearted Eurylochus.

[208] "So he set out, and with him went two-and-twenty comrades, all weeping; and they left us behind, lamenting. Within the forest glades they found the house of Circe, built of polished stone in a place of wide outlook, and round about it were mountain wolves and lions, whom Circe herself had bewitched; for she gave them evil drugs. Yet these beasts did not rush upon my men, but pranced about them fawningly, wagging their long tails. And as when hounds fawn around their master as he comes from a feast, for he ever brings them bits to soothe their temper, so about them fawned the stout-clawed wolves and lions; but they were seized with fear, as they saw the dread monsters. So they stood in the gateway of the fair-tressed goddess, and within they heard Circe singing with sweet voice, as she went to and fro before a great imperishable web, such as is the handiwork of goddesses, finely-woven and beautiful, and glorious. Then among them spoke Polites, a leader of men, dearest to me of my comrades, and trustiest: `Friends, within someone goes to and fro before a great web, singing sweetly, so that the entire floor echoes; some goddess it is, or some woman. Come, let us quickly call to her.’

[229] “So he spoke, and they cried aloud, and called to her. And she straightway came forth and opened the bright doors, and bade them in; and all went with her in their folly. Only Eurylochus remained behind, for he suspected that there was a snare. She brought them in and made them sit on chairs and seats, and made for them a potion of cheese and barley meal

and yellow honey with Pramnian wine; but in the food she mixed baneful drugs that they might utterly forget their native land. Now when she had given them the potion, and they had drunk it off, then she presently smote them with her wand, and penned them in the sties. And they had the heads, and voice, and bristles, and shape of swine, but their minds remained unchanged even as before. So they were penned there weeping, and before them Circe flung mast and acorns, and the fruit of the cornel tree, to eat, such things as wallowing swine are wont to feed upon.

[244] "But Eurylochus came back straightway to the swift, black ship, to bring tiding of his comrades and their shameful doom. Not a word could he utter, for all his desire, so stricken to the heart was he with great distress, and his eyes were filled with tears, and his spirit was set on lamentation. But when we questioned him in amazement, then he told the fate of the others, his comrades. `We went through the thickets, as thou badest, noble Odysseus. We found in the forest glades a fair palace, built of polished stones, in a place of wide outlook. There someone was going to and fro before a great web, and singing with clear voice, some goddess or some woman, and they cried aloud, and called to her. And she came forth straightway, and opened the bright doors, and bade them in; and they all went with her in their folly. But I remained behind, for I suspected that there was a snare. Then they all vanished together, nor did one of them appear again, though I sat long and watched.'

[261] "So he spoke, and I cast my silver-studded sword about my shoulders, a great sword of bronze, and slung my bow about me, and bade him lead me back by the self-same road. But he clasped me with both hands, and be sought me by my knees, and with wailing he spoke to me winged words: `Lead me not thither against my will, O thou fostered of Zeus, but leave me here. For I know that thou wilt neither come back thyself, nor bring anyone of thy comrades. Nay, with these

that are here let us flee with all speed, for still we may haply escape the evil day.'

[270] "So he spoke, but I answered him, and said: `Eurylochus, do thou stay here in this place, eating and drinking by the hollow, black ship; but I will go, for strong necessity is laid upon me.'

[274] "So saying, I went up from the ship and the sea. But when, as I went through the sacred glades, I was about to come to the great house of the sorceress, Circe, then Hermes, of the golden wand, met me as I went toward the house, in the likeness of a young man with the first down upon his lip, in whom the charm of youth is fairest. He clasped my hand, and spoke, and addressed me: `Whither now again, hapless man, dost thou go alone through the hills, knowing naught of the country? Lo, thy comrades yonder in the house of Circe are penned like swine in close-barred sties. And art thou come to release them? Nay, I tell thee, thou shalt not thyself return, but shalt remain there with the others. But come, I will free thee from harm, and save thee. Here, take this potent herb, and go to the house of Circe, and it shall ward off from thy head the evil day. And I will tell thee all the baneful wiles of Circe. She will mix thee a potion, and cast drugs into the food; but even so she shall not be able to bewitch thee, for the potent herb that I shall give thee will not suffer it. And I will tell thee all. When Circe shall smite thee with her long wand, then do thou draw thy sharp sword from beside thy thigh, and rush upon Circe, as though thou wouldst slay her. And she will be seized with fear, and will bid thee lie with her. Then do not thou thereafter refuse the couch of the goddess, that she may set free thy comrades, and give entertainment to thee. But bid her swear a great oath by the blessed gods that she will not plot against thee any fresh mischief to thy hurt, lest when she has thee stripped she may render thee a weakling and unmanned.'

[302] "So saying, Argeiphontes gave me the herb, drawing it from the ground, and showed me its nature. At the root it was

black, but its flower was like milk. Moly the gods call it, and it is hard for mortal men to dig; but with the gods all things are possible. Hermes then departed to high Olympus through the wooded isle, and I went my way to the house of Circe, and many things did my heart darkly ponder as I went. So I stood at the gates of the fair-tressed goddess. There I stood and called, and the goddess heard my voice. Straightway then she came forth, and opened the bright doors, and bade me in; and I went with her, my heart sore troubled. She brought me in and made me sit on a silver-studded chair, a beautiful chair, richly wrought, and beneath was a foot-stool for the feet. And she prepared me a potion in a golden cup that I might drink, and put therein a drug, with evil purpose in her heart. But when she had given it me, and I had drunk it off, yet was not bewitched, she smote me with her wand, and spoke, and addressed me: `Begone now to the sty, and lie with the rest of thy comrades.'

[321] "So she spoke, but I, drawing my sharp sword from beside my thigh, rushed upon Circe, as though I would slay her. But she, with a loud cry, ran beneath, and clasped my knees, and with wailing she spoke to me winged words: `Who art thou among men, and from whence? Where is thy city, and where thy parents? Amazement holds me that thou hast drunk this charm and wast in no wise bewitched. For no man else soever hath withstood this charm, when once he has drunk it, and it has passed the barrier of his teeth. Nay, but the mind in thy breast is one not to be beguiled. Surely thou art Odysseus, the man of ready device, who Argeiphontes of the golden wand ever said to me would come hither on his way home from Troy with his swift, black ship. Nay, come, put up thy sword in its sheath, and let us two then go up into my bed, that couched together in love we may put trust in each other.'

[336] "So she spoke, but I answered her, and said: `Circe, how canst thou bid me be gentle to thee, who hast turned my comrades into swine in thy halls, and now keepest me here, and with guileful purpose biddest me go to thy chamber, and

go up into thy bed, that when thou hast me stripped thou mayest render me a weakling and unmanned? Nay, verily, it is not I that shall be fain to go up into thy bed, unless thou, goddess, wilt consent to swear a mighty oath that thou wilt not plot against me any fresh mischief to my hurt.'

[345] "So I spoke, and she straightway swore the oath to do me no harm, as I bade her. But when she had sworn, and made an end of the oath, then I went up to the beautiful bed of Circe. But her handmaids meanwhile were busied in the halls, four maidens who are her serving-women in the house. Children are they of the springs and groves, and of the sacred rivers that flow forth to the sea, and of them one threw upon chairs fair rugs of purple above, and spread beneath them a linen cloth; another drew up before the chairs tables of silver, and set upon them golden baskets; and the third mixed sweet, honey-hearted wine in a bowl of silver, and served out golden cups; and the fourth brought water, and kindled a great fire beneath a large cauldron, and the water grew warm. But when the water boiled in the bright bronze, she set me in a bath, and bathed me with water from out the great cauldron, mixing it to my liking, and pouring it over my head and shoulders, till she took from my limbs soul-consuming weariness. But when she had bathed me, and anointed me richly with oil, and had cast about me a fair cloak and a tunic, she brought me into the hall, and made me sit upon a silver-studded chair—a beautiful chair, richly wrought, and beneath was a foot-stool for the feet. Then a handmaid brought water for the hands in a fair pitcher of gold, and poured it over a silver basin for me to wash, and beside me drew up a polished table. And the grave housewife brought and set before me bread, and therewith meats in abundance, granting freely of her store. Then she bade me eat, but my heart inclined not thereto. Rather, I sat with other thoughts, and my spirit boded ill.

[375] "Now when Circe noted that I sat thus, and did not put forth my hands to the food, but was burdened with sore grief, she came close to me, and spoke winged words: `Why,

Odysseus, dost thou sit thus like one that is dumb, eating thy heart, and dost not touch food or drink? Dost thou haply forbode some other guile? Nay, thou needest in no wise fear, for already have I sworn a mighty oath to do thee no harm.'

[383] "So she spoke, but I answered her, and said: `Circe, what man that is right-minded could bring himself to taste of food or drink, ere yet he had won freedom for his comrades, and beheld them before his face? But if thou of a ready heart dost bid me eat and drink, set them free, that mine eyes may behold my trusty comrades.'

[388] "So I spoke, and Circe went forth through the hall holding her wand in her hand, and opened the doors of the sty, and drove them out in the form of swine of nine years old. So they stood there before her, and she went through the midst of them, and anointed each man with another charm. Then from their limbs the bristles fell away which the baneful drug that queenly Circe gave them had before made to grow, and they became men again, younger than they were before, and far comelier and taller to look upon. They knew me, and clung to my hands, each man of them, and upon them all came a passionate sobbing, and the house about them rang wondrously, and the goddess herself was moved to pity.

[400] "Then the beautiful goddess drew near me, and said: `Son of Laertes, sprung from Zeus, Odysseus of many devices, go now to thy swift ship and to the shore of the sea. First of all do ye draw the ship up on the land, and store your goods and all the tackling in caves. Then come back thyself, and bring thy trusty comrades.'

[406] "So she spoke, and my proud heart consented. I went my way to the swift ship and the shore of the sea, and there I found my trusty comrades by the swift ship, wailing piteously, shedding big tears. And as when calves in a farmstead sport about the droves of cattle returning to the yard, when they have had their fill of grazing—all together they frisk before

them, and the pens no longer hold them, but with constant lowing they run about their mothers—so those men, when their eyes beheld me, thronged about me weeping, and it seemed to their hearts as though they had got to their native land, and the very city of rugged Ithaca, where they were bred and born. And with wailing they spoke to me winged words: `At thy return, O thou fostered of Zeus, we are as glad as though we had returned to Ithaca, our native land. But come, tell the fate of the others, our comrades.'

[422] "So they spoke, and I answered them with gentle words: `First of all let us draw the ship up on the land, and store our goods and all the tackling in caves. Then haste you, one and all, to go with me that you may see your comrades in the sacred halls of Circe, drinking and eating, for they have unfailing store.'

[428] "So I spoke, and they quickly hearkened to my words. Eurylochus alone sought to hold back all my comrades, and he spoke, and addressed them with winged words: `Ah, wretched men, whither are we going? Why are you so enamored of these woes, as to go down to the house of Circe, who will change us all to swine, or wolves, or lions, that so we may guard her great house perforce? Even so did the Cyclops, when our comrades went to his fold, and with them went this reckless Odysseus. For it was through this man's folly that they too perished.'

[439] "So he spoke, and I pondered in heart, whether to draw my long sword from beside my stout thigh, and therewith strike off his head, and bring it to the ground, near kinsman of mine by marriage though he was; but my comrades one after another sought to check me with gentle words: `O thou sprung from Zeus, as for this man, we will leave him, if thou so biddest, to abide here by the ship, and to guard the ship, but as for us, do thou lead us to the sacred house of Circe.'

[446] “So saying, they went up from the ship and the sea. Nor was Eurylochus left beside the hollow ship, but he went with us, for he feared my dread reproof. Meanwhile in her halls Circe bathed the rest of my comrades with kindly care, and anointed them richly with oil, and cast about them fleecy cloaks and tunics; and we found them all feasting bountifully in the halls. But when they saw and recognized one another, face to face, they wept and wailed, and the house rang around. Then the beautiful goddess drew near me, and said: `No longer now do ye rouse this plenteous lamenting. Of myself I know both all the woes you have suffered on the teeming deep, and all the wrong that cruel men have done you on the land. Nay, come, eat food and drink wine, until you once more get spirit in your breasts such as when at the first you left your native land of rugged Ithaca; but now ye are withered and spiritless, ever thinking of your weary wanderings, nor are your hearts ever joyful, for verily ye have suffered much.’

[466] “So she spoke, and our proud hearts consented. So there day after day for a full year we abode, feasting on abundant flesh and sweet wine. But when a year was gone and the seasons turned, as the months waned and the long days were brought in their course, then my trusty comrades called me forth, and said: `Strange man, bethink thee now at last of thy native land, if it is fated for thee to be saved, and to reach thy high-roofed house and thy native land.’

[475] “So they spoke, and my proud heart consented. So then all day long till set of sun we sat feasting on abundant flesh and sweet wine. But when the sun set and darkness came on, they lay down to sleep throughout the shadowy halls, but I went up to the beautiful bed of Circe, and besought her by her knees; and the goddess heard my voice, and I spoke, and addressed her with winged words: `Circe, fulfill for me the promise which thou gavest to send me home; for my spirit is now eager to be gone, and the spirit of my comrades, who make my heart to pine, as they sit about me mourning, whenever thou haply art not at hand.’

[487] “So I spoke, and the beautiful goddess straightway made answer: `Son of Laertes, sprung from Zeus, Odysseus of many devices, abide ye now no longer in my house against your will; but you must first complete another journey, and come to the house of Hades and dread Persephone, to seek soothsaying of the spirit of Theban Tiresias, the blind seer, whose mind abides steadfast. To him even in death Persephone has granted reason, that he alone should have understanding; but the others flit about as shadows.’

[496] “So she spoke, and my spirit was broken within me, and I wept as I sat on the bed, nor had my heart any longer desire to live and behold the light of the sun. But when I had my fill of weeping and writhing, then I made answer, and addressed her, saying: `O Circe, who will guide us on this journey? To Hades no man ever yet went in a black ship.’

[503] “So I spoke, and the beautiful goddess straightway made answer: `Son of Laertes, sprung from Zeus, Odysseus of many devices, let there be in thy mind no concern for a pilot to guide thy ship, but set up thy mast, and spread the white sail, and sit thee down; and the breath of the North Wind will bear her onward. But when in thy ship thou hast now crossed the stream of Oceanus, where is a level shore and the groves of Persephone —tall poplars, and willows that shed their fruit—there do thou beach thy ship by the deep eddying Oceanus, but go thyself to the dank house of Hades. There into Acheron flow Periphlegethon and Cocytus, which is a branch of the water of the Styx; and there is a rock, and the meeting place of the two roaring rivers. Thither, prince, do thou draw nigh, as I bid thee, and dig a pit of a cubit's length this way and that, and around it pour a libation to all the dead, first with milk and honey, thereafter with sweet wine, and in the third place with water, and sprinkle thereon white barley meal. And do thou earnestly entreat the powerless heads of the dead, vowing that when thou comest to Ithaca thou wilt sacrifice in thy halls a barren heifer, the best thou hast, and wilt fill the altar with rich

gifts; and that to Tiresias alone thou wilt sacrifice separately a ram, wholly black, the goodliest of thy flock. But when with prayers thou hast made supplication to the glorious tribes of the dead, then sacrifice a ram and a black ewe, turning their heads toward Erebus but thyself turning backward, and setting thy face towards the streams of the river. Then many ghosts of men that are dead will come forth. But do thou thereafter call to thy comrades, and bid them flay and burn the sheep that lie there, slain by the pitiless bronze, and make prayer to the gods, to mighty Hades and to dread Persephone. And do thou thyself draw thy sharp sword from beside thy thigh, and sit there, not suffering the powerless heads of the dead to draw near to the blood, till thou hast enquired of Tiresias. Then the seer will presently come to thee, leader of men, and he will tell thee thy way and the measures of thy path, and of thy return, how thou mayest go over the teeming deep.'

[541] "So she spoke, and straightway came golden-throned Dawn. Round about me then she cast a cloak and tunic as raiment, and the nymph clothed herself in a long white robe, finely-woven and beautiful, and about her waist she cast a fair girdle of gold, and upon her head she put a veil. But I went through the halls, and roused my men with gentle words, coming up to each man in turn. `No longer now sleep ye, and drowse in sweet slumber, but let us go; lo! queenly Circe has told me all.'

[550] "So I spoke, and their proud hearts consented. But not even from thence could I lead my men unscathed. There was one, Elpenor, the youngest of all, not over valiant in war nor sound of understanding, who had laid him down apart from his comrades in the sacred house of Circe, seeking the cool air, for he was heavy with wine. He heard the noise and the bustle of his comrades as they moved about, and suddenly sprang up, and forgot to go to the long ladder that he might come down again, but fell headlong from the roof, and his neck was broken away from the spine, and his spirit went down to the house of Hades.

[561] "But as my men were going on their way I spoke among them, saying:`Ye think, forsooth, that ye are going to your dear native land; but Circe has pointed out for us another journey, even to the house of Hades and dread Persephone, to consult the spirit of Theban Tiresias.'

[566] "So I spoke, and their spirit was broken within them, and sitting down right where they were, they wept and tore their hair. But no good came of their lamenting. But when we were on our way to the swift ship and the shore of the sea, sorrowing and shedding big tears, meanwhile Circe had gone forth and made fast beside the black ship a ram and a black ewe, for easily had she passed us by. Who with his eyes could behold a god against his will, whether going to or fro?

BOOK 11 OF THE *ODYSSEY*

[1] "But when we had come down to the ship and to the sea, first of all we drew the ship down to the bright sea, and set the mast and sail in the black ship, and took the sheep and put them aboard, and ourselves embarked, sorrowing, and shedding big tears. And for our aid in the wake of our dark-prowed ship a fair wind that filled the sail, a goodly comrade, was sent by fair-tressed Circe, dread goddess of human speech. So when we had made fast all the tackling throughout the ship, we sat down, and the wind and the helms man made straight her course. All the day long her sail was stretched as she sped over the sea; and the sun set and all the ways grew dark.

[13] "She came to deep-flowing Oceanus, that bounds the Earth, where is the land and city of the Cimmerians, wrapped in mist and cloud. Never does the bright sun look down on them with his rays either when he mounts the starry heaven or when he turns again to earth from heaven, but baneful night is spread over wretched mortals. Thither we came and beached

our ship, and took out the sheep, and ourselves went beside the stream of Oceanus until we came to the place of which Circe had told us.

[24] "Here Perimedes and Eurylochus held the victims, while I drew my sharp sword from beside my thigh, and dug a pit of a cubit's length this way and that, and around it poured a libation to all the dead, first with milk and honey, thereafter with sweet wine, and in the third place with water, and I sprinkled thereon white barley meal. And I earnestly entreated the powerless heads of the dead, vowing that when I came to Ithaca I would sacrifice in my halls a barren heifer, the best I had, and pile the altar with goodly gifts, and to Tiresias alone would sacrifice separately a ram, wholly black, the goodliest of my flocks. But when with vows and prayers I had made supplication to the tribes of the dead, I took the sheep and cut their throats over the pit, and the dark blood ran forth.

[37] "Then there gathered from out of Erebus the spirits of those that are dead, brides, and unwedded youths, and toil-worn old men, and tender maidens with hearts yet new to sorrow, and many, too, that had been wounded with bronze-tipped spears, men slain in fight, wearing their blood-stained armor. These came thronging in crowds about the pit from every side, with a wondrous cry; and pale fear seized me. Then I called to my comrades and bade them flay and burn the sheep that lay there slain with the pitiless bronze, and to make prayer to the gods, to mighty Hades and dread Persephone. And I myself drew my sharp sword from beside my thigh and sat there, and would not suffer the powerless heads of the dead to draw near to the blood until I had enquired of Tiresias.

[51] "The first to come was the spirit of my comrade Elpenor. Not yet had he been buried beneath the broad-wayed earth, for we had left his corpse behind us in the hall of Circe, unwept and unburied, since another task was then urging us on. When I saw him I wept, and my heart had compassion on him; and I spoke and addressed him with winged words: `Elpenor, how

didst thou come beneath the murky darkness? Thou coming on foot hast out-stripped me in my black ship.'

[59] "So I spoke, and with a groan he answered me and said: 'Son of Laertes, sprung from Zeus, Odysseus of many devices, and an evil doom of some god was my undoing, and measureless wine. When I had lain down to sleep in the house of Circe I did not think to go to the long ladder that I might come down again, but fell headlong from the roof, and my neck was broken away from the spine and my spirit went down to the house of Hades. Now I beseech thee by those whom we left behind, who are not present with us, by thy wife and thy father who reared thee when a babe, and by Telemachus whom thou didst leave an only son in thy halls; for I know that as thou goest hence from the house of Hades thou wilt touch at the Aeaean isle with thy well-built ship. There, then, O prince, I bid thee remember me. Leave me not behind thee unwept and unburied as thou goest thence, and turn not away from me, lest haply I bring the wrath of the gods upon thee. Nay, burn me with my armor, all that is mine, and heap up a mound for me on the shore of the grey sea, in memory of an unhappy man, that men yet to be may learn of me. Fulfill this my prayer, and fix upon the mound my oar wherewith I rowed in life when I was among my comrades.'

[79] "So he spoke, and I made answer and said: `All this, unhappy man, will I perform and do.' Thus we two sat and held sad converse one with the other, I on one side holding my sword over the blood, while on the other side the phantom of my comrade spoke at large.

[84] "Then there came up the spirit of my dead mother, Anticleia, the daughter of great-hearted Autolycus, whom I had left alive when I departed for sacred Ilios. At sight of her I wept, and my heart had compassion on her, but even so I would not suffer her to come near the blood, for all my great sorrow, until I had enquired of Tiresias.

[90] "Then there came up the spirit of the Theban Tiresias, bearing his golden staff in his hand, and he knew me and spoke to me: `Son of Laertes, sprung from Zeus, Odysseus of many devices, what now, hapless man? Why hast thou left the light of the sun and come hither to behold the dead and a region where is no joy? Nay, give place from the pit and draw back thy sharp sword, that I may drink of the blood and tell thee sooth.'

[97] "So he spoke, and I gave place and thrust my silver-studded sword into its sheath, and when he had drunk the dark blood, then the blameless seer spoke to me and said: 'Thou askest of thy honey-sweet return, glorious Odysseus, but this shall a god make grievous unto thee; for I think not that thou shalt elude the Earth-shaker, seeing that he has laid up wrath in his heart against thee, angered that thou didst blind his dear son. Yet even so ye may reach home, though in evil plight, if thou wilt curb thine own spirit and that of thy comrades, as soon as thou shalt bring thy well-built ship to the island Thrinacia, escaping from the violet sea, and ye find grazing there the cattle and goodly flocks of Helios, who over sees and overhears all things. If thou leavest these unharmed and heedest thy homeward way, verily ye may yet reach Ithaca, though in evil plight. But if thou harmest them, then I foresee ruin for thy ship and thy comrades, and even if thou shalt thyself escape, late shalt thou come home and in evil case, after losing all thy comrades, in a ship that is another's, and thou shalt find woes in thy house—proud men that devour thy livelihood, wooing thy godlike wife, and offering wooers' gifts. Yet verily on their violent deeds shalt thou take vengeance when thou comest.

[119] "`But when thou hast slain the wooers in thy halls, whether by guile or openly with the sharp sword, then do thou go forth, taking a shapely oar, until thou comest to men that know naught of the sea and eat not of food mingled with salt, aye, and they know naught of ships with purple cheeks, or of shapely oars that are as wings unto ships. And I will tell thee a

sign right manifest, which will not escape thee. When another wayfarer, on meeting thee, shall say that thou hast a winnowing-fan on thy stout shoulder, then do thou fix in the earth thy shapely oar and make goodly offerings to lord Poseidon—a ram, and a bull, and a boar that mates with sows—and depart for thy home and offer sacred hecatombs to the immortal gods who hold broad heaven, to each one in due order. And death shall come to thee thyself far from the sea, a death so gentle, that shall lay thee low when thou art overcome with sleek old age, and thy people shall dwell in prosperity around thee. In this have I told thee sooth.'

[138] "So he spoke, and I made answer and said: `Tiresias, of all this, I ween, the gods themselves have spun the thread. But come, tell me this, and declare it truly. I see here the spirit of my dead mother; she sits in silence near the blood, and deigns not to look upon the face of her own son or to speak to him. Tell me, prince, how she may recognize that I am he?'

[145] "So I spoke, and he straightway made answer, and said: `Easy is the word that I shall say and put in thy mind. Whomsoever of those that are dead and gone thou shalt suffer to draw near the blood, he will tell thee sooth; but whomsoever thou refusest, he surely will go back again.'

[150] "So saying the spirit of the prince, Tiresias, went back into the house of Hades, when he had declared his prophecies; but I remained there steadfastly until my mother came up and drank the dark blood. At once then she knew me, and with wailing she spoke to me winged words: `My child, how didst thou come beneath the murky darkness, being still alive? Hard is it for those that live to behold these realms, for between are great rivers and dread streams; Oceanus first, which one may in no wise cross on foot, but only if one have a well-built ship. Art thou but now come hither from Troy after long wanderings with thy ship and thy companions? and hast thou not yet reached Ithaca, nor seen thy wife in thy halls?'

[163] "So she spoke, and I made answer and said: `My mother, necessity brought me down to the house of Hades, to seek soothsaying of the spirit of Theban Tiresias. For not yet have I come near to the shore of Achaea, nor have I as yet set foot on my own land, but have ever been wandering, laden with woe, from the day when first I went with goodly Agamemnon to Ilios, famed for its horses, to fight with the Trojans. But come, tell me this, and declare it truly. What fate of grievous death overcame thee? Was it long disease, or did the archer, Artemis, assail thee with her gentle shafts, and slay thee? And tell me of my father and my son, whom I left behind me. Does the honor that was mine still abide with them, or does some other man now possess it, and do they say that I shall no more return? And tell me of my wedded wife, of her purpose and of her mind. Does she abide with her son, and keep all things safe? or has one already wedded her, whosoever is best of the Achaeans?'

[180] "So I spoke, and my honored mother straightway answered: `Aye verily she abides with steadfast heart in thy halls, and ever sorrowfully for her do the nights and the days wane, as she weeps. But the fair honor that was thine no man yet possesses, but Telemachus holds thy demesne unharassed, and feasts an equal banquets, such as it is fitting that one who deals judgment should share, for all men invite him. But thy father abides there in the tilled land, and comes not to the city, nor has he, for bedding, bed and cloaks and bright coverlets, but through the winter he sleeps in the house, where the slaves sleep, in the ashes by the fire, and wears upon his body mean raiment. But when summer comes and rich autumn, then all about the slope of his vineyard plot are strewn his lowly beds of fallen leaves. There he lies sorrowing, and nurses his great grief in his heart, in longing for thy return, and heavy old age has come upon him. Even so did I too perish and meet my fate. Neither did the keen-sighted archer goddess assail me in my halls with her gentle shafts, and slay me, nor did any disease come upon me, such as oftenest through grievous wasting takes the spirit from the limbs; nay, it was longing for

thee, and for thy counsels, glorious Odysseus, and for thy tender-heartedness, that robbed me of honey-sweet life.'

[204] "So she spoke, and I pondered in heart, and was fain to clasp the spirit of my dead mother. Thrice I sprang towards her, and my heart bade me clasp her, and thrice she flitted from my arms like a shadow or a dream, and pain grew ever sharper at my heart. And I spoke and addressed her with winged words: `My mother, why dost thou not stay for me, who am eager to clasp thee, that even in the house of Hades we two may cast our arms each about the other, and take our fill of chill lamenting. Is this but a phantom that august Persephone has sent me that I may lament and groan the more?'

[215] "So I spoke, and my honored mother straightway answered: `Ah me, my child, ill-fated above all men, in no wise does Persephone, the daughter of Zeus, deceive thee, but this is the appointed way with mortals when one dies. For the sinews no longer hold the flesh and the bones together, but the strong might of blazing fire destroys these, as soon as the life leaves the white bones, and the spirit, like a dream, flits away, and hovers to and fro. But haste thee to the light with what speed thou mayest, and bear all these things in mind, that thou mayest hereafter tell them to thy wife.'

[225] "Thus we two talked with one another; and the women came, for august Persephone sent them forth, even all those that had been the wives and the daughters of chieftains. These flocked in throngs about the dark blood, and I considered how I might question each; and this seemed to my mind the best counsel. I drew my long sword from beside my stout thigh, and would not suffer them to drink of the dark blood all at one time. So they drew near, one after the other, and each declared her birth, and I questioned them all.

[235] "Then verily the first that I saw was high-born Tyro, who said that she was the daughter of noble Salmoneus, and

declared herself to be the wife of Cretheus, son of Aeolus. She became enamored of the river, divine Enipeus, who is far the fairest of rivers that send forth their streams upon the earth, and she was wont to resort to the fair waters of Enipeus. But the Enfolder and Shaker of the earth took his form, and lay with her at the mouths of the eddying river. And the dark wave stood about them like a mountain, vaulted-over, and hid the god and the mortal woman. And he loosed her maiden girdle, and shed sleep upon her. But when the god had ended his work of love, he clasped her hand, and spoke, and addressed her: `Be glad, woman, in our love, and as the year goes on its course thou shalt bear glorious children, for not weak are the embraces of a god. These do thou tend and rear. But now go to thy house, and hold thy peace, and tell no man; but know that I am Poseidon, the shaker of the earth.' So saying, he plunged beneath the surging sea. But she conceived and bore Pelias and Neleus, who both became strong servants of great Zeus; and Pelias dwelt in spacious Iolcus, and was rich in flocks, and the other dwelt in sandy Pylos. But her other children she, the queenly among women, bore to Cretheus, even Aeson, and Pheres, and Amythaon, who fought from chariots.

[260] "And after her I saw Antiope, daughter of Asopus, who boasted that she had slept even in the arms of Zeus, and she bore two sons, Amphion and Zethus, who first established the seat of seven-gated Thebe, and fenced it in with walls, for they could not dwell in spacious Thebe unfenced, how mighty soever they were. And after her I saw Alcmene, wife of Amphitryon, who lay in the arms of great Zeus, and bore Heracles, staunch in fight, the lion-hearted. And Megara I saw, daughter of Creon, high-of-heart, whom the son of Amphitryon, ever stubborn in might, had to wife.

[271] "And I saw the mother of Oedipus, fair Epicaste, who wrought a monstrous deed in ignorance of mind, in that she wedded her own son, and he, when he had slain his own father, wedded her, and straightway the gods made these things known among men. Howbeit he abode as lord of the

Cadmeans in lovely Thebe, suffering woes through the baneful counsels of the gods, but she went down to the house of Hades, the strong warder. She made fast a noose on high from a lofty beam, overpowered by her sorrow, but for him she left behind woes full many, even all that the Avengers of a mother bring to pass.

[281] "And I saw beauteous Chloris, whom once Neleus wedded because of her beauty, when he had brought countless gifts of wooing. Youngest daughter was she of Amphion, son of Iasus, who once ruled mightily in Orchomenus of the Minyae. And she was queen of Pylos, and bore to her husband glorious children, Nestor, and Chromius, and lordly Periclymenus, and besides these she bore noble Pero, a wonder to men. Her all that dwelt about sought in marriage, but Neleus would give her to no man, save to him who should drive from Phylace the cattle of mighty Iphicles, sleek and broad of brow; and hard they were to drive. These the blameless seer alone undertook to drive off; but a grievous fate of the gods ensnared him, even hard bonds and the herdsmen of the field. Howbeit when at length the months and the days were being brought to fulfillment, as the year rolled round, and the seasons came on, then verily mighty Iphicles released him, when he had told all the oracles; and the will of Zeus was fulfilled.

[299] "And I saw Lede, the wife of Tyndareus, who bore to Tyndareus two sons, stout of heart, Castor the tamer of horses, and the boxer Polydeuces. These two the earth, the giver of life, covers, albeit alive, and even in the world below they have honor from Zeus. One day they live in turn, and one day they are dead; and they have won honor like unto that of the gods.

[305] "And after her I saw Iphimedeia, wife of Aloeus, who declared that she had lain with Poseidon. She bore two sons, but short of life were they, godlike Otus, and far-famed Ephialtes—men whom the earth, the giver of grain, reared as

the tallest, and far the comeliest, after the famous Orion. For at nine years they were nine cubits in breadth and in height nine fathoms. Yea, and they threatened to raise the din of furious war against the immortals in Olympus. They were fain to pile Ossa on Olympus, and Pelion, with its waving forests, on Ossa, that so heaven might be scaled. And this they would have accomplished, if they had reached the measure of manhood; but the son of Zeus, whom fair-haired Leto bore, slew them both before the down blossomed beneath their temples and covered their chins with a full growth of beard.

[321] "And Phaedra and Procris I saw, and fair Ariadne, the daughter of Minos of baneful mind, whom once Theseus was fain to bear from Crete to the hill of sacred Athens; but he had no joy of her, for ere that Artemis slew her in sea-girt Dia because of the witness of Dionysus.

[326] "And Maera and Clymene I saw, and hateful Eriphyle, who took precious gold as the price of the life of her own lord. But I cannot tell or name all the wives and daughters of heroes that I saw; ere that immortal night would wane. Nay, it is now time to sleep, either when I have gone to the swift ship and the crew, or here. My sending shall rest with the gods, and with you."

[334] So he spoke, and they were all hushed in silence, and were held spell-bound throughout the shadowy halls. Then among them white-armed Arete was the first to speak: "Phaeacians, how seems this man to you for comeliness and stature, and for the balanced spirit within him? And moreover he is my guest, though each of you has a share in this honor. Wherefore be not in haste to send him away, nor stint your gifts to one in such need; for many are the treasures which lie stored in your halls by the favor of the gods."

[342] Then among them spoke also the old lord Echeneus, who was an elder among the Phaeacians: "Friends, verily not wide of the mark or of our own thought are the words of our

wise queen. Nay, do you give heed to them. Yet it is on Alcinous here that deed and word depend."

[347] Then again Alcinous answered him and said: "This word of hers shall verily hold, as surely as I live and am lord over the Phaeacians, lovers of the oar. But let our guest, for all his great longing to return, nevertheless endure to remain until tomorrow, till I shall make all our gift complete. His sending shall rest with the men, with all, but most of all with me; for mine is the control in the land."

[354] Then Odysseus of many wiles answered him and said: "Lord Alcinous, renowned above all men, if you should bid me abide here even for a year, and should further my sending, and give glorious gifts, even that would I choose; and it would be better far to come with a fuller hand to my dear native land. Aye, and I should win more respect and love from all men who should see me when I had returned to Ithaca."

[361] Then again Alcinous made answer and said: "Odysseus, in no wise as we look on thee do we deem this of thee, that thou art a cheat and a dissembler, such as are many whom the dark earth breeds scattered far and wide, men that fashion lies out of what no man can even see. But upon thee is grace of words, and within thee is a heart of wisdom, and thy tale thou hast told with skill, as doth a minstrel, even the grievous woes of all the Argives and of thine own self. But come, tell me this, and declare it truly, whether thou sawest any of thy godlike comrades, who went to Ilios together with thee, and there met their fate. The night is before us, long, aye, wondrous long, and it is not yet the time for sleep in the hall. Tell on, I pray thee, the tale of these wondrous deeds. Verily I could abide until bright dawn, so thou wouldest be willing to tell in the hall of these woes of thine."

[377] Then Odysseus of many wiles answered him and said: "Lord Alcinous, renowned above all men, there is a time for many words and there is a time also for sleep. But if thou art

fain still to listen, I would not begrudge to tell thee of other things more pitiful still than these, even the woes of my comrades, who perished afterward, who escaped from the dread battle-cry of the Trojans, but perished on their return through the will of an evil woman.

[385] "When then holy Persephone had scattered this way and that the spirits of the women, there came up the spirit of Agamemnon, son of Atreus, sorrowing; and round about him others were gathered, spirits of all those who were slain with him in the house of Aegisthus, and met their fate. He knew me straightway, when he had drunk the dark blood, and he wept aloud, and shed big tears, and stretched forth his hands toward me eager to reach me. But no longer had he aught of strength or might remaining such as of old was in his supple limbs. When I saw him I wept, and my heart had compassion on him, and I spoke, and addressed him with winged words: `Most glorious son of Atreus, king of men, Agamemnon, what fate of grievous death overcame thee? Did Poseidon smite thee on board thy ships, when he had roused a furious blast of cruel winds? Or did foemen work thee harm on the land, while thou wast cutting off their cattle and fair flocks of sheep, or wast fighting to win their city and their women?'

[404] "So I spoke, and he straightway made answer and said: `Son of Laertes, sprung from Zeus, Odysseus of many devices, neither did Poseidon smite me on board my ships, when he had roused a furious blast of cruel winds, nor did foemen work me harm on the land, but Aegisthus wrought for me death and fate, and slew me with the aid of my accursed wife, when he had bidden me to his house and made me a feast, even as one slays an ox at the stall. So I died by a most pitiful death, and round about me the rest of my comrades were slain unceasingly like white-tusked swine, which are slaughtered in the house of a rich man of great might at a marriage feast, or a joint meal, or a rich drinking-bout. Ere now thou hast been present at the slaying of many men, killed in single combat or in the press of the fight, but in heart thou wouldst have felt

most pity hadst thou seen that sight, how about the mixing bowl and the laden tables we lay in the hall, and the floor all swam with blood. But the most piteous cry that I heard was that of the daughter of Priam, Cassandra, whom guileful Clytemnestra slew by my side. And I sought to raise my hands and smite down the murderess, dying though I was, pierced through with the sword. But she, the shameless one, turned her back upon me, and even though I was going to the house of Hades deigned neither to draw down my eyelids with her fingers nor to close my mouth. So true is it that there is nothing more dread or more shameless than a woman who puts into her heart such deeds, even as she too devised a monstrous thing, contriving death for her wedded husband. Verily I thought that I should come home welcome to my children and to my slaves; but she, with her heart set on utter wickedness, has shed shame on herself and on women yet to be, even upon her that doeth uprightly.'

[435] "So he spoke, and I made answer and said: `Ah, verily has Zeus, whose voice is borne afar, visited wondrous hatred on the race of Atreus from the first because of the counsels of women. For Helen's sake many of us perished, and against thee Clytemnestra spread a snare whilst thou wast afar.'

[440] "So I spoke, and he straightway made answer and said: `Wherefore in thine own case be thou never gentle even to thy wife. Declare not to her all the thoughts of thy heart, but tell her somewhat, and let somewhat also be hidden. Yet not upon thee, Odysseus, shall death come from thy wife, for very prudent and of an understanding heart is the daughter of Icarius, wise Penelope. Verily we left her a bride newlywed, when we went to the war, and a boy was at her breast, a babe, who now, I ween, sits in the ranks of men, happy in that his dear father will behold him when he comes, and he will greet his father as is meet. But my wife did not let me sate my eyes even with sight of my own son. Nay, ere that she slew even me, her husband. And another thing will I tell thee, and do thou lay it to heart: in secret and not openly do thou bring thy

ship to the shore of thy dear native land; for no longer is there faith in women. But, come, tell me this, and declare it truly, whether haply ye hear of my son as yet alive in Orchomenus it may be, or in sandy Pylos, or yet with Menelaus in wide Sparta; for not yet has goodly Orestes perished on the earth.'

[462] "So he spoke, and I made answer and said: 'Son of Atreus, wherefore dost thou question me of this? I know not at all whether he be alive or dead, and it is an ill thing to speak words vain as wind.'

[465] "Thus we two stood and held sad converse with one another, sorrowing and shedding big tears; and there came up the spirit of Achilles, son of Peleus, and those of Patroclus and of peerless Antilochus and of Aias, who in comeliness and form was the goodliest of all the Danaans after the peerless son of Peleus. And the spirit of the swift-footed son of Aeacus recognized me, and weeping, spoke to me winged words: `Son of Laertes, sprung from Zeus, Odysseus of many devices, rash man, what deed yet greater than this wilt thou devise in thy heart? How didst thou dare to come down to Hades, where dwell the unheeding dead, the phantoms of men outworn.'

[477] "So he spoke, and I made answer and said: `Achilles, son of Peleus, far the mightiest of the Achaeans, I came through need of Tiresias, if haply he would tell me some plan whereby I might reach rugged Ithaca. For not yet have I come near to the land of Achaea, nor have I as yet set foot on my own country, but am ever suffering woes; whereas than thou, Achilles, no man aforetime was more blessed nor shall ever be hereafter. For of old, when thou wast alive, we Argives honored thee even as the gods, and now that thou art here, thou rulest mightily among the dead. Wherefore grieve not at all that thou art dead, Achilles.'

[486] "So I spoke, and he straightway made answer and said: `Nay, seek not to speak soothingly to me of death, glorious Odysseus. I should choose, so I might live on earth, to serve as

the hireling of another, of some portionless man whose livelihood was but small, rather than to be lord over all the dead that have perished. But come, tell me tidings of my son, that lordly youth, whether or not he followed to the war to be a leader. And tell me of noble Peleus, if thou hast heard aught, whether he still has honor among the host of the Myrmidons, or whether men do him dishonor throughout Hellas and Phthia, because old age binds him hand and foot. For I am not there to bear him aid beneath the rays of the sun in such strength as once was mine in wide Troy, when I slew the best of the host in defense of the Argives. If but in such strength I could come, were it but for an hour, to my father's house, I would give many a one of those who do him violence and keep him from his honor, cause to rue my strength and my invincible hands.'

[504] "So he spoke, and I made answer and said: 'Verily of noble Peleus have I heard naught, but as touching thy dear son, Neoptolemus, I will tell thee all the truth, as thou biddest me. I it was, myself, who brought him from Scyros in my shapely, hollow ship to join the host of the well-greaved Archaeans. And verily, as often as we took counsel around the city of Troy, he was ever the first to speak, and made no miss of words; godlike Nestor and I alone surpassed him. But as often as we fought with the bronze on the Trojan plain, he would never remain behind in the throng or press of men, but would ever run forth far to the front, yielding to none in his might; and many men he slew in dread combat. All of them I could not tell or name, all the host that he slew in defense of the Argives; but what a warrior was that son of Telephus whom he slew with the sword, the prince Eurypylus! Aye, and many of his comrades, the Ceteians, were slain about him, because of gifts a woman craved. He verily was the comeliest man I saw, next to goodly Memnon. And again, when we, the best of the Argives, were about to go down into the horse which Epeus made, and the command of all was laid upon me, both to open and to close the door of our stout-built ambush, then the other leaders and counselors of the Danaans would

wipe away tears from their eyes, and each man's limbs shook beneath him, but never did my eyes see his fair face grow pale at all, nor see him wiping tears from his cheeks; but he earnestly besought me to let him go forth from the horse, and kept handling his sword-hilt and his spear heavy with bronze, and was eager to work harm to the Trojans. But after we had sacked the lofty city of Priam, he went on board his ship with his share of the spoil and a goodly prize—all unscathed he was, neither smitten with the sharp spear nor wounded in close fight, as often befalls in war; for Ares rages confusedly.'

[538] "So I spoke, and the spirit of the son of Aeacus departed with long strides over the field of asphodel, joyful in that I said that his son was preeminent. And other spirits of those dead and gone stood sorrowing, and each asked of those dear to him. Alone of them all the spirit of Aias, son of Telamon, stood apart, still full of wrath for the victory that I had won over him in the contest by the ships for the arms of Achilles, whose honored mother had set them for a prize; and the judges were the sons of the Trojans and Pallas Athena. I would that I had never won in the contest for such a prize, over so noble a head did the earth close because of those arms, even over Aias, who in comeliness and in deeds of war was above all the other Achaeans, next to the peerless son of Peleus. To him I spoke with soothing words: `Aias, son of peerless Telamon, wast thou then not even in death to forget thy wrath against me because of those accursed arms? Surely the gods set them to be a bane to the Argives: such a tower of strength was lost to them in thee; and for thee in death we Achaeans sorrow unceasingly, even as for the life of Achilles, son of Peleus. Yet no other is to blame but Zeus, who bore terrible hatred against the host of Danaan spearmen, and brought on thee thy doom. Nay, come hither, prince, that thou mayest hear my word and my speech; and subdue thy wrath and thy proud spirit.'

[563] "So I spoke, but he answered me not a word, but went his way to Erebus to join the other spirits of those dead and gone. Then would he nevertheless have spoken to me for his

entire wrath, or I to him, but the heart in my breast was fain to see the spirits of those others that are dead.

[567] "There then I saw Minos, the glorious son of Zeus, golden scepter in hand, giving judgment to the dead from his seat, while they sat and stood about the king through the wide-gated house of Hades, and asked of him judgment.

[572] "And after him I marked huge Orion driving together over the field of asphodel wild beasts which he himself had slain on the lonely hills, and in his hands he held a club all of bronze, ever unbroken.

[576] "And I saw Tityos, son of glorious Gaea, lying on the ground. Over nine roods he stretched, and two vultures sat, one on either side, and tore his liver, plunging their beaks into his bowels, nor could he beat them off with his hands. For he had offered violence to Leto, the glorious wife of Zeus, as she went toward Pytho through Panopeus with its lovely lawns.

[582] "Aye, and I saw Tantalus in violent torment, standing in a pool, and the water came nigh unto his chin. He seemed as one athirst, but could not take and drink; for as often as that old man stooped down, eager to drink, so often would the water be swallowed up and vanish away, and at his feet the black earth would appear, for some god made all dry. And trees, high and leafy, let stream their fruits above his head, pears, and pomegranates, and apple trees with their bright fruit, and sweet figs, and luxuriant olives. But as often as that old man would reach out toward these, to clutch them with his hands, the wind would toss them to the shadowy clouds.

[593] "Aye, and I saw Sisyphus in violent torment, seeking to raise a monstrous stone with both his hands. Verily he would brace himself with hands and feet, and thrust the stone toward the crest of a hill, but as often as he was about to heave it over the top, the weight would turn it back, and then down again to the plain would come rolling the ruthless stone. But he would

strain again and thrust it back, and the sweat flowed down from his limbs, and dust rose up from his head.

[601] "And after him I marked the mighty Heracles—his phantom; for he himself among the immortal gods takes his joy in the feast, and has to wife Hebe, of the fair ankles, daughter of great Zeus and of Here, of the golden sandals. About him rose a clamor from the dead, as of birds flying everywhere in terror; and he like dark night, with his bow bare and with arrow on the string, glared about him terribly, like one in act to shoot. Awful was the belt about his breast, a baldric of gold, whereon wondrous things were fashioned, bears and wild boars, and lions with flashing eyes, and conflicts, and battles, and murders, and slayings of men. May he never have designed, or hereafter design such another, even he who stored up in his craft the device of that belt.

[615] "He in turn knew me when his eyes beheld me, and weeping spoke to me winged words: `Son of Laertes, sprung from Zeus, Odysseus of many devices, ah, wretched man, dost thou, too, drag out an evil lot such as I once bore beneath the rays of the sun? I was the son of Zeus, son of Cronus, but I had woe beyond measure; for to a man far worse than I was I made subject, and he laid on me hard labors. Yea, he once sent me hither to fetch the hound of Hades, for he could devise for me no other task mightier than this. The hound I carried off and led forth from the house of Hades; and Hermes was my guide, and flashing-eyed Athena.'

[627] "So saying, he went his way again into the house of Hades, but I abode there steadfastly, in the hope that some other haply might still come forth of the warrior heroes who died in the days of old. And I should have seen yet others of the men of former time, whom I was fain to behold, even Theseus and Peirithous, glorious children of the gods, but ere that the myriad tribes of the dead came thronging up with a wondrous cry, and pale fear seized me, lest august Persephone

might send forth upon me from out the house of Hades the head of the Gorgon, that awful monster.

[637] "Straightway then I went to the ship and bade my comrades themselves to embark, and to loose the stern cables. So they went on board quickly and sat down upon the benches. And the ship was borne down the stream Oceanus by the swelling flood, first with our rowing, and afterwards the wind was fair.

BOOK 12 OF THE *ODYSSEY*

[1] "Now after our ship had left the stream of the river Oceanus and had come to the wave of the broad sea, and the Aeaean isle, where is the dwelling of early Dawn and her dancing-lawns, and the risings of the sun, there on our coming we beached our ship on the sands, and ourselves went forth upon the shore of the sea, and there we fell asleep, and waited for the bright Dawn.

[8] "As soon as early Dawn appeared, the rosy-fingered, then I sent forth my comrades to the house of Circe to fetch the body of the dead Elpenor. Straightway then we cut billets of wood and gave him burial where the headland runs furthest out to sea, sorrowing and shedding big tears. But when the dead man was burned, and the armor of the dead, we heaped up a mound and dragged on to it a pillar, and on the top of the mound we planted his shapely oar.

[16] "We then were busied with these several tasks, howbeit Circe was not unaware of our coming forth from the house of Hades, but speedily she arrayed herself and came, and her handmaids brought with her bread and meat in abundance and flaming red wine. And the beautiful goddess stood in our midst, and spoke among us, saying: `Rash men, who have gone down alive to the house of Hades to meet death twice, while other men die but once. Nay, come, eat food and drink

wine here this whole day through; but at the coming of Dawn ye shall set sail, and I will point out the way and declare to you each thing, in order that ye may not suffer pain and woes through wretched ill-contriving either by sea or on land.'

[28] "So she spoke, and our proud hearts consented. So then all day long till set of sun we sat feasting on abundant flesh and sweet wine. But when the sun set and darkness came on, they lay down to rest beside the stern cables of the ship; but Circe took me by the hand, and leading me apart from my dear comrades, made me to sit, and herself lay down close at hand and asked me all the tale. And I told her all in due order.

[36] "Then queenly Circe spoke to me and said: `All these things have thus found an end; but do thou hearken as I shall tell thee, and a god shall himself bring it to thy mind. To the Sirens first shalt thou come, who beguile all men whosoever comes to them. Whoso in ignorance draws near to them and hears the Sirens' voice, he nevermore returns, that his wife and little children may stand at his side rejoicing, but the Sirens beguile him with their clear-toned song, as they sit in a meadow, and about them is a great heap of bones of moldering men, and round the bones the skin is shriveling. But do thou row past them, and anoint the ears of thy comrades with sweet wax, which thou hast kneaded, lest any of the rest may hear. But if thou thyself hast a will to listen, let them bind thee in the swift ship hand and foot upright in the step of the mast, and let the ropes be made fast at the ends to the mast itself, that with delight thou mayest listen to the voice of the two Sirens. And if thou shalt implore and bid thy comrades to loose thee, then let them bind thee with yet more bonds.

[55] "`But when thy comrades shall have rowed past these, thereafter I shall not fully say on which side thy course is to lie, but do thou thyself ponder it in mind, and I will tell thee of both ways. For on the one hand are beetling crags, and against them roars the great wave of dark-eyed Amphitrite; the Planctae do the blessed gods call these. Thereby not even

winged things may pass, no, not the timorous doves that bear ambrosia to father Zeus, but the smooth rock ever snatches away one even of these, and the father sends in another to make up the tale. And thereby has no ship of men ever yet escaped that has come thither, but the planks of ships and bodies of men are whirled confusedly by the waves of the sea and the blasts of baneful fire. One seafaring ship alone has passed thereby, that Argo famed of all, on her voyage from Aeetes, and even her the wave would speedily have dashed there against the great crags, had not Here sent her through, for that Jason was dear to her.

[73] "'Now on the other path are two cliffs, one of which reaches with its sharp peak to the broad heaven, and a dark cloud surrounds it. This never melts away, nor does clear sky ever surround that peak in summer or in harvest time. No mortal man could scale it or set foot upon the top, not though he had twenty hands and feet; for the rock is smooth, as if it were polished. And in the midst of the cliff is a dim cave, turned to the West, toward Erebus, even where you shall steer your hollow ship, glorious Odysseus. Not even a man of might could shoot an arrow from the hollow ship so as to reach into that vaulted cave. Therein dwells Scylla, yelping terribly. Her voice is indeed but as the voice of a new-born whelp, but she herself is an evil monster, nor would anyone be glad at sight of her, no, not though it were a god that met her. Verily she has twelve feet, all misshapen, and six necks, exceeding long, and on each one an awful head, and therein three rows of teeth, thick and close, and full of black death. Up to her middle she is hidden in the hollow cave, but she holds her head out beyond the dread chasm, and fishes there, eagerly searching around the rock for dolphins and sea-dogs and whatever greater beast she may haply catch, such creatures as deep-moaning Amphitrite rears in multitudes past counting. By her no sailors yet may boast that they have fled unscathed in their ship, for with each head she carries off a man, snatching him from the dark-prowed ship.

[101] "`But the other cliff, thou wilt note, Odysseus, is lower—they are close to each other; thou couldst even shoot an arrow across—and on it is a great fig tree with rich foliage, but beneath this divine Charybdis sucks down the black water. Thrice a day she belches it forth, and thrice she sucks it down terribly. Mayest thou not be there when she sucks it down, for no one could save thee from ruin, no, not the Earth-shaker. Nay, draw very close to Scylla's cliff, and drive thy ship past quickly; for it is better far to mourn six comrades in thy ship than all together.'

[111] "So she spoke, but I made answer and said: `Come, I pray thee, goddess, tell me this thing truly, if in any wise I might escape from fell Charybids, and ward off that other, when she works harm to my comrades.'

[115] "So I spoke, and the beautiful goddess answered and said: `Rash man, lo, now again thy heart is set on the deeds of war and on toil. Wilt thou not yield even to the immortal gods? She is not mortal, but an immortal bane, dread, and dire, and fierce, and not to be fought with; there is no defense; to flee from her is bravest. For if thou tarriest to arm thyself by the cliff, I fear lest she may again dart forth and attack thee with as many heads and seize as many men as before. Nay, row past with all thy might, and call upon Crataiis, the mother of Scylla, who bore her for a bane to mortals. Then will she keep her from darting forth again.

[127] "`And thou wilt come to the isle Thrinacia. There in great numbers feed the cattle of Helios and his goodly flocks, seven herds of cattle and as many fair flocks of sheep, and fifty in each. These bear no young, nor do they ever die, and goddesses are their shepherds, fair-tressed nymphs, Phaethusa and Lampetie, whom beautiful Neaera bore to Helios Hyperion. These their honored mother, when she had born and reared them, sent to the isle Thrinacia to dwell afar, and keep the flocks of their father and his sleek cattle. If thou leavest these unharmed and heedest thy homeward way, verily ye may

yet reach Ithaca, though in evil plight. But if thou harmest them, then I foretell ruin for thy ship and for thy comrades, and even if thou shalt thyself escape, late shalt thou come home and in evil case, after losing all thy comrades.'

[143] "So she spoke, and presently came golden-throned Dawn. Then the beautiful goddess departed up the island, but I went to the ship and roused my comrades themselves to embark and to loose the stern cables. So they went on board straightway and sat down upon the benches, and sitting well in order smote the grey sea with their oars. And for our aid in the wake of our dark-prowed ship a fair wind that filled the sail, a goodly comrade, was sent by fair-tressed Circe, dread goddess of human speech. So when we had straightway made fast all the tackling throughout the ship we sat down, but the wind and the helmsman guided the ship.

[153] "Then verily I spoke among my comrades, grieved at heart: `Friends, since it is not right that one or two alone should know the oracles that Circe, the beautiful goddess, told me, therefore will I tell them, in order that knowing them we may either die or, shunning death and fate, escape. First she bade us avoid the voice of the wondrous Sirens, and their flowery meadow. Me alone she bade to listen to their voice; but do ye bind me with grievous bonds, that I may abide fast where I am, upright in the step of the mast, and let the ropes be made fast at the ends to the mast itself; and if I implore and bid you to loose me, then do ye tie me fast with yet more bonds.'

[165] "Thus I rehearsed all these things and told them to my comrades. Meanwhile the well-built ship speedily came to the isle of the two Sirens, for a fair and gentle wind bore her on. Then presently the wind ceased and there was a windless calm, and a god lulled the waves to sleep. But my comrades rose up and furled the sail and stowed it in the hollow ship, and thereafter sat at the oars and made the water white with their polished oars of fir. But I with my sharp sword cut into

small bits a great round cake of wax, and kneaded it with my strong hands, and soon the wax grew warm, forced by the strong pressure and the rays of the lord Helios Hyperion. Then I anointed with this the ears of all my comrades in turn; and they bound me in the ship hand and foot, upright in the step of the mast, and made the ropes fast at the ends to the mast itself; and themselves sitting down smote the grey sea with their oars. But when we were as far distant as a man can make himself heard when he shouts, driving swiftly on our way, the Sirens failed not to note the swift ship as it drew near, and they raised their clear-toned song: `Come hither, as thou farest, renowned Odysseus, great glory of the Achaeans; stay thy ship that thou mayest listen to the voice of us two. For never yet has any man rowed past this isle in his black ship until he has heard the sweet voice from our lips. Nay, he has joy of it, and goes his way a wiser man. For we know all the toils that in wide Troy the Argives and Trojans endured through the will of the gods, and we know all things that come to pass upon the fruitful earth.'

[192] "So they spoke, sending forth their beautiful voice, and my heart was fain to listen, and I bade my comrades loose me, nodding to them with my brows; but they fell to their oars and rowed on. And presently Perimedes and Eurylochus arose and bound me with yet more bonds and drew them tighter. But when they had rowed past the Sirens, and we could no more hear their voice or their song, then straightway my trusty comrades took away the wax with which I had anointed their ears and loosed me from my bonds.

[201] "But when we had left the island, I presently saw smoke and a great billow, and heard a booming. Then from the hands of my men in their terror the oars flew, and splashed one and all in the swirl, and the ship stood still where it was, when they no longer plied with their hands the tapering oars. But I went through the ship and cheered my men with gentle words, coming up to each man in turn: `Friends, hitherto we have been in no wise ignorant of sorrow; surely this evil that besets

us now is no greater than when the Cyclops penned us in his hollow cave by brutal strength; yet even thence we made our escape through my valor and counsel and wit; these dangers, too, methinks we shall someday remember. But now come, as I bid, let us all obey. Do you keep your seats on the benches and smite with your oars the deep surf of the sea, in the hope that Zeus may grant us to escape and avoid this death. And to thee, steersman, I give this command, and do thou lay it to heart, since thou wieldest the steering oar of the hollow ship. From this smoke and surf keep the ship well away and hug the cliff, lest, ere thou know it, the ship swerve off to the other side and thou cast us into destruction.'

[222] "So I spoke, and they quickly hearkened to my words. But of Scylla I went not on to speak, a cureless bane, lest haply my comrades, seized with fear, should cease from rowing and huddle together in the hold. Then verily I forgot the hard command of Circe, whereas she bade me in no wise to arm myself; but when I had put on my glorious armor and grasped in my hand two long spears, I went to the fore-deck of the ship, whence I deemed that Scylla of the rock would first be seen, who was to bring ruin upon my comrades. But nowhere could I descry her, and my eyes grew weary as I gazed everywhere toward the misty rock.

[234] "We then sailed on up the narrow strait with wailing. For on one side lay Scylla and on the other divine Charybdis terribly sucked down the salt water of the sea. Verily whenever she belched it forth, like a cauldron on a great fire she would seethe and bubble in utter turmoil, and high overhead the spray would fall on the tops of both the cliffs. But as often as she sucked down the salt water of the sea, within she could all be seen in utter turmoil, and round about the rock roared terribly, while beneath the earth appeared black with sand; and pale fear seized my men. So we looked toward her and feared destruction; but meanwhile Scylla seized from out the hollow ship six of my comrades who were the best in strength and in might. Turning my eyes to the swift

ship and to the company of my men, even then I noted above me their feet and hands as they were raised aloft. To me they cried aloud, calling upon me by name for that last time in anguish of heart. And as a fisher on a jutting rock, when he casts in his baits as a snare to the little fishes, with his long pole lets down into the sea the horn of an ox of the steading, and then as he catches a fish flings it writhing ashore, even so were they drawn writhing up towards the cliffs. Then at her doors she devoured them shrieking and stretching out their hands toward me in their awful death-struggle. Most piteous did mine eyes behold that thing of all that I bore while I explored the paths of the sea.

[260] "Now when we had escaped the rocks, and dread Charybdis and Scylla, presently then we came to the goodly island of the god, where were the fair cattle, broad of brow, and the many goodly flocks of Helios Hyperion. Then while I was still out at sea in my black ship, I heard the lowing of the cattle that were being stalled and the bleating of the sheep, and upon my mind fell the words of the blind seer, Theban Tiresias, and of Aeaean Circe, who very straitly charged me to shun the island of Helios, who gives joy to mortals. Then verily I spoke among my comrades, grieved at heart: `Hear my words, comrades, for your entire evil plight, that I may tell you the oracles of Tiresias and of Aeaean Circe, who very straitly charged me to shun the island of Helios, who gives joy to mortals; for there, she said, was our most terrible bane. Nay, row the black ship out past the island.'

[277] "So I spoke, but their spirit was broken within them, and straightway Eurylochus answered me with hateful words: `Hardy art thou, Odysseus; thou hast strength beyond that of other men and thy limbs never grow weary. Verily thou art wholly wrought of iron, seeing that thou sufferest not thy comrades, worn out with toil and drowsiness, to set foot on shore, where on this sea-girt isle we might once more make ready a savory supper; but thou biddest us even as we are to wander on through the swift night, driven away from the

island over the misty deep. It is from the night that fierce winds are born, wreckers of ships. How could one escape utter destruction, if haply there should suddenly come a blast of the South Wind or the blustering West Wind, which oftenest wreck ships in despite of the sovereign gods? Nay, verily for this time let us yield to black night and make ready our supper, remaining by the swift ship, and in the morning we will go aboard, and put out into the broad sea.'

[294] "So spoke Eurylochus, and the rest of my comrades gave assent. Then verily I knew that some god was assuredly devising ill, and I spoke and addressed him with winged words: `Eurylochus, verily ye constrain me, who stand alone. But come now, do ye all swear to me a mighty oath, to the end that, if we haply find a herd of cattle or a great flock of sheep, no man may slay either cow or sheep in the blind folly of his mind; but be content to eat the food which immortal Circe gave.'

[302] "So I spoke; and they straightway swore that they would not, even as I bade them. But when they had sworn and made an end of the oath, we moored our well-built ship in the hollow harbor near a spring of sweet water, and my comrades went forth from the ship and skillfully made ready their supper. But when they had put from them the desire of food and drink, then they fell to weeping, as they remembered their dear comrades whom Scylla had snatched from out the hollow ship and devoured; and sweet sleep came upon them as they wept. But when it was the third watch of the night, and the stars had turned their course, Zeus, the cloud-gatherer, roused against us a fierce wind with a wondrous tempest, and hid with clouds the land and sea alike, and night rushed down from heaven. And as soon as early Dawn appeared, the rosy-fingered, we dragged our ship, and made her fast in a hollow cave, where were the fair dancing-floors and seats of the nymphs. Then I called my men together and spoke among them: `Friends, in our swift ship is meat and drink; let us therefore keep our hands from those cattle lest we come to

harm, for these are the cattle and goodly sheep of a dread god, even of Helios, who oversees all things and overhears all things.'

[324] "So I spoke, and their proud hearts consented. Then for a full month the South Wind blew unceasingly, nor did any other wind arise except the East and the South.

[327] "Now so long as my men had grain and red wine they kept their hands from the cattle, for they were eager to save their lives. But when all the stores had been consumed from out the ship, and now they must needs roam about in search of game, fishes, and fowl, and whatever might come to their hands—fishing with bent hooks, for hunger pinched their bellies—then I went apart up the island that I might pray to the gods in the hope that one of them might show me a way to go. And when, as I went through the island, I had got away from my comrades, I washed my hands in a place where there was shelter from the wind, and prayed to all the gods that hold Olympus; but they shed sweet sleep upon my eyelids.

[339] And meanwhile Eurylochus began to give evil counsel to my comrades: `Hear my words, comrades, for your entire evil plight. All forms of death are hateful to wretched mortals, but to die of hunger, and so meet one's doom, is the most pitiful. Nay, come, let us drive off the best of the cattle of Helios and offer sacrifice to the immortals who hold broad heaven. And if we ever reach Ithaca, our native land, we will straightway build a rich temple to Helios Hyperion and put therein many goodly offerings. And if haply he be wroth at all because of his straight-horned cattle, and be minded to destroy our ship, and the other gods consent, rather would I lose my life once for all with a gulp at the wave, than pine slowly away in a desert isle.'

[352] "So spoke Eurylochus, and the rest of my comrades gave assent. Straightway they drove off the best of the cattle of Helios from near at hand, for not far from the dark-prowed

ship were grazing the fair, sleek cattle, broad of brow. Around these, then, they stood and made prayer to the gods, plucking the tender leaves from off a high-crested oak; for they had no white barley on board the well-benched ship. Now when they had prayed and had cut the throats of the cattle and flayed them, they cut out the thigh-pieces and covered them with a double layer of fat and laid raw flesh upon them. They had no wine to pour over the blazing sacrifice, but they made libations with water, and roasted all the entrails over the fire.

[364] "Now when the thighs were wholly burned and they had tasted the inner parts, they cut up the rest and spitted it. Then it was that sweet sleep fled from my eyelids, and I went my way to the swift ship and the shore of the sea. But when, as I went, I drew near to the curved ship, then verily the hot savor of the fat was wafted about me, and I groaned and cried aloud to the immortal gods: `Father Zeus and ye other blessed gods that are forever, verily it was for my ruin that ye lulled me in pitiless sleep, while my comrades remaining behind have contrived a monstrous deed.'

[374] "Swiftly then to Helios Hyperion came Lampetie of the long robes, bearing tidings that we had slain his cattle; and straightway he spoke among the immortals, wroth at heart: `Father Zeus and ye other blessed gods that are forever, take vengeance now on the comrades of Odysseus, son of Laertes, who have insolently slain my cattle, in which I ever took delight, when I went toward the starry heaven and when I turned back again to earth from heaven. If they do not pay me fit atonement for the cattle I will go down to Hades and shine among the dead.'

[384] "Then Zeus, the cloud-gatherer, answered him and said: `Helios, do thou verily shine on among the immortals and among mortal men upon the earth, the giver of grain. As for these men I will soon smite their swift ship with my bright thunder-bolt, and shatter it to pieces in the midst of the wine-dark sea.'

[389] "This I heard from fair-haired Calypso, and she said that she herself had heard it from the messenger Hermes. But when I had come down to the ship and to the sea I upbraided my men, coming up to each in turn, but we could find no remedy—the cattle were already dead. For my men, then, the gods straightway showed forth portents. The hides crawled, the flesh, both roast and raw, bellowed upon the spits, and there was a lowing as of cattle.

[397] "For six days, then, my trusty comrades feasted on the best of the cattle of Helios which they had driven off. But when Zeus, the son of Cronus, brought upon us the seventh day, then the wind ceased to blow tempestuously, and we straightway went on board, and put out into the broad sea when we had set up the mast and hoisted the white sail.

[404] "But when we had left that island and no other land appeared, but only sky and sea, then verily the son of Cronus set a black cloud above the hollow ship, and the sea grew dark beneath it. She ran on for no long time, for straightway came the shrieking West Wind, blowing with a furious tempest, and the blast of the wind snapped both the fore-stays of the mast, so that the mast fell backward and all its tackling was strewn in the bilge. On the stern of the ship the mast struck the head of the pilot and crushed all the bones of his skull together, and like a diver he fell from the deck and his proud spirit left his bones. Therewith Zeus thundered and hurled his bolt upon the ship, and she quivered from stem to stern, smitten by the bolt of Zeus, and was filled with sulphurous smoke, and my comrades fell from out the ship. Like sea-crows they were borne on the waves about the black ship, and the god took from them their returning. But I kept pacing up and down the ship till the surge tore the sides from the keel, and the wave bore her on dismantled and snapped the mast off at the keel; but over the mast had been flung the back-stay fashioned of ox-hide; with this I lashed the two together, both keel and mast, and sitting on these was borne by the direful winds.

[426] "Then verily the West Wind ceased to blow tempestuously, and swiftly the South Wind came, bringing sorrow to my heart, that I might traverse again the way to baneful Charybdis. All night long was I borne, and at the rising of the sun I came to the cliff of Scylla and to dread Charybdis. She verily sucked down the salt water of the sea, but I, springing up to the tall fig-tree, laid hold of it, and clung to it like a bat. Yet I could in no wise plant my feet firmly or climb upon the tree, for its roots spread far below and its branches hung out of reach above, long and great, and overshadowed Charybdis. There I clung steadfastly until she should vomit forth mast and keel again, and to my joy they came at length. At the hour when a man rises from the assembly for his supper, one that decides the many quarrels of young men that seek judgment, even at that hour those spars appeared from out Charybdis. And I let go hands and feet from above and plunged down into the waters out beyond the long spars, and sitting on these I rowed onward with my hands. But as for Scylla, the father of gods and men did not suffer her again to catch sight of me, else should I never have escaped utter destruction.

[447] "Thence for nine days was I borne, and on the tenth night the gods brought me to Ogygia, where the fair-tressed Calypso dwells, dread goddess of human speech, who gave me welcome and attendance. But why should I tell thee this tale? For it was but yesterday that I told it in thy hall to thyself and to thy noble wife. It is an irksome thing, me seems, to tell again a plain-told tale."

"MYTH OF ER" BY PLATO, FROM THE REPUBLIC

Plato, ; Benjamin Jowett. *Dialogues*. New York: C. Scribner's sons, 1871. Print.

Well, I said, I will tell you a tale; not one of the tales which Odysseus tells to the hero Alcinous, yet this too is a tale of a hero, Er the son of Armenius, a Pamphylian by birth. He was slain in battle, and ten days afterwards, when the bodies of the dead were taken up already in a state of corruption, his body was found unaffected by decay, and carried away home to be buried. And on the twelfth day, as he was lying on the funeral pile, he returned to life and told them what he had seen in the other world. He said that when his soul left the body he went on a journey with a great company, and that they came to a mysterious place at which there were two openings in the earth; they were near together, and over against them were two other openings in the heaven above. In the intermediate space there were judges seated, who commanded the just, after they had given judgment on them and had bound their sentences in front of them, to ascend by the heavenly way on the right hand; and in like manner the unjust were bidden by them to descend by the lower way on the left hand; these also bore the symbols of their deeds, but fastened on their backs. He drew near, and they told him that he was to be the messenger who would carry the report of the other world to men, and they bade him hear and see all that was to be heard and seen in that place. Then he beheld and saw on one side the souls departing at either opening of heaven and earth when sentence had been given on them; and at the two other openings other souls, some ascending out of the earth dusty and worn with travel, some descending out of heaven clean and bright. And arriving ever and anon they seemed to have come from a long journey, and they went forth with gladness into the meadow, where they encamped as at a festival; and those who knew one another embraced and conversed, the souls which came from earth curiously enquiring about the things above, and the souls which came from heaven about the things beneath. And they told one another of what had happened by the way, those from below weeping and sorrowing at the remembrance of the things which they had endured and seen in their journey beneath the earth (now the journey lasted a thousand years), while those from above were describing heavenly delights and visions of inconceivable beauty. The story, Glaucon, would take too long to tell; but the sum was this:—He said that for every wrong which they had done to any one they suffered tenfold; or once in a hundred years—such being reckoned to be the length of man's life, and the penalty being thus paid ten times in a thousand years. If, for example, there were any who had been the cause of many deaths, or had betrayed or enslaved cities or armies, or been guilty of any other evil behavior, for each and all of their offences they received punishment ten times over, and the rewards of beneficence and justice and holiness were in the same proportion. I need hardly repeat what he said concerning young children dying almost as soon as they were born. Of piety and impiety to gods and parents, and of murderers, there were retributions other and greater far which he described. He mentioned that he was present when one of the spirits asked another, 'Where is Ardiaeus the Great?' (Now this Ardiaeus lived a thousand years before the time of Er: he had been the tyrant of some city of Pamphylia, and had murdered his aged father and his elder brother, and was said to have committed many other abominable crimes.) The answer of the other spirit was: 'He comes not hither and will never come. And this,' said he, 'was one of the dreadful sights which we ourselves witnessed. We were at the mouth of the cavern, and, having completed all our experiences, were about to reascend, when of a sudden Ardiaeus appeared and several others, most of whom were tyrants; and there were also besides the tyrants private individuals who had been great criminals: they were just, as they fancied, about to return into the upper world, but the mouth, instead of admitting them, gave a roar, whenever any of these incurable sinners or someone who had not been sufficiently punished tried to ascend; and then wild men of fiery aspect, who were standing by and heard the sound, seized and carried them off; and Ardiaeus and others they bound head and foot and hand, and threw them down and flayed them with scourges, and dragged them along the road at the side, carding them on thorns like wool, and declaring to the passers-by what were their crimes, and that they were being taken away to be cast into hell.' And of all the many terrors which they had endured, he said that there was none like the terror which each of them felt at that moment, lest they should hear the voice; and when there was silence, one by one they ascended with exceeding joy. These, said Er, were the penalties and retributions, and there were blessings as great.

Now when the spirits which were in the meadow had tarried seven days, on the eighth they were obliged to proceed on their journey, and, on the fourth day after, he said that they came to a place where they could see from above a line of light, straight as a column, extending right through the whole heaven and through the earth, in color resembling the rainbow, only brighter and purer; another day's journey brought them to the place, and there, in the midst of the light, they saw the ends of the chains of heaven let down from above: for this light is the belt of heaven, and holds together the circle of the universe, like the undergirders of a trireme. From these ends is extended the spindle of Necessity, on which all the revolutions turn. The shaft and hook of this spindle are made of steel, and the whorl is made partly of steel and also partly of other materials. Now the whorl is in form like the whorl used on earth; and the description of it implied that there is one large hollow whorl which is quite scooped out, and into this is fitted another lesser one, and another, and another, and four others, making eight in all, like vessels which fit into one another; the whorls show their edges on the upper side, and on their lower side all together form one continuous whorl. This is pierced by the spindle, which is driven home through the center of the eighth. The first and outermost whorl has the rim broadest, and the seven inner whorls are narrower, in the following proportions—the sixth is next to the first in size, the fourth next to the sixth; then comes the eighth; the seventh is fifth, the fifth is sixth, the third is seventh, last and eighth comes the second. The largest [or fixed stars] is spangled, and the seventh [or sun] is brightest; the eighth [or moon] colored by the reflected light of the seventh; the second and fifth [Saturn and Mercury] are in color like one another, and yellower than the preceding; the third [Venus] has the whitest light; the fourth [Mars] is reddish; the sixth [Jupiter] is in whiteness second. Now the whole spindle has the same motion; but, as the whole revolves in one direction, the seven inner circles move slowly in the other, and of these the swiftest is the eighth; next in swiftness are the seventh, sixth, and fifth, which move together; third in swiftness appeared to move according to the law of this reversed motion the fourth; the third appeared fourth and the second fifth. The spindle turns on the knees of Necessity; and on the upper surface of each circle is a siren, who goes round with them, hymning a single tone or note. The eight together form one harmony; and roundabout, at equal intervals, there is another band, three in number, each sitting upon her throne: these are the Fates, daughters of Necessity, who are clothed in white robes and have chaplets upon their heads, Lachesis and Clotho and Atropos, who accompany with their voices the harmony of the sirens—Lachesis singing of the past, Clotho of the present, Atropos of the future; Clotho from time to time assisting with a touch of her right hand the revolution of the outer circle of the whorl or spindle, and Atropos with her left hand touching and guiding the inner ones, and Lachesis laying hold of either in turn, first with one hand and then with the other.

When Er and the spirits arrived, their duty was to go at once to Lachesis; but first of all there came a prophet who arranged them in order; then he took from the knees of Lachesis lots and samples of lives, and having mounted a high pulpit, spoke as follows: 'Hear the word of Lachesis, the daughter of Necessity. Mortal souls, behold a new cycle of life and mortality. Your genius will not be allotted to you, but you will choose your genius; and let him who draws the first lot have the first choice, and the life which he chooses shall be his destiny. Virtue is free, and as a man honors or dishonors her he will have more or less of her; the responsibility is with the chooser—God is justified.' When the Interpreter had thus spoken he scattered lots indifferently among them all, and each of them took up the lot which fell near him, all but Er himself (he was not allowed), and each as he took his lot perceived the number which he had obtained. Then the Interpreter placed on the ground before them the samples of lives; and there were many more lives than the souls present, and they were of all sorts. There were lives of every animal and of man in every condition. And there were tyrannies among them, some lasting out the tyrant's life, others which broke off in the middle and came to an end in poverty and exile and beggary; and there were lives of famous men, some who were famous for their form and beauty as well as for their strength and success in games, or, again, for their birth and the qualities of their ancestors; and some who were the reverse of famous for the opposite qualities. And of women likewise; there was not, however, any definite character in them, because the soul, when choosing a new life, must of necessity become different. But there was every other quality, and they all mingled with one another, and also with elements of wealth and poverty, and disease and health; and there were mean states also. And here, my dear Glaucon, is the supreme peril of our human state; and therefore the utmost care should be taken. Let each one of us leave every other kind of knowledge and seek and follow one thing only, if peradventure he may be able to learn and may find someone who will make him able to learn and discern between good and evil, and so to choose always and everywhere the better life as he has opportunity. He should consider the bearing of all these things which have been mentioned severally and collectively upon virtue; he should know what the effect of beauty is when combined with poverty or wealth in a particular soul, and what are the good and evil consequences of noble and humble birth, of private and public station, of strength and weakness, of cleverness and dullness, and of all the natural and acquired gifts of the soul, and the operation of them when conjoined; he will then look at the nature of the soul, and from the consideration of all these qualities he will be able to determine which is the better and which is the worse; and so he will choose, giving the name of evil to the life which will make his soul more unjust, and good to the life which will make his soul more just; all else he will disregard. For we have seen and know that this is the best choice both in life and after death. A man must take with him into the world below an adamantine faith in truth and right, that there too he may be undazzled by the desire of wealth or the other allurements of evil, lest, coming upon tyrannies and similar villainies, he do irremediable wrongs to others and suffer yet worse himself; but let him know how to choose the mean and avoid the extremes on either side, as far as possible, not only in this life but in all that which is to come. For this is the way of happiness.

And according to the report of the messenger from the other world this was what the prophet said at the time: 'Even for the last comer, if he chooses wisely and will live diligently, there is appointed a happy and not undesirable existence. Let not him who chooses first be careless, and let not the last despair.' And when he had spoken, he who had the first choice came forward and in a moment chose the greatest tyranny; his mind having been darkened by folly and sensuality, he had not thought out the whole matter before he chose, and did not at first sight perceive that he was fated, among other evils, to devour his own children. But when he had time to reflect, and saw what was in the lot, he began to beat his breast and lament over his choice, forgetting the proclamation of the prophet; for, instead of throwing the blame of his misfortune on himself, he accused chance and the gods, and everything rather than himself. Now he was one of those who came from heaven, and in a former life had dwelt in a well-ordered State, but his virtue was a matter of habit only, and he had no philosophy. And it was true of others who were similarly overtaken, that the greater number of them came from heaven and therefore they had never been schooled by trial, whereas the pilgrims who came from earth having themselves suffered and seen others suffer were not in a hurry to choose. And owing to this inexperience of theirs, and also because the lot was a chance, many of the souls exchanged a good destiny for an evil or an evil for a good. For if a man had always on his arrival in this world dedicated himself from the first to sound philosophy, and had been moderately fortunate in the number of the lot, he might, as the messenger reported, be happy here, and also his journey to another life and return to this, instead of being rough and underground, would be smooth and heavenly. Most curious, he said, was the spectacle—sad and laughable and strange; for the choice of the souls was in most cases based on their experience of a previous life. There he saw the soul which had once been Orpheus choosing the life of a swan out of enmity to the race of women, hating to be born of a woman because they had been his murderers; he beheld also the soul of Thamyras choosing the life of a nightingale; birds, on the other hand, like the swan and other musicians, wanting to be men. The soul which obtained the twentieth lot chose the life of a lion, and this was the soul of Ajax the son of Telamon, who would not be a man, remembering the injustice which was done him in the judgment about the arms. The next was Agamemnon, who took the life of an eagle, because, like Ajax, he hated human nature by reason of his sufferings. About the middle came the lot of Atalanta; she, seeing the great fame of an athlete, was unable to resist the temptation: and after her there followed the soul of Epeus the son of Panopeus passing into the nature of a woman cunning in the arts; and far away among the last who chose, the soul of the jester Thersites was putting on the form of a monkey. There came also the soul of Odysseus having yet to make a choice, and his lot happened to be the last of them all. Now the recollection of former toils had disenchanted him of ambition, and he went about for a considerable time in search of the life of a private man who had no cares; he had some difficulty in finding this, which was lying about and had been neglected by everybody else; and when he saw it, he said that he would have done the same had his lot been first instead of last, and that he was delighted to have it. And not only did men pass into animals, but I must also mention that there were animals tame and wild who changed into one another and into corresponding human natures—the good into the gentle and the evil into the savage, in all sorts of combinations.

All the souls had now chosen their lives, and they went in the order of their choice to Lachesis, who sent with them the genius whom they had severally chosen, to be the guardian of their lives and the fulfiller of the choice: this genius led the souls first to Clotho, and drew them within the revolution of the spindle impelled by her hand, thus ratifying the destiny of each; and then, when they were fastened to this, carried them to Atropos, who spun the threads and made them irreversible, whence without turning round they passed beneath the throne of Necessity; and when they had all passed, they marched on in a scorching heat to the plain of Forgetfulness, which was a barren waste destitute of trees and verdure; and then towards evening they encamped by the river of Unmindfulness, whose water no vessel can hold; of this they were all obliged to drink a certain quantity, and those who were not saved by wisdom drank more than was necessary; and each one as he drank forgot all things. Now after they had gone to rest, about the middle of the night there was a thunderstorm and earthquake, and then in an instant they were driven upwards in all manner of ways to their birth, like stars shooting. He himself was hindered from drinking the water. But in what manner or by what means he returned to the body he could not say; only, in the morning, awaking suddenly, he found himself lying on the pyre.

And thus, Glaucon, the tale has been saved and has not perished, and will save us if we are obedient to the word spoken; and we shall pass safely over the river of

Forgetfulness and our soul will not be defiled. Wherefore my counsel is, that we hold fast ever to the heavenly way and follow after justice and virtue always, considering that the soul is immortal and able to endure every sort of good and every sort of evil. Thus shall we live dear to one another and to the gods, both while remaining here and when, like conquerors in the games who go round to gather gifts, we receive our reward. And it shall be well with us both in this life and in the pilgrimage of a thousand years which we have been describing.

HISTORIES BY HERODOTUS

SCYTHIAN LOGOI – BOOK 4

Herodotus, , George Rawlinson, Henry C. Rawlinson, and John G. Wilkinson. *The History of Herodotus*. New York: D. Appleton and Co, 1885. Print.

2. Now the Scythians blind all their slaves, to use them in preparing their milk. The plan they follow is to thrust tubes made of bone, not unlike our musical pipes, up the vulva of the mare, and then to blow into the tubes with their mouths, some milking while the others blow. They say that they do this because when the veins of the animal are full of air, the udder is forced down. The milk thus obtained is poured into deep wooden casks, about which the blind slaves are placed, and then the milk is stirred round. That which rises to the top is drawn off, and considered the best part; the under portion is of less account. Such is the reason why the Scythians blind all those whom they take in war; it arises from their not being tillers of the ground, but a pastoral race.

3. When therefore the children sprung from these slaves and the Scythian women grew to manhood, and understood the circumstances of their birth, they resolved to oppose the army which was returning from Media. And, first of all, they cut off a tract of country from the rest of Scythia by digging a broad dyke from the Tauric mountains to the vast lake of the Maeotis. Afterwards, when the Scythians tried to force an entrance, they marched out and engaged them. Many battles were fought, and the Scythians gained no advantage, until at last one of them thus addressed the remainder: "What are we doing, Scythians? We are fighting our slaves, diminishing our own number when we fall, and the number of those that

belong to us when they fall by our hands. Take my advice- lay spear and bow aside, and let each man fetch his horsewhip, and go boldly up to them. So long as they see us with arms in our hands, they imagine themselves our equals in birth and bravery; but let them behold us with no other weapon but the whip, and they will feel that they are our slaves, and flee before us."

4. The Scythians followed this counsel, and the slaves were so astounded, that they forgot to fight, and immediately ran away. Such was the mode in which the Scythians, after being for a time the lords of Asia, and being forced to quit it by the Medes, returned and settled in their own country. This inroad of theirs it was that Darius was anxious to avenge, and such was the purpose for which he was now collecting an army to invade them.

5. According to the account which the Scythians themselves give, they are the youngest of all nations. Their tradition is as follows. A certain Targitaus was the first man who ever lived in their country, which before his time was a desert without inhabitants. He was a child- I do not believe the tale, but it is told nevertheless- of Jove and a daughter of the Borysthenes. Targitaus, thus descended, begat three sons, Leipoxais, Arpoxais, and Colaxais, who was the youngest born of the three. While they still ruled the land, there fell from the sky four implements, all of gold- a plough, a yoke, a battle-axe, and a drinking-cup. The eldest of the brothers perceived them first, and approached to pick them up; when lo! as he came near, the gold took fire, and blazed. He therefore went his way, and the second coming forward made the attempt, but the same thing happened again. The gold rejected both the eldest and the second brother. Last of the entire youngest brother approached, and immediately the flames were extinguished; so he picked up the gold, and carried it to his home. Then the two elder agreed together, and made the whole kingdom over to the youngest born.

6. From Leipoxais sprang the Scythians of the race called Auchatae; from Arpoxais, the middle brother, those known as the Catiari and Traspians; from Colaxais, the youngest, the Royal Scythians, or Paralatae. All together they are named Scoloti, after one of their kings: the Greeks, however, call them Scythians.

7. Such is the account which the Scythians give of their origin. They add that from the time of Targitaus, their first king, to the invasion of their country by Darius, is a period of one thousand years, neither less nor more. The Royal Scythians guard the sacred gold with most especial care, and year by year offer great sacrifices in its honor. At this feast, if the man who has the custody of the gold should fall asleep in the open air, he is sure (the Scythians say) not to outlive the year. His pay therefore is as much land as he can ride round on horseback in a day. As the extent of Scythia is very great, Colaxais gave each of his three sons a separate kingdom, one of which was of ampler size than the other two: in this the gold was preserved. Above, to the northward of the farthest dwellers in Scythia, the country is said to be concealed from sight and made impassable by reason of the feathers which are shed abroad abundantly. The earth and air are alike full of them, and this it is which prevents the eye from obtaining any view of the region.

8. Such is the account which the Scythians give of themselves, and of the country which lies above them. The Greeks who dwell about the Pontus tell a different story. According to Hercules, when he was carrying off the cattle of Geryon, arrived in the region which is now inhabited by the Scyths, but which was then a desert. Geryon lived outside the Pontus, in an island called by the Greeks Erytheia, near Gades, which is beyond the Pillars of Hercules upon the Ocean. Now some say that the Ocean begins in the east, and runs the whole way round the world; but they give no proof that this is really so. Hercules came from thence into the region now called Scythia, and, being overtaken by storm and frost, drew his lion's skin

about him, and fell fast asleep. While he slept, his mares, which he had loosed from his chariot to graze, by some wonderful chance disappeared.

9. On waking, he went in quest of them, and, after wandering over the whole country, came at last to the district called "the Woodland," where he found in a cave a strange being, between a maiden and a serpent, whose form from the waist upwards was like that of a woman, while all below was like a snake. He looked at her wonderingly; but nevertheless inquired, whether she had chanced to see his strayed mares anywhere. She answered him, "Yes, and they were now in her keeping; but never would she consent to give them back, unless he took her for his mistress." So Hercules, to get his mares back, agreed; but afterwards she put him off and delayed restoring the mares, since she wished to keep him with her as long as possible. He, on the other hand, was only anxious to secure them and to get away. At last, when she gave them up, she said to him, "When thy mares strayed hither, it was I who saved them for thee: now thou hast paid their salvage; for lo! I bear in my womb three sons of thine. Tell me therefore when thy sons grow up, what must I do with them? Wouldst thou wish that I should settle them here in this land, whereof I am mistress, or shall I send them to thee?" Thus questioned, they say, Hercules answered, "When the lads have grown to manhood, do thus, and assuredly thou wilt not err. Watch them, and when thou seest one of them bend this bow as I now bend it, and gird himself with this girdle thus, choose him to remain in the land. Those who fail in the trial, send away. Thus wilt thou at once please thyself and obey me."

10. Hereupon he strung one of his bows- up to that time he had carried two- and showed her how to fasten the belt. Then he gave both bow and belt into her hands. Now the belt had a golden goblet attached to its clasp. So after he had given them to her, he went his way; and the woman, when her children grew to manhood, first gave them severally their names. One

she called Agathyrsus, one Gelonus, and the other, who was the youngest, Scythes. Then she remembered the instructions she had received from Hercules, and, in obedience to his orders, she put her sons to the test. Two of them, Agathyrsus and Gelonus, proving unequal to the task enjoined, their mother sent them out of the land; Scythes, the youngest, succeeded, and so he was allowed to remain. From Scythes, the son of Hercules, were descended the after kings of Scythia; and from the circumstance of the goblet which hung from the belt, the Scythians to this day wear goblets at their girdles. This was the only thing which the mother of Scythes did for him. Such is the tale told by the Greeks who dwell around the Pontus.

11. There is also another different story, now to be related, in which I am more inclined to put faith than in any other. It is that the wandering Scythians once dwelt in Asia, and there warred with the Massagetae, but with ill success; they therefore quitted their homes, crossed the Araxes, and entered the land of Cimmeria. For the land which is now inhabited by the Scyths was formerly the country of the Cimmerians. On their coming, the natives, who heard how numerous the invading army was, held a council. At this meeting opinion was divided, and both parties stiffly maintained their own view; but the counsel of the Royal tribe was the braver. For the others urged that the best thing to be done was to leave the country, and avoid a contest with so vast a host; but the Royal tribe advised remaining and fighting for the soil to the last. As neither party chose to give way, the one determined to retire without a blow and yield their lands to the invaders; but the other, remembering the good things which they had enjoyed in their homes, and picturing to themselves the evils which they had to expect if they gave them up, resolved not to flee, but rather to die and at least be buried in their fatherland. Having thus decided, they drew apart in two bodies, the one as numerous as the other, and fought together. All of the Royal tribe were slain, and the people buried them near the river Tyras, where their grave is still to be seen. Then the rest of the

Cimmerians departed, and the Scythians, on their coming, took possession of a deserted land.

12. Scythia still retains traces of the Cimmerians; there are Cimmerian castles, and a Cimmerian ferry, also a tract called Cimmeria, and a Cimmerian Bosphorus. It appears likewise that the Cimmerians, when they fled into Asia to escape the Scyths, made a settlement in the peninsula where the Greek city of Sinope was afterwards built. The Scyths, it is plain, pursued them, and missing their road, poured into Media. For the Cimmerians kept the line which led along the sea-shore, but the Scyths in their pursuit held the Caucasus upon their right, thus proceeding inland, and falling upon Media. This account is one which is common both to Greeks and barbarians.

13. Aristeas also, son of Caystrobius, a native of Proconnesus, says in the course of his poem that wrapped in Bacchic fury he went as far as the Issedones. Above them dwelt the Arimaspi, men with one eye; still further, the gold-guarding griffins; and beyond these, the Hyperboreans, who extended to the sea. Except the Hyperboreans, all these nations, beginning with the Arimaspi, were continually encroaching upon their neighbors. Hence it came to pass that the Arimaspi drove the Issedonians from their country, while the Issedonians dispossessed the Scyths; and the Scyths, pressing upon the Cimmerians, who dwelt on the shores of the Southern Sea, forced them to leave their land. Thus even Aristeas does not agree in his account of this region with the Scythians.

14. The birthplace of Aristeas, the poet who sung of these things, I have already mentioned. I will now relate a tale which I heard concerning him both at Proconnesus and at Cyzicus. Aristeas, they said, who belonged to one of the noblest families in the island, had entered one day into a fuller's shop, when he suddenly dropt down dead. Hereupon the fuller shut up his shop, and went to tell Aristeas' kindred what had happened. The report of the death had just spread

through the town, when a certain Cyzicenian, lately arrived from Artaca, contradicted the rumor, affirming that he had met Aristeas on his road to Cyzicus, and had spoken with him. This man, therefore, strenuously denied the rumor; the relations, however, proceeded to the fuller's shop with all things necessary for the funeral, intending to carry the body away. But on the shop being opened, no Aristeas was found, either dead or alive. Seven years afterwards he reappeared, they told me, in Proconnesus, and wrote the poem called by the Greeks The Arimaspeia, after which he disappeared a second time. This is the tale current in the two cities above-mentioned.

15. What follows I know to have happened to the Metapontines of Italy, three hundred and forty years after the second disappearance of Aristeas, as I collect by comparing the accounts given me at Proconnesus and Metapontum. Aristeas then, as the Metapontines affirm, appeared to them in their own country, and ordered them to set up an altar in honor of Apollo, and to place near it a statue to be called that of Aristeas the Proconnesian. "Apollo," he told them, "had come to their country once, though he had visited no other Italiots; and he had been with Apollo at the time, not however in his present form, but in the shape of a crow." Having said so much, he vanished. Then the Metapontines, as they relate, sent to Delphi, and inquired of the god in what light they were to regard the appearance of this ghost of a man. The Pythoness, in reply, bade them attend to what the specter said, "for so it would go best with them." Thus advised, they did as they had been directed: and there is now a statue bearing the name of Aristeas, close by the image of Apollo in the market-place of Metapontum, with bay-trees standing around it. But enough has been said concerning Aristeas.

16. With regard to the regions which lie above the country whereof this portion of my history treats, there is no one who possesses any exact knowledge. Not a single person can I find who professes to be acquainted with them by actual

observation. Even Aristeas, the traveler of whom I lately spoke, does not claim- and he is writing poetry- to have reached any farther than the Issedonians. What he relates concerning the regions beyond is, he confesses, mere hearsay, being the account which the Issedonians gave him of those countries. However, I shall proceed to mention all that I have learnt of these parts by the most exact inquiries which I have been able to make concerning them.

17. Above the mart of the Borysthenites, which is situated in the very center of the whole sea-coast of Scythia, the first people who inhabit the land are the Callipedae, a Greco-Scythic race. Next to them, as you go inland, dwell the people called the Alazonians. These two nations in other respects resemble the Scythians in their usages, but sow and eat corn, also onions, garlic, lentils, and millet. Beyond the Alazonians reside Scythian cultivators, who grow corn, not for their own use, but for sale. Still higher up are the Neuri. Northwards of the Neuri the continent, as far as it is known to us, is uninhabited. These are the nations along the course of the river Hypanis, west of the Borysthenes.

18. Across the Borysthenes, the first country after you leave the coast is Hylaea (the Woodland). Above this dwell the Scythian Husbandmen, whom the Greeks living near the Hypanis call Borysthenites, while they call themselves Olbiopolites. These Husbandmen extend eastward a distance of three days' journey to a river bearing the name of Panticapes, while northward the country is theirs for eleven days' sail up the course of the Borysthenes. Further inland there is a vast tract which is uninhabited. Above this desolate region dwell the Cannibals, who are a people apart, much unlike the Scythians. Above them the country becomes an utter desert; not a single tribe, so far as we know, inhabits it.

19. Crossing the Panticapes, and proceeding eastward of the Husbandmen, we come upon the wandering Scythians, who neither plough nor sow. Their country, and the whole of this

region, except Hylaea, is quite bare of trees. They extend towards the east a distance of fourteen' days' journey, occupying a tract which reaches to the river Gerrhus.

20. On the opposite side of the Gerrhus is the Royal district, as it is called: here dwells the largest and bravest of the Scythian tribes, which looks upon all the other tribes in the light of slaves. Its country reaches on the south to Taurica, on the east to the trench dug by the sons of the blind slaves, the mart upon the Palus Maeotis, called Cremni (the Cliffs), and in part to the river Tanais. North of the country of the Royal Scythians are the Melanchaeni (Black-Robes), a people of quite a different race from the Scythians. Beyond them lie marshes and a region without inhabitants, so far as our knowledge reaches.

21. When one crosses the Tanais, one is no longer in Scythia; the first region on crossing is that of the Sauromatae, who, beginning at the upper end of the Palus Maeotis, stretch northward a distance of fifteen days' journey, inhabiting a country which is entirely bare of trees, whether wild or cultivated. Above them, possessing the second region, dwell the Budini, whose territory is thickly wooded with trees of every kind.

22. Beyond the Budini, as one goes northward, first there is a desert, seven days' journey across; after which, if one inclines somewhat to the east, the Thyssagetae are reached, a numerous nation quite distinct from any other, and living by the chase. Adjoining them, and within the limits of the same region, are the people who bear the name of Iyrcae; they also support themselves by hunting, which they practice in the following manner. The hunter climbs a tree, the whole country abounding in wood, and there sets himself in ambush; he has a dog at hand, and a horse, trained to lie down upon its belly, and thus make itself low; the hunter keeps watch, and when he sees his game, lets fly an arrow; then mounting his horse, he gives the beast chase, his dog following hard all the while. Beyond these people, a little to the east, dwells a distinct tribe

of Scyths, who revolted once from the Royal Scythians, and migrated into these parts.

23. As far as their country, the tract of land whereof I have been speaking is all a smooth plain, and the soil deep; beyond you enter on a region which is rugged and stony. Passing over a great extent of this rough country, you come to a people dwelling at the foot of lofty mountains, who are said to be all- both men and women- bald from their birth, to have flat noses, and very long chins. These people speak a language of their own,. the dress which they wear is the same as the Scythian. They live on the fruit of a certain tree, the name of which is Ponticum; in size it is about equal to our fig-tree, and it bears a fruit like a bean, with a stone inside. When the fruit is ripe, they strain it through cloths; the juice which runs off is black and thick, and is called by the natives "aschy." They lap this up with their tongues, and also mix it with milk for a drink; while they make the lees, which are solid, into cakes, and eat them instead of meat; for they have but few sheep in their country, in which there is no good pasturage. Each of them dwells under a tree, and they cover the tree in winter with a cloth of thick white felt, but take off the covering in the summer-time. No one harms these people, for they are looked upon as sacred- they do not even possess any warlike weapons. When their neighbors fall out, they make up the quarrel; and when one flies to them for refuge, he is safe from all hurt. They are called the Argippaeans.

24. Up to this point the territory of which we are speaking is very completely explored, and all the nations between the coast and the bald-headed men are well known to us. For some of the Scythians are accustomed to penetrate as far, of whom inquiry may easily be made, and Greeks also go there from the mart on the Borysthenes, and from the other marts along the Euxine. The Scythians who make this journey communicate with the inhabitants by means of seven interpreters and seven languages.

25. Thus far, therefore, the land is known; but beyond the bald-headed men lies a region of which no one can give any exact account. Lofty and precipitous mountains, which are never crossed, bar further progress. The bald men say, but it does not seem to me credible, that the people who live in these mountains have feet like goats; and that after passing them you find another race of men, who sleep during one half of the year. This latter statement appears to me quite unworthy of credit. The region east of the bald-headed men is well known to be inhabited by the Issedonians, but the tract that lies to the north of these two nations is entirely unknown, except by the accounts which they give of it.

26. The Issedonians are said to have the following customs. When a man's father dies, all the near relatives bring sheep to the house; which are sacrificed, and their flesh cut in pieces, while at the same time the dead body undergoes the like treatment. The two sorts of flesh are afterwards mixed together, and the whole is served up at a banquet. The head of the dead man is treated differently: it is stripped bare, cleansed, and set in gold. It then becomes an ornament on which they pride themselves, and is brought out year by year at the great festival which sons keep in honor of their fathers' death, just as the Greeks keep their Genesia. In other respects the Issedonians are reputed to be observers of justice: and it is to be remarked that their women have equal authority with the men. Thus our knowledge extends as far as this nation.

27. The regions beyond are known only from the accounts of the Issedonians, by whom the stories are told of the one-eyed race of men and the gold-guarding griffins. These stories are received by the Scythians from the Issedonians, and by them passed on to us Greeks: whence it arises that we give the one-eyed race the Scythian name of Arimaspi, "arima" being the Scythic word for "one," and "spu" for "the eye."

28. The whole district whereof we have here discoursed has winters of exceeding rigor. During eight months the frost is so

intense that water poured upon the ground does not form mud, but if a fire be lighted on it mud is produced. The sea freezes, and the Cimmerian Bosphorus is frozen over. At that season the Scythians who dwell inside the trench make warlike expeditions upon the ice, and even drive their wagons across to the country of the Sindians. Such is the intensity of the cold during eight months out of the twelve; and even in the remaining four the climate is still cool. The character of the winter likewise is unlike that of the same season in any other country; for at that time, when the rains ought to fall in Scythia, there is scarcely any rain worth mentioning, while in summer it never gives over raining; and thunder, which elsewhere is frequent then, in Scythia is unknown in that part of the year, coming only in summer, when it is very heavy. Thunder in the winter-time is there accounted a prodigy; as also are earthquakes, whether they happen in winter or summer. Horses bear the winter well, cold as it is, but mules and asses are quite unable to bear it; whereas in other countries mules and asses are found to endure the cold, while horses, if they stand still, are frost-bitten.

29. To me it seems that the cold may likewise be the cause which prevents the oxen in Scythia from having horns. There is a line of Homer's in the Odyssey which gives a support to my opinion:-

Libya too, where horns bud quick on the foreheads of lambkins.

He means to say what is quite true, that in warm countries the horns come early. So too in countries where the cold is severe animals either have no horns, or grow them with difficulty- the cold being the cause in this instance.

30. Here I must express my wonder- additions being what my work always from the very first affected- that in Elis, where the cold is not remarkable, and there is nothing else to account for it, mules are never produced. The Eleans say it is in

consequence of a curse; and their habit is, when the breeding-time comes, to take their mares into one of the adjoining countries, and there keep them till they are in foal, when they bring them back again into Elis.

31. With respect to the feathers which are said by the Scythians to fill the air, and to prevent persons from penetrating into the remoter parts of the continent, even having any view of those regions, my opinion is that in the countries above Scythia it always snows- less, of course, in the summer than in the wintertime. Now snow when it falls looks like feathers, as everyone is aware who has seen it come down close to him. These northern regions, therefore, are uninhabitable by reason of the severity of the winter; and the Scythians, with their neighbors, call the snow-flakes feathers because, I think, of the likeness which they bear to them. I have now related what is said of the most distant parts of this continent whereof any account is given.

32. Of the Hyperboreans nothing is said either by the Scythians or by any of the other dwellers in these regions, unless it be the Issedonians. But in my opinion, even the Issedonians are silent concerning them; otherwise the Scythians would have repeated their statements, as they do those concerning the one-eyed men. Hesiod, however, mentions them, and Homer also in the Epigoni, if that be really a work of his.

33. But the persons who have by far the most to say on this subject are the Delians. They declare that certain offerings, packed in wheaten straw, were brought from the country of the Hyperboreans into Scythia, and that the Scythians received them and passed them on to their neighbors upon the west, who continued to pass them on until at last they reached the Adriatic. From hence they were sent southward, and when they came to Greece, were received first of all by the Dodonaeans. Thence they descended to the Maliac Gulf, from which they were carried across into Euboea, where the people

handed them on from city to city, till they came at length to Carystus. The Carystians took them over to Tenos, without stopping at Andros; and the Tenians brought them finally to Delos. Such, according to their own account, was the road by which the offerings reached the Delians. Two damsels, they say, named Hyperoche and Laodice, brought the first offerings from the Hyperboreans; and with them the Hyperboreans sent five men to keep them from all harm by the way; these are the persons whom the Delians call "Perpherees," and to whom great honors are paid at Delos. Afterwards the Hyperboreans, when they found that their messengers did not return, thinking it would be a grievous thing always to be liable to lose the envoys they should send, adopted the following plan:- they wrapped their offerings in the wheaten straw, and bearing them to their borders, charged their neighbors to send them forward from one nation to another, which was done accordingly, and in this way the offerings reached Delos. I myself know of a practice like this, which obtains with the women of Thrace and Paeonia. They in their sacrifices to the queenly Diana bring wheaten straw always with their offerings. Of my own knowledge I can testify that this is so.

34. The damsels sent by the Hyperboreans died in Delos; and in their honor all the Delian girls and youths are wont to cut off their hair. The girls, before their marriage-day, cut off a curl, and twining it round a distaff, lay it upon the grave of the strangers. This grave is on the left as one enters the precinct of Diana, and has an olive-tree growing on it. The youths wind some of their hair round a kind of grass, and, like the girls, place it upon the tomb. Such are the honors paid to these damsels by the Delians.

35. They add that, once before, there came to Delos by the same road as Hyperoche and Laodice, two other virgins from the Hyperboreans, whose names were Arge and Opis. Hyperoche and Laodice came to bring to Ilithyia the offering which they had laid upon themselves, in acknowledgment of their quick labors; but Arge and Opis came at the same time as

the gods of Delos, and are honored by the Delians in a different way. For the Delian women make collections in these maidens' names, and invoke them in the hymn which Olen, a Lycian, composed for them; and the rest of the islanders, and even the Ionians, have been taught by the Delians to do the like. This Olen, who came from Lycia, made the other old hymns also which are sung in Delos. The Delians add that the ashes from the thigh-bones burnt upon the altar are scattered over the tomb of Opis and Arge. Their tomb lies behind the temple of Diana, facing the east, near the banqueting-hall of the Ceians. Thus much then, and no more, concerning the Hyperboreans.

36. As for the tale of Abaris, who is said to have been a Hyperborean, and to have gone with his arrow all round the world without once eating, I shall pass it by in silence. Thus much, however, is clear: if there are Hyperboreans, there must also be Hypernotians. For my part, I cannot but laugh when I see numbers of persons drawing maps of the world without having any reason to guide them; making, as they do, the ocean-stream to run all round the earth, and the earth itself to be an exact circle, as if described by a pair of compasses, with Europe and Asia just of the same size. The truth in this matter I will now proceed to explain in a very few words, making it clear what the real size of each region is, and what shape should be given them.

[...]

46. The Euxine sea, where Darius now went to war, has nations dwelling around it, with the one exception of the Scythians, more unpolished than those of any other region that we know of. For, setting aside Anacharsis and the Scythian people, there is not within this region a single nation which can be put forward as having any claims to wisdom, or which has produced a single person of any high repute. The Scythians indeed have in one respect, and that the very most important of all those that fall under man's control, shown

themselves wiser than any nation upon the face of the earth. Their customs otherwise are not such as I admire. The one thing of which I speak is the contrivance whereby they make it impossible for the enemy who invades them to escape destruction, while they themselves are entirely out of his reach, unless it please them to engage with him. Having neither cities nor forts, and carrying their dwellings with them wherever they go; accustomed, moreover, one and all of them, to shoot from horseback; and living not by husbandry but on their cattle, their wagons the only houses that they possess, how can they fail of being unconquerable, and unassailable even?

47. The nature of their country, and the rivers by which it is intersected, greatly favor this mode of resisting attacks. For the land is level, well watered, and abounding in pasture; while the rivers which traverse it are almost equal in number to the canals of Egypt. Of these I shall only mention the most famous and such as are navigable to some distance from the sea. They are, the Ister, which has five mouths; the Tyras, the Hypanis, the Borysthenes, the Panticapes, the Hypacyris, the Gerrhus, and the Tanais. The courses of these streams I shall now proceed to describe.

48. The Ister is of all the rivers with which we are acquainted the mightiest. It never varies in height, but continues at the same level summer and winter. Counting from the west it is the first of the Scythian rivers, and the reason of its being the greatest is that it receives the water of several tributaries. Now the tributaries which swell its flood are the following: first, on the side of Scythia, these five- the stream called by the Scythians Porata, and by the Greeks Pyretus, the Tiarantus, the Ararus, the Naparis, and the Ordessus. The first mentioned is a great stream, and is the easternmost of the tributaries. The Tiarantus is of less volume, and more to the west. The Ararus, Naparis, and Ordessus fall into the Ister between these two. All the above mentioned are genuine Scythian rivers, and go to swell the current of the Ister.

49. From the country of the Agathyrsi comes down another river, the Maris, which empties itself into the same; and from the heights of Haemus descend with a northern course three mighty streams, the Atlas, the Auras, and the Tibisis, and pour their waters into it. Thrace gives it three tributaries, the Athrys, the Noes, and the Artanes, which all pass through the country of the Crobyzian Thracians. Another tributary is furnished by Paeonia, namely, the Scius; this river, rising near Mount Rhodope, forces its way through the chain of Haemus, and so reaches the Ister. From Illyria comes another stream, the Angrus, which has a course from south to north, and after watering the Triballian plain, falls into the Brongus, which falls into the Ister. So the Ister is augmented by these two streams, both considerable. Besides all these, the Ister receives also the waters of the Carpis and the Alpis, two rivers running in a northerly direction from the country above the Umbrians. For the Ister flows through the whole extent of Europe, rising in the country of the Celts (the most westerly of all the nations of Europe, excepting the Cynetians), and thence running across the continent till it reaches Scythia, whereof it washes the flanks.

50. All these streams, then, and many others, add their waters to swell the flood of the Ister, which thus increased becomes the mightiest of rivers; for undoubtedly if we compare the stream of the Nile with the single stream of the Ister, we must give the preference to the Nile, of which no tributary river, nor even rivulet, augments the volume. The Ister remains at the same level both summer and winter- owing to the following reasons, as I believe. During the winter it runs at its natural height, or a very little higher, because in those countries there is scarcely any rain in winter, but constant snow. When summer comes, this snow, which is of great depth, begins to melt, and flows into the Ister, which is swelled at that season, not only by this cause but also by the rains, which are heavy and frequent at that part of the year. Thus the various streams which go to form the Ister are higher in summer than in

winter, and just so much higher as the sun's power and attraction are greater; so that these two causes counteract each other, and the effect is to produce a balance, whereby the Ister remains always at the same level.

51. This, then, is one of the great Scythian rivers; the next to it is the Tyras, which rises from a great lake separating Scythia from the land of the Neuri, and runs with a southerly course to the sea. Greeks dwell at the mouth of the river, who are called Tyritae.

52. The third river is the Hypanis. This stream rises within the limits of Scythia, and has its source in another vast lake, around which wild white horses graze. The lake is called, properly enough, the Mother of the Hypanis. The Hypanis, rising here, during the distance of five days' navigation is a shallow stream, and the water sweet and pure; thence, however, to the sea, which is a distance of four days, it is exceedingly bitter. This change is caused by its receiving into it at that point a brook the waters of which are so bitter that, although it is but a tiny rivulet, it nevertheless taints the entire Hypanis, which is a large stream among those of the second order. The source of this bitter spring is on the borders of the Scythian Husbandmen, where they adjoin upon the Alazonians; and the place where it rises is called in the Scythic tongue Exampaeus, which means in our language, "The Sacred Ways." The spring itself bears the same name. The Tyras and the Hypanis approach each other in the country of the Alazonians, but afterwards separate, and leave a wide space between their streams.

53. The fourth of the Scythian rivers is the Borysthenes. Next to the Ister, it is the greatest of them all; and, in my judgment, it is the most productive river, not merely in Scythia, but in the whole world, excepting only the Nile, with which no stream can possibly compare. It has upon its banks the loveliest and most excellent pasturages for cattle; it contains abundance of the most delicious fish; its water is most pleasant to the taste;

its stream is limpid, while all the other rivers near it are muddy; the richest harvests spring up along its course, and where the ground is not sown, the heaviest crops of grass; while salt forms in great plenty about its mouth without human aid, and large fish are taken in it of the sort called Antacaei, without any prickly bones, and good for pickling. Nor are these the whole of its marvels. As far inland as the place named Gerrhus, which is distant forty days' voyage from the sea, its course is known, and its direction is from north to south; but above this no one has traced it, so as to say through what countries it flows. It enters the territory of the Scythian Husbandmen after running for some time across a desert region, and continues for ten days' navigation to pass through the land which they inhabit. It is the only river besides the Nile the sources of which are unknown to me, as they are also (I believe) to all the other Greeks. Not long before it reaches the sea, the Borysthenes is joined by the Hypanis, which pours its waters into the same lake. The land that lies between them, a narrow point like the beak of a ship, is called Cape Hippolaus. Here is a temple dedicated to Ceres, and opposite the temple upon the Hypanis is the dwelling-place of the Borysthenites. But enough has been said of these streams.

54. Next in succession comes the fifth river, called the Panticapes, which has, like the Borysthenes, a course from north to south, and rises from a lake. The space between this river and the Borysthenes is occupied by the Scythians who are engaged in husbandry. After watering their country, the Panticapes flows through Hylaea, and empties itself into the Borysthenes.

55. The sixth stream is the Hypacyris, a river rising from a lake, and running directly through the middle of the Nomadic Scythians. It falls into the sea near the city of Carcinitis, leaving Hylaea and the course of Achilles to the right.

56. The seventh river is the Gerrhus, which is a branch thrown out by the Borysthenes at the point where the course of that stream first begins to be known, to wit, the region called by

the same name as the stream itself, viz. Gerrhus. This river on its passage towards the sea divides the country of the Nomadic from that of the Royal Scyths. It runs into the Hypacyris.

57. The eighth river is the Tanais, a stream which has its source, far up the country, in a lake of vast size, and which empties itself into another still larger lake, the Palus Maeotis, whereby the country of the Royal Scythians is divided from that of the Sauromatae. The Tanais receives the waters of a tributary stream, called the Hyrgis.

58. Such then are the rivers of chief note in Scythia. The grass which the land produces is more apt to generate gall in the beasts that feed on it than any other grass which is known to us, as plainly appears on the opening of their carcasses.

59. Thus abundantly are the Scythians provided with the most important necessaries. Their manners and customs come now to be described. They worship only the following gods, namely, Vesta, whom they reverence beyond all the rest, Jupiter, and Tellus, whom they consider to be the wife of Jupiter; and after these Apollo, Celestial Venus, Hercules, and Mars. These gods are worshipped by the whole nation: the Royal Scythians offer sacrifice likewise to Neptune. In the Scythic tongue Vesta is called Tabiti, Jupiter (very properly, in my judgment) Papaeus, Tellus Apia, Apollo Oetosyrus, Celestial Venus Artimpasa, and Neptune Thamimasadas. They use no images, altars, or temples, except in the worship of Mars; but in his worship they do use them.

60. The manner of their sacrifices is everywhere and in every case the same; the victim stands with its two fore-feet bound together by a cord, and the person who is about to offer, taking his station behind the victim, gives the rope a pull, and thereby throws the animal down; as it falls he invokes the god to whom he is offering; after which he puts a noose round the animal's neck, and, inserting a small stick, twists it round, and so strangles him. No fire is lighted, there is no consecration,

and no pouring out of drink-offerings; but directly that the beast is strangled the sacrificer flays him, and then sets to work to boil the flesh.

61. As Scythia, however, is utterly barren of firewood, a plan has had to be contrived for boiling the flesh, which is the following. After flaying the beasts, they take out all the bones, and (if they possess such gear) put the flesh into boilers made in the country, which are very like the cauldrons of the Lesbians, except that they are of a much larger size; then placing the bones of the animals beneath the cauldron, they set them alight, and so boil the meat. If they do not happen to possess a cauldron, they make the animal's paunch hold the flesh, and pouring in at the same time a little water, lay the bones under and light them. The bones burn beautifully; and the paunch easily contains all the flesh when it is stripped from the bones, so that by this plan your ox is made to boil himself, and other victims also to do the like. When the meat is all cooked, the sacrificer offers a portion of the flesh and of the entrails, by casting it on the ground before him. They sacrifice all sorts of cattle, but most commonly horses.

62. Such are the victims offered to the other gods, and such is the mode in which they are sacrificed; but the rites paid to Mars are different. In every district, at the seat of government, there stands a temple of this god, whereof the following is a description. It is a pile of brushwood, made of a vast quantity of fagots, in length and breadth three furlongs; in height somewhat less, having a square platform upon the top, three sides of which are precipitous, while the fourth slopes so that men may walk up it. Each year a hundred and fifty wagon-loads of brushwood are added to the pile, which sinks continually by reason of the rains. An antique iron sword is planted on the top of every such mound, and serves as the image of Mars: yearly sacrifices of cattle and of horses are made to it, and more victims are offered thus than to all the rest of their gods. When prisoners arc taken in war, out of every hundred men they sacrifice one, not however with the

same rites as the cattle, but with different. Libations of wine are first poured upon their heads, after which they are slaughtered over a vessel; the vessel is then carried up to the top of the pile, and the blood poured upon the scymitar. While this takes place at the top of the mound, below, by the side of the temple, the right hands and arms of the slaughtered prisoners are cut off, and tossed on high into the air. Then the other victims are slain, and those who have offered the sacrifice depart, leaving the hands and arms where they may chance to have fallen, and the bodies also, separate.

63. Such are the observances of the Scythians with respect to sacrifice. They never use swine for the purpose, nor indeed is it their wont to breed them in any part of their country.

64. In what concerns war, their customs are the following. The Scythian soldier drinks the blood of the first man he overthrows in battle. Whatever number he slays, he cuts off all their heads, and carries them to the king; since he is thus entitled to a share of the booty, whereto he forfeits all claim if he does not produce a head. In order to strip the skull of its covering, he makes a cut round the head above the ears, and, laying hold of the scalp, shakes the skull out; then with the rib of an ox he scrapes the scalp clean of flesh, and softening it by rubbing between the hands, uses it thenceforth as a napkin. The Scyth is proud of these scalps, and hangs them from his bridle-rein; the greater the number of such napkins that a man can show, the more highly is he esteemed among them. Many make themselves cloaks, like the capotes of our peasants, by sewing a quantity of these scalps together. Others flay the right arms of their dead enemies, and make of the skin, which stripped off with the nails hanging to it, a covering for their quivers. Now the skin of a man is thick and glossy, and would in whiteness surpass almost all other hides. Some even flay the entire body of their enemy, and stretching it upon a frame carry it about with them wherever they ride. Such are the Scythian customs with respect to scalps and skins.

65. The skulls of their enemies, not indeed of all, but of those whom they most detest, they treat as follows. Having sawn off the portion below the eyebrows, and cleaned out the inside, they cover the outside with leather. When a man is poor, this is all that he does; but if he is rich, he also lines the inside with gold: in either case the skull is used as a drinking-cup. They do the same with the skulls of their own kith and kin if they have been at feud with them, and have vanquished them in the presence of the king. When strangers whom they deem of any account come to visit them, these skulls are handed round, and the host tells how that these were his relations who made war upon him, and how that he got the better of them; all this being looked upon as proof of bravery.

66. Once a year the governor of each district, at a set place in his own province, mingles a bowl of wine, of which all Scythians have a right to drink by whom foes have been slain; while they who have slain no enemy are not allowed to taste of the bowl, but sit aloof in disgrace. No greater shame than this can happen to them. Such as have slain a very large number of foes, have two cups instead of one, and drink from both.

67. Scythia has an abundance of soothsayers, who foretell the future by means of a number of willow wands. A large bundle of these wands is brought and laid on the ground. The soothsayer unties the bundle, and places each wand by itself, at the same time uttering his prophecy: then, while he is still speaking, he gathers the rods together again, and makes them up once more into a bundle. This mode of divination is of home growth in Scythia. The Enarees, or woman-like men, have another method, which they say Venus taught them. It is done with the inner bark of the linden-tree. They take a piece of this bark, and, splitting it into three strips, keep twining the strips about their fingers, and untwining them, while they prophesy.

68. Whenever the Scythian king falls sick, he sends for the three soothsayers of most renown at the time, who come and make trial of their art in the mode above described. Generally they say that the king is ill because such or such a person, mentioning his name, has sworn falsely by the royal hearth. This is the usual oath among the Scythians, when they wish to swear with very great solemnity. Then the man accused of having foresworn himself is arrested and brought before the king. The soothsayers tell him that by their art it is clear he has sworn a false oath by the royal hearth, and so caused the illness of the king- he denies the charge, protests that he has sworn no false oath, and loudly complains of the wrong done to him. Upon this the king sends for six new soothsayers, who try the matter by soothsaying. If they too find the man guilty of the offence, straightway he is beheaded by those who first accused him, and his goods are parted among them: if, on the contrary, they acquit him, other soothsayers, and again others, are sent for, to try the case. Should the greater number decide in favor of the man's innocence, then they who first accused him forfeit their lives.

69. The mode of their execution is the following: a wagon is loaded with brushwood, and oxen are harnessed to it; the soothsayers, with their feet tied together, their hands bound behind their backs, and their mouths gagged, are thrust into the midst of the brushwood; finally the wood is set alight, and the oxen, being startled, are made to rush off with the wagon. It often happens that the oxen and the soothsayers are both consumed together, but sometimes the pole of the wagon is burnt through, and the oxen escape with a scorching. Diviners- lying diviners, they call them- are burnt in the way described, for other causes besides the one here spoken of. When the king puts one of them to death, he takes care not to let any of his sons survive: all the male offspring are slain with the father, only the females being allowed to live.

70. Oaths among the Scyths are accompanied with the following ceremonies: a large earthern bowl is filled with

wine, and the parties to the oath, wounding themselves slightly with a knife or an awl, drop some of their blood into the wine; then they plunge into the mixture a scymitar, some arrows, a battle-axe, and a javelin, all the while repeating prayers; lastly the two contracting parties drink each a draught from the bowl, as do also the chief men among their followers.

71. The tombs of their kings are in the land of the Gerrhi, who dwell at the point where the Borysthenes is first navigable. Here, when the king dies, they dig a grave, which is square in shape, and of great size. When it is ready, they take the king's corpse, and, having opened the belly, and cleaned out the inside, fill the cavity with a preparation of chopped cypress, frankincense, parsley-seed, and anise-seed, after which they sew up the opening, enclose the body in wax, and, placing it on a wagon, carry it about through all the different tribes. On this procession each tribe, when it receives the corpse, imitates the example which is first set by the Royal Scythians; every man chops off a piece of his ear, crops his hair close, and makes a cut all round his arm, lacerates his forehead and his nose, and thrusts an arrow through his left hand. Then they who have the care of the corpse carry it with them to another of the tribes which are under the Scythian rule, followed by those whom they first visited. On completing the circuit of all the tribes under their sway, they find themselves in the country of the Gerrhi, who are the most remote of all, and so they come to the tombs of the kings. There the body of the dead king is laid in the grave prepared for it, stretched upon a mattress; spears are fixed in the ground on either side of the corpse, and beams stretched across above it to form a roof, which is covered with a thatching of osier twigs. In the open space around the body of the king they bury one of his concubines, first killing her by strangling, and also his cup-bearer, his cook, his groom, his lacquey, his messenger, some of his horses, firstlings of all his other possessions, and some golden cups; for they use neither silver nor brass. After this they set to work, and raise a vast mound above the grave, all

of them vying with each other and seeking to make it as tall as possible.

72. When a year is gone by, further ceremonies take place. Fifty of the best of the late king's attendants are taken, all native Scythians- for, as bought slaves are unknown in the country, the Scythian kings choose any of their subjects that they like, to wait on them- fifty of these are taken and strangled, with fifty of the most beautiful horses. When they are dead, their bowels are taken out, and the cavity cleaned, filled full of chaff, and straightway sewn up again. This done, a number of posts are driven into the ground, in sets of two pairs each, and on every pair half the felly of a wheel is placed archwise; then strong stakes are run lengthways through the bodies of the horses from tail to neck, and they are mounted up upon the fellies, so that the felly in front supports the shoulders of the horse, while that behind sustains the belly and quarters, the legs dangling in mid-air; each horse is furnished with a bit and bridle, which latter is stretched out in front of the horse, and fastened to a peg. The fifty strangled youths are then mounted severally on the fifty horses. To effect this, a second stake is passed through their bodies along the course of the spine to the neck; the lower end of which projects from the body, and is fixed into a socket, made in the stake that runs lengthwise down the horse. The fifty riders are thus ranged in a circle round the tomb, and so left.

73. Such, then, is the mode in which the kings are buried: as for the people, when any one dies, his nearest of kin lay him upon a wagon and take him round to all his friends in succession: each receives them in turn and entertains them with a banquet, whereat the dead man is served with a portion of all that is set before the others; this is done for forty days, at the end of which time the burial takes place. After the burial, those engaged in it have to purify themselves, which they do in the following way. First they well soap and wash their heads; then, in order to cleanse their bodies, they act as follows: they make a booth by fixing in the ground three sticks

inclined towards one another, and stretching around them woollen felts, which they arrange so as to fit as close as possible: inside the booth a dish is placed upon the ground, into which they put a number of red-hot stones, and then add some hemp-seed.

74. Hemp grows in Scythia: it is very like flax; only that it is a much coarser and taller plant: some grows wild about the country, some is produced by cultivation: the Thracians make garments of it which closely resemble linen; so much so, indeed, that if a person has never seen hemp he is sure to think they are linen, and if he has, unless he is very experienced in such matters, he will not know of which material they are.

75. The Scythians, as I said, take some of this hemp-seed, and, creeping under the felt coverings, throw it upon the red-hot stones; immediately it smokes, and gives out such a vapor as no Grecian vapor-bath can exceed; the Scyths, delighted, shout for joy, and this vapor serves them instead of a water-bath; for they never by any chance wash their bodies with water. Their women make a mixture of cypress, cedar, and frankincense wood, which they pound into a paste upon a rough piece of stone, adding a little water to it. With this substance, which is of a thick consistency, they plaster their faces all over, and indeed their whole bodies. A sweet odor is thereby imparted to them, and when they take off the plaster on the day following, their skin is clean and glossy.

76. The Scythians have an extreme hatred of all foreign customs, particularly of those in use among the Greeks, as the instances of Anacharsis, and, more lately, of Scylas, have fully shown. The former, after he had travelled over a great portion of the world, and displayed wherever he went many proofs of wisdom, as he sailed through the Hellespont on his return to Scythia touched at Cyzicus. There he found the inhabitants celebrating with much pomp and magnificence a festival to the Mother of the Gods, and was himself induced to make a vow to the goddess, whereby he engaged, if he got back safe and

sound to his home, that he would give her a festival and a night-procession in all respects like those which he had seen in Cyzicus. When, therefore, he arrived in Scythia, he betook himself to the district called the Woodland, which lies opposite the course of Achilles, and is covered with trees of all manner of different kinds, and there went through all the sacred rites with the tabour in his hand, and the images tied to him. While thus employed, he was noticed by one of the Scythians, who went and told king Saulius what he had seen. Then king Saulius came in person, and when he perceived what Anacharsis was about, he shot at him with an arrow and killed him. To this day, if you ask the Scyths about Anacharsis, they pretend ignorance of him, because of his Grecian travels and adoption of the customs of foreigners. I learnt, however, from Timnes, the steward of Ariapithes, that Anacharsis was paternal uncle to the Scythian king Idanthyrsus, being the son of Gnurus, who was the son of Lycus and the grandson of Spargapithes. If Anacharsis were really of this house, it must have been by his own brother that he was slain, for Idanthyrsus was a son of the Saulius who put Anacharsis to death.

77. I have heard, however, another tale, very different from this, which is told by the Peloponnesians: they say, that Anacharsis was sent by the king of the Scyths to make acquaintance with Greece- that he went, and on his return home reported that the Greeks were all occupied in the pursuit of every kind of knowledge, except the Lacedaemonians; who, however, alone knew how to converse sensibly. A silly tale this, which the Greeks have invented for their amusement! There is no doubt that Anacharsis suffered death in the mode already related, on account of his attachment to foreign customs, and the intercourse which he held with the Greeks.

78. Scylas, likewise, the son of Ariapithes, many years later, met with almost the very same fate. Ariapithes, the Scythian king, had several sons, among them this Scylas, who was the child, not of a native Scyth, but of a woman of Istria. Bred up

by her, Scylas gained an acquaintance with the Greek language and letters. Sometime afterwards, Ariapithes was treacherously slain by Spargapithes, king of the Agathyrsi; whereupon Scylas succeeded to the throne, and married one of his father's wives, a woman named Opoea. This Opoea was a Scythian by birth, and had brought Ariapithes a son called Oricus. Now when Scylas found himself king of Scythia, as he disliked the Scythic mode of life, and was attached, by his bringing up, to the manners of the Greeks, he made it his usual practice, whenever he came with his army to the town of the Borysthenites, who, according to their own account, are colonists of the Milesians- he made it his practice, I say, to leave the army before the city, and, having entered within the walls by himself, and carefully closed the gates, to exchange his Scythian dress for Grecian garments, and in this attire to walk about the forum, without guards or retinue. The Borysthenites kept watch at the gates, that no Scythian might see the king thus appareled. Scylas, meanwhile, lived exactly as the Greeks, and even offered sacrifices to the gods according to the Grecian rites. In this way he would pass a month, or more, with the Borysthenites, after which he would clothe himself again in his Scythian dress, and so take his departure. This he did repeatedly, and even built himself a house in Borysthenes, and married a wife there who was a native of the place.

79. But when the time came that was ordained to bring him woe, the occasion of his ruin was the following. He wanted to be initiated in the Bacchic mysteries, and was on the point of obtaining admission to the rites, when a most strange prodigy occurred to him. The house which he possessed, as I mentioned a short time back, in the city of the Borysthenites, a building of great extent and erected at a vast cost, round which there stood a number of sphinxes and griffins carved in white marble, was struck by lightning from on high, and burnt to the ground. Scylas, nevertheless, went on and received the initiation. Now the Scythians are wont to reproach the Greeks with their Bacchanal rage, and to say that it is not reasonable

to imagine there is a god who impels men to madness. No sooner, therefore, was Scylas initiated in the Bacchic mysteries than one of the Borysthenites went and carried the news to the Scythians "You Scyths laugh at us" he said, "because we rave when the god seizes us. But now our god has seized upon your king, who raves like us, and is maddened by the influence. If you think I do not tell you true, come with me, and I will show him to you." The chiefs of the Scythians went with the man accordingly, and the Borysthenite, conducting them into the city, placed them secretly on one of the towers. Presently Scylas passed by with the band of revelers, raving like the rest, and was seen by the watchers. Regarding the matter as a very great misfortune they instantly departed, and came and told the army what they had witnessed.

80. When, therefore, Scylas, after leaving Borysthenes, was about returning home, the Scythians broke out into revolt. They put at their head Octamasadas, grandson (on the mother's side) of Teres. Then Scylas, when he learned the danger with which he was threatened, and the reason of the disturbance, made his escape to Thrace. Octamasadas, discovering whither he had fled, marched after him, and had reached the Ister, when he was met by the forces of the Thracians. The two armies were about to engage, but before they joined battle, Sitalces sent a message to Octamasadas to this effect- "Why should there be trial of arms betwixt thee and me? Thou art my own sister's son, and thou hast in thy keeping my brother. Surrender him into my hands, and I will give thy Scylas back to thee. So neither thou nor I will risk our armies." Sitalces sent this message to Octamasadas, by a herald, and Octamasadas, with whom a brother of Sitalces had formerly taken refuge, accepted the terms. He surrendered his own uncle to Sitalces, and obtained in exchange his brother Scylas. Sitalces took his brother with him and withdrew; but Octamasadas beheaded Scylas upon the spot. Thus rigidly do the Scythians maintain their own customs, and thus severely do they punish such as adopt foreign usages.

81. What the population of Scythia is I was not able to learn with certainty; the accounts which I received varied from one another. I heard from some that they were very numerous indeed; others made their numbers but scanty for such a nation as the Scyths. Thus much, however, I witnessed with my own eyes. There is a tract called Exampaeus between the Borysthenes and the Hypanis. I made some mention of it in a former place, where I spoke of the bitter stream which rising there flows into the Hypanis, and renders the water of that river undrinkable. Here then stands a brazen bowl, six times as big as that at the entrance of the Euxine, which Pausanias, the son of Cleombrotus, set up. Such as have never seen that vessel may understand me better if I say that the Scythian bowl holds with ease six hundred amphorae, and is of the thickness of six fingers' breadth. The natives gave me the following account of the manner in which it was made. One of their kings, by name Ariantas, wishing to know the number of his subjects, ordered them all to bring him, on pain of death, the point off one of their arrows. They obeyed; and he collected thereby a vast heap of arrow-heads, which he resolved to form into a memorial that might go down to posterity. Accordingly he made of them this bowl, and dedicated it at Exampaeus. This was all that I could learn concerning the number of the Scythians.

82. The country has no marvels except its rivers, which are larger and more numerous than those of any other land. These, and the vastness of the great plain, are worthy of note, and one thing besides, which I am about to mention. They show a footmark of Hercules, impressed on a rock, in shape like the print of a man's foot, but two cubits in length. It is in the neighborhood of the Tyras. Having described this, I return to the subject on which I originally proposed to discourse.

Herodotus, , and G C. Macaulay. *The History of Herodotus*. London: Macmillan and Co, 1890. Print.

97. These were the provinces and the assessments of tribute: and the Persian land alone has not been mentioned by me as paying a contribution, for the Persians have their land to dwell in free from payment. The following moreover had no tribute fixed for them to pay, but brought gifts, namely the Ethiopians who border upon Egypt, whom Cambyses subdued as he marched against the Long-lived Ethiopians, those who dwell about Nysa, which is called "sacred," and who celebrate the festivals in honor of Dionysos: these Ethiopians and those who dwell near them have the same kind of seed as the Callantian Indians, and they have underground dwellings. These both together brought every other year, and continue to bring even to my own time, two quart measures of unmelted gold and two hundred blocks of ebony and five Ethiopian boys and twenty large elephant tusks. The Colchians also had set themselves among those who brought gifts, and with them those who border upon them extending as far as the range of the Caucasus (for the Persian rule extends as far as these mountains, but those who dwell in the parts beyond Caucasus toward the North Wind regard the Persians no longer),--these, I say, continued to bring the gifts which they had fixed for themselves every four years even down to my own time, that is to say, a hundred boys and a hundred maidens. Finally, the Arabians brought a thousand talents of frankincense every year. Such were the gifts which these brought to the king apart from the tribute.

98. Now this great quantity of gold, out of which the Indians bring in to the king the gold-dust which has been mentioned, is obtained by them in a manner which I shall tell:--That part of the Indian land which is towards the rising sun is sand; for of all the peoples in Asia of which we know or about which any certain report is given, the Indians dwell furthest away towards the East and the sunrising; seeing that the country to the East of the Indians is desert on account of the sand. Now

there are many tribes of Indians, and they do not agree with one another in language; and some of them are pastoral and others not so, and some dwell in the swamps of the river and feed upon raw fish, which they catch by fishing from boats made of cane; and each boat is made of one joint of cane. These Indians of which I speak wear clothing made of rushes: they gather and cut the rushes from the river and then weave them together into a kind of mat and put it on like a corslet.

99. Others of the Indians, dwelling to the East of these, are pastoral and eat raw flesh: these are called Padaians, and they practice the following customs:--whenever any of their tribe falls ill, whether it be a woman or a man, if a man then the men who are his nearest associates put him to death, saying that he is wasting away with the disease and his flesh is being spoilt for them: and meanwhile he denies stoutly and says that he is not ill, but they do not agree with him; and after they have killed him they feast upon his flesh: but if it be a woman who falls ill, the women who are her greatest intimates do to her in the same manner as the men do in the other case. For in fact even if a man has come to old age they slay him and feast upon him; but very few of them come to be reckoned as old, for they kill everyone who falls into sickness, before he reaches old age.

100. Other Indians have on the contrary a manner of life as follows:--they neither kill any living thing nor do they sow any crops nor is it their custom to possess houses; but they feed on herbs, and they have a grain of the size of millet, in a sheath, which grows of itself from the ground; this they gather and boil with the sheath, and make it their food: and whenever any of them falls into sickness, he goes to the desert country and lies there, and none of them pay any attention either to one who is dead or to one who is sick.

101. The sexual intercourse of all these Indians of whom I have spoken is open like that of cattle, and they have all one color of skin, resembling that of the Ethiopians: moreover the

seed which they emit is not white like that of other races, but black like their skin; and the Ethiopians also are similar in this respect. These tribes of Indians dwell further off than the Persian power extends, and towards the South Wind, and they never became subjects of Dareios.

102. Others however of the Indians are on the borders of the city of Caspatyros and the country of Pactyïke, dwelling towards the North of the other Indians; and they have a manner of living nearly the same as that of the Bactrians: these are the most warlike of the Indians, and these are they who make expeditions for the gold. For in the parts where they live it is desert on account of the sand; and in this desert and sandy tract are produced ants, which are in size smaller than dogs but larger than foxes, for there are some of them kept at the residence of the king of Persia, which are caught here. These ants then make their dwelling underground and carry up the sand just in the same manner as the ants found in the land of the Hellenes, which they themselves also very much resemble in form; and the sand which is brought up contains gold. To obtain this sand the Indians make expeditions into the desert, each one having yoked together three camels, placing a female in the middle and a male like a trace-horse to draw by each side. On this female he mounts himself, having arranged carefully that she shall be taken to be yoked from young ones, the more lately born the better. For their female camels are not inferior to horses in speed, and moreover they are much more capable of bearing weights.

103. As to the form of the camel, I do not here describe it, since the Hellenes for whom I write are already acquainted with it, but I shall tell that which is not commonly known about it, which is this:--the camel has in the hind legs four thighs and four knees, and its organs of generation are between the hind legs, turned towards the tail.

104. The Indians, I say, ride out to get the gold in the manner and with the kind of yoking which I have described, making

calculations so that they may be engaged in carrying it off at the time when the greatest heat prevails; for the heat causes the ants to disappear underground. Now among these nations the sun is hottest in the morning hours, not at midday as with others, but from sunrise to the time of closing the market: and during this time it produces much greater heat than at midday in Hellas, so that it is said that then they drench themselves with water. Midday however has about equal degree of heat with the Indians as with other men, while after midday their sun becomes like the morning sun with other men, and after this, as it goes further away, it produces still greater coolness, until at last at sunset it makes the air very cool indeed.

105. When the Indians have come to the place with bags, they fill them with the sand and ride away back as quickly as they can, for forthwith the ants, perceiving, as the Persians allege, by the smell, begin to pursue them: and this animal, they say, is superior to every other creature in swiftness, so that unless the Indians got a start in their course, while the ants were gathering together, not one of them would escape. So then the male camels, for they are inferior in speed of running to the females, if they drag behind are even let loose from the side of the female, one after the other; the females however, remembering the young which they left behind, do not show any slackness in their course. Thus it is that the Indians get most part of the gold, as the Persians say; there is however other gold also in their land obtained by digging, but in smaller quantities.

106. It seems indeed that the extremities of the inhabited world had allotted to them by nature the fairest things, just as it was the lot of Hellas to have its seasons far more fairly tempered than other lands: for first, India is the most distant of inhabited lands towards the East, as I have said a little above, and in this land not only the animals, birds as well as four-footed beasts, are much larger than in other places (except the horses, which are surpassed by those of Media called Nessaian), but also there is gold in abundance there, some got

by digging, some brought down by rivers, and some carried off as I explained just now: and there also the trees which grow wild produce wool which surpasses in beauty and excellence that from sheep, and the Indians wear clothing obtained from these trees.

ARABIAN LOGOI – BOOK 3

Herodotus, , and G C. Macaulay. *The History of Herodotus.* London: Macmillan and Co, 1890. Print.

107. Then again Arabia is the furthest of inhabited lands in the direction of the midday, and in it alone of all lands grow frankincense and myrrh and cassia and cinnamon and gum-mastich. All these except myrrh are got with difficulty by the Arabians. Frankincense they collect by burning the storax, which is brought thence to the Hellenes by the Phoenicians, by burning this, I say, so as to produce smoke they take it; for these trees which produce frankincense are guarded by winged serpents, small in size and of various colors, which watch in great numbers about each tree, of the same kind as those which attempt to invade Egypt: and they cannot be driven away from the trees by any other thing but only the smoke of storax.

108. The Arabians say also that all the world would have been by this time filled with these serpents, if that did not happen with regard to them which I knew happened with regard to vipers: and it seems that the Divine Providence, as indeed was to be expected, seeing that it is wise, has made all those animals prolific which are of cowardly spirit and good for food, in order that they may not be all eaten up and their race fail, whereas it has made those which are bold and noxious to have small progeny. For example, because the hare is hunted by every beast and bird as well as by man, therefore it is so very prolific as it is: and this is the only one of all beasts which becomes pregnant again before the former young are

born, and has in its womb some of its young covered with fur and others bare; and while one is just being shaped in the matrix, another is being conceived. Thus it is in this case; whereas the lioness, which is the strongest and most courageous of creatures, produces one cub once only in her life; for when she produces young she casts out her womb together with her young; and the cause of it is this:--when the cub being within the mother begins to move about, then having claws by far sharper than those of any other beast he tears the womb, and as he grows larger he proceeds much further in his scratching: at last the time of birth approaches and there is now nothing at all left of it in a sound condition.

109. Just so also, if vipers and the winged serpents of the Arabians were produced in the ordinary course of their nature, man would not be able to live upon the earth; but as it is, when they couple with one another and the male is in the act of generation, as he lets go from him the seed, the female seizes hold of his neck, and fastening on to it does not relax her hold till she has eaten it through. The male then dies in the manner which I have said, but the female pays the penalty of retribution for the male in this manner:--the young while they are still in the womb take vengeance for their father by eating through their mother, and having eaten through her belly they thus make their way out for themselves. Other serpents however, which are not hurtful to man, produce eggs and hatch from them a very large number of offspring. Now vipers are distributed over all the earth; but the others, which are winged, are found in great numbers together in Arabia and in no other land: therefore it is that they appear to be numerous.

110. This frankincense then is obtained thus by the Arabians; and cassia is obtained as follows:-- they bind up in cattle'-hide and other kinds of skins all their body and their face except only the eyes, and then go to get the cassia. This grows in a pool not very deep, and round the pool and in it lodge, it seems, winged beasts nearly resembling bats, and they squeak

horribly and are courageous in fight. These they must keep off from their eyes, and so cut the cassia.

111. Cinnamon they collect in a yet more marvelous manner than this: for where it grows and what land produces it they are not able to tell, except only that some say (and it is a probable account) that it grows in those regions where Dionysos was brought up; and they say that large birds carry those dried sticks which we have learnt from the Phoenicians to call cinnamon, carry them, I say, to nests which are made of clay and stuck on to precipitous sides of mountains, which man can find no means of scaling. With regard to this then the Arabians practice the following contrivance:-- they divide up the limbs of the oxen and asses that die and of their other beasts of burden, into pieces as large as convenient, and convey them to these places, and when they have laid them down not far from the nests, they withdraw to a distance from them: and the birds fly down and carry the limbs of the beasts of burden off to their nests; and these are not able to bear them, but break down and fall to the earth; and the men come up to them and collect the cinnamon. Thus cinnamon is collected and comes from this nation to the other countries of the world.

112. Gum-mastich however, which the Arabians call ladanon, comes in a still more extraordinary manner; for though it is the most sweet-scented of all things, it comes in the most evil-scented thing, since it is found in the beards of he-goats, produced there like resin from wood: this is of use for the making of many perfumes, and the Arabians use it more than anything else as incense.

113. Let what we have said suffice with regard to spices; and from the land of Arabia there blows a scent of them most marvelously sweet. They have also two kinds of sheep which are worthy of admiration and are not found in any other land: the one kind has the tail long, not less than three cubits in length; and if one should allow these to drag these after them,

they would have sores from their tails being worn away against the ground; but as it is, every one of the shepherds knows enough of carpentering to make little cars, which they tie under the tails, fastening the tail of each animal to a separate little car. The other kind of sheep has the tail broad, even as much as a cubit in breadth.

LIBYAN LOGOI – BOOK 4

Herodotus, , and G C. Macaulay. *The History of Herodotus.* London: Macmillan and Co, 1890. Print.

168. Now the Libyans have their dwelling as follows:-- Beginning from Egypt, first of the Libyans are settled the Adyrmachidai, who practice for the most part the same customs as the Egyptians, but wear clothing similar to that of the other Libyans. Their women wear a bronze ring upon each leg, and they have long hair on their heads, and when they catch their lice, each one bites her own in retaliation and then throws them away. These are the only people of the Libyans who do this; and they alone display to the king their maidens when they are about to be married, and whosoever of them proves to be pleasing to the king is deflowered by him. These Adyrmachidai extend along the coast from Egypt as far as the port which is called Plynos.

169. Next after these come the Giligamai, occupying the country towards the West as far as the island of Aphrodisias. In the space within this limit lies off the coast the island of Platea, where the Kyrenians made their settlement; and on the coast of the mainland there is Port Menelaos, and Aziris, where the Kyrenians used to dwell. From this point begins the silphion and it extends along the coast from the island of Platea as far as the entrance of the Syrtis. This nation practices customs nearly resembling those of the rest.

170. Next to the Giligamai on the West are the Asbystai: these dwell above Kyrene, and the Asbystai do not reach down the sea, for the region along the sea is occupied by Kyrenians. These most of all the Libyans are drivers of four-horse chariots, and in the greater number of their customs they endeavor to imitate the Kyrenians.

171. Next after the Asbystai on the West come the Auchisai: these dwell above Barca and reach down to the sea by Euesperides: and in the middle of the country of the Auchisai dwell the Bacales, a small tribe, who reach down to the sea by the city of Taucheira in the territory of Barca: these practice the same customs as those above Kyrene.

172. Next after these Auschisai towards the West come the Nasamonians, a numerous race, who in the summer leave their flocks behind by the sea and go up to the region of Augila to gather the fruit of the date- palms, which grow in great numbers and very large and are all fruit- bearing: these hunt the wingless locusts, and they dry them in the sun and then pound them up, and after that they sprinkle them upon milk and drink them. Their custom is for each man to have many wives, and they make their intercourse with them common in nearly the same manner as the Massagetai, that is they set up a staff in front of the door and so have intercourse. When a Nasamonian man marries his first wife, the custom is for the bride on the first night to go through the whole number of the guests having intercourse with them, and each man when he has laid with her gives a gift, whatsoever he has brought with him from his house. The forms of oath and of divination which they use are as follows:--they swear by the men among themselves who are reported to have been the most righteous and brave, by these, I say, laying hands upon their tombs; and they divine by visiting the sepulchral mounds of their ancestors and lying down to sleep upon them after having prayed; and whatsoever thing the man sees in his dream, this he accepts. They practice also the exchange of pledges in the following manner, that is to say, one gives the other to drink

from his hand, and drinks himself from the hand of the other; and if they have no liquid, they take of the dust from the ground and lick it.
173. Adjoining the Nasamonians is the country of the Psylloi. These have perished utterly in the following manner:--The South Wind blowing upon them dried up all their cisterns of water, and their land was waterless, lying all within the Syrtis. They then having taken a resolve by common consent, marched in arms against the South Wind (I report that which is reported by the Libyans), and when they had arrived at the sandy tract, the South Wind blew and buried them in the sand. These then having utterly perished, the Nasamonians from that time forward possess their land.

174. Above these towards the South Wind in the region of wild beasts dwell the Garamantians, who fly from every man and avoid the company of all; and they neither possess any weapon of war, nor know how to defend themselves against enemies.

175. These dwell above the Nasamonians; and next to the Nasamonians along the sea coast towards the West come the Macai, who shave their hair so as to leave tufts, letting the middle of their hair grow long, but round this on all sides shaving it close to the skin; and for fighting they carry shields made of ostrich skins. Through their land the river Kinyps runs out into the sea, flowing from a hill called the "Hill of the Charites." This Hill of the Charites is overgrown thickly with wood, while the rest of Libya which has been spoken of before is bare of trees; and the distance from the sea to this hill is two hundred furlongs.

176. Next to these Macai are the Gindanes, whose women wear each of them a number of anklets made of the skins of animals, for the following reason, as it is said:--for every man who has commerce with her she binds on an anklet, and the woman who has most is esteemed the best, since she has been loved by the greatest number of men.

177. In a peninsula which stands out into the sea from the land of these Gindanes dwell the Lotophagoi, who live by eating the fruit of the lotos only. Now the fruit of the lotos is in size like that of the mastich-tree, and in flavor it resembles that of the date-palm. Of this fruit the Lotophagoi even make for themselves wine.

178. Next after the Lotophagoi along the sea-coast are the Machlyans, who also make use of the lotos, but less than those above mentioned. These extend to a great river named the river Triton, and this runs out into a great lake called Tritonis, in which there is an island named Phla. About this island they say there was an oracle given to the Lacedemonians that they should make a settlement in it.

179. The following moreover is also told, namely that Jason, when the Argo had been completed by him under Mount Pelion, put into it a hecatomb and with it also a tripod of bronze, and sailed round Peloponnese, desiring to come to Delphi; and when in sailing he got near Malea, a North Wind seized his ship and carried it off to Libya, and before he caught sight of land he had come to be in the shoals of the lake Tritonis. Then as he was at a loss how he should bring his ship forth, the story goes that Triton appeared to him and bade Jason give him the tripod, saying that he would show them the right course and let them go away without hurt: and when Jason consented to it, then Triton showed them the passage out between the shoals and set the tripod in his own temple, after having first uttered a prophecy over the tripod and having declared to Jason and his company the whole matter, namely that whenever one of the descendants of those who sailed with him in the Argo should carry away this tripod, then it was determined by fate that a hundred cities of Hellenes should be established about the lake Tritonis. Having heard this native Libyans concealed the tripod.

180. Next to these Machlyans are the Auseans. These and the Machlyans dwell round the lake Tritonis, and the river Triton is the boundary between them: and while the Machlyans grow their hair long at the back of the head, the Auseans do so in front. At a yearly festival of Athene their maidens take their stand in two parties and fight against one another with stones and staves, and they say that in doing so they are fulfilling the rites handed down by their fathers for the divinity who was sprung from that land, whom we call Athene: and those of the maidens who die of the wounds received they call "false-maidens." But before they let them begin the fight they do this:--all join together and equip the maiden who is judged to be the fairest on each occasion, with a Corinthian helmet and with full Hellenic armor, and then causing her to go up into a chariot they conduct her round the lake. Now I cannot tell with what they equipped the maidens in old time, before the Hellenes were settled near them; but I suppose that they used to be equipped with Egyptian armor, for it is from Egypt that both the shield and the helmet have come to the Hellenes, as I affirm. They say moreover that Athene is the daughter of Poseidon and of the lake Tritonis, and that she had some cause of complaint against her father and therefore gave herself to Zeus, and Zeus made her his own daughter. Such is the story which these tell; and they have their intercourse with women in common, not marrying but having intercourse like cattle: and when the child of any woman has grown big, he is brought before a meeting of the men held within three months of that time, and whomsoever of the men the child resembles, his son he is accounted to be.

181. Thus then have been mentioned those nomad Libyans who live along the sea-coast: and above these inland is the region of Libya which has wild beasts; and above the wild-beast region there stretches a raised belt of sand, extending from Thebes of the Egyptians to the Pillars of Heracles. In this belt at intervals of about ten days' journey there are fragments of salt in great lumps forming hills, and at the top of each hill there shoots up from the middle of the salt a spring of water

cold and sweet; and about the spring dwell men, at the furthest limit towards the desert, and above the wild-beast region. First, at a distance of ten days' journey from Thebes, are the Ammonians, whose temple is derived from that of the Theban Zeus, for the image of Zeus in Thebes also, as I have said before, has the head of a ram. These, as it chances, have also other water of a spring, which in the early morning is warm; at the time when the market fills, cooler; when midday comes, it is quite cold, and then they water their gardens; but as the day declines, it abates from its coldness, until at last, when the sun sets, the water is warm; and it continues to increase in heat still more until it reaches midnight, when it boils and throws up bubbles; and when midnight passes, it becomes cooler gradually till dawn of day. This spring is called the fountain of the Sun.

182. After the Ammonians, as you go on along the belt of sand, at an interval again of ten days' journey there is a hill of salt like that of the Ammonians, and a spring of water, with men dwelling about it; and the name of this place is Augila. To this the Nasamonians come year by year to gather the fruit of the date-palms.

183. From Augila at a distance again of ten days' journey there is another hill of salt and spring of water and a great number of fruit-bearing date-palms, as there are also in the other places: and men dwell here who are called the Garmantians, a very great nation, who carry earth to lay over the salt and then sow crops. From this point is the shortest way to the Lotophagoi, for from these it is a journey of thirty days to the country of the Garmantians. Among them also are produced the cattle which feed backwards; and they feed backwards for this reason, because they have their horns bent down forwards, and therefore they walk backwards as they feed; for forwards they cannot go, because the horns run into the ground in front of them; but in nothing else do they differ from other cattle except in this and in the thickness and firmness to the touch of their hide. These Garamantians of whom I speak hunt the

"Cave-dwelling" Ethiopians with their four-horse chariots, for the Cave-dwelling Ethiopians are the swiftest of foot of all men about whom we hear report made: and the Cave-dwellers feed upon serpents and lizards and such creeping things, and they use a language which resembles no other, for in it they squeak just like bats.

184. From the Garmantians at a distance again of ten days' journey there is another hill of salt and spring of water, and men dwell round it called Atarantians, who alone of all men about whom we know are nameless; for while all taken together have the name Atarantians, each separate man of them has no name given to him. These utter curses against the Sun when he is at his height, and moreover revile him with all manner of foul terms, because he oppresses them by his burning heat, both themselves and their land. After this at a distance of ten days' journey there is another hill of salt and spring of water, and men dwell round it. Near this salt hill is a mountain named Atlas, which is small in circuit and rounded on every side; and so exceedingly lofty is it said to be, and that it is not possible to see its summits, for clouds never leave them either in the summer or in the winter. This natives say is the pillar of the heaven. After this mountain these men got their name, for they are called Atlantians; and it is said that they neither eat anything that has life nor have any dreams.

185. As far as these Atlantians I am able to mention in order the names of those who are settled in the belt of sand; but for the parts beyond these I can do so no more. However, the belt extends as far as the Pillars of Heracles and also in the parts outside them: and there is a mine of salt in it at a distance of ten days' journey from the Atlantians, and men dwelling there; and these all have their houses built of the lumps of salt, since these parts of Libya which we have now reached are without rain; for if it rained, the walls being made of salt would not be able to last: and the salt is dug up there both white and purple in color. Above the sand-belt, in the parts which are in the direction of the South Wind and towards the interior of Libya,

the country is uninhabited, without water and without wild beasts, rainless and treeless, and there is no trace of moisture in it.

186. I have said that from Egypt as far as the lake Tritonis Libyans dwell who are nomads, eating flesh and drinking milk; and these do not taste at all of the flesh of cattle, for the same reason as the Egyptians also abstain from it, nor do they keep swine. Moreover the women of the Kyrenians too think it not right to eat cattle' flesh, because of the Egyptian Isis, and they even keep fasts and celebrate festivals for her; and the women of Barca, in addition from cattle' flesh, do not taste of swine either.

187. Thus it is with these matters: but in the region to the West of lake Tritonis the Libyans cease to be nomads, and they do not practice the same customs, nor do to their children anything like that which the nomads are wont to do; for the nomad Libyans, whether all of them I cannot say for certain, but many of them, do as follows:--when their children are four years old, they burn with a greasy piece of sheep's wool the veins in the crowns of their heads, and some of them burn the veins of the temples, so that for all their lives to come the cold humor may not run down from their heads and do them hurt: and for this reason it is (they say) that they are so healthy; for the Libyans are in truth the most healthy of all races concerning which we have knowledge, whether for this reason or not I cannot say for certain, but the most healthy they certainly are: and if, when they burn the children, a convulsion comes on, they have found out a remedy for this; for they pour upon them the water of a he-goat and so save them. I report that which is reported by the Libyans themselves.

188. The following is the manner of sacrifice which the nomads have:--they cut off a part of the animal's ear as a first offering and throw it over the house and having done this they twist its neck. They sacrifice only to the Sun and the Moon; that is to say, to these all the Libyans sacrifice, but those who

dwell round the lake Tritonis sacrifice most of all to Athene, and next to Triton and Poseidon.

189. It would appear also that the Hellenes made the dress and the aigis of the images of Athene after the model of the Libyan women; for except that the dress of the Libyan women is of leather, and the tassels which hang from their aigis are not formed of serpents but of leather thongs, in all other respects Athene is dressed like them. Moreover the name too declares that the dress of the figures of Pallas has come from Libya, for the Libyan women wear over their other garments bare goat-skins (aigeas) with tasseled fringes and colored over with red madder, and from the name of these goat-skins the Hellenes formed the name aigis. I think also that in these regions first arose the practice of crying aloud during the performance of sacred rites, for the Libyan women do this very well. The Hellenes learnt from the Libyans also the yoking together of four horses.

190. The nomads bury those who die just in the same manner as the Hellenes, except only the Nasamonians: these bury bodies in a sitting posture, taking care at the moment when the man expires to place him sitting and not to let him die lying down on his back. They have dwellings composed of the stems of asphodel entwined with rushes, and so made that they can be carried about. Such are the customs followed by these tribes.

191. On the West of the river Triton next after the Auseans come Libyans who are tillers of the soil, and whose custom it is to possess fixed habitations; and they are called Maxyans. They grow their hair long on the right side of their heads and cut it short upon the left, and smear their bodies over with red ochre. These say that they are of the men who came from Troy.

This country and the rest of Libya which is towards the West is both much more frequented by wild beasts and much more thickly wooded than the country of the nomads: for whereas the part of Libya which is situated towards the East, where the nomads dwell, is low-lying and sandy up to the river Triton, that which succeeds it towards the West, the country of those who till the soil, is exceedingly mountainous and thickly-wooded and full of wild beasts: for in the land of these are found both the monstrous serpent and the lion and the elephant, and bears and venomous snakes and horned asses, besides the dog-headed men, and the headless men with their eyes set in their breasts (at least so say the Libyans about them), and the wild men and wild women, and a great multitude of other beasts which are not fabulous like these.

192. In the land of the nomads however there exist none of these, but other animals as follows:--white-rump antelopes, gazelles, buffaloes, asses, not the horned kind but others which go without water (for in fact these never drink), oryes, whose horns are made into the sides of the Phoenician lyre (this animal is in size about equal to an ox), small foxes, hyenas, porcupines, wild rams, wolves, jackals, panthers, boryes, land-crocodiles about three cubits in length and very much resembling lizards, ostriches, and small snakes, each with one horn: these wild animals there are in this country, as well as those which exist elsewhere, except the stag and the wild-boar; but Libya has no stags nor wild boars at all. Also there are in this country three kinds of mice, one is called the "two- legged" mouse, another the zegeris (a name which is Libyan and signifies in the Hellenic tongue a "hill"), and a third the "prickly" mouse. There are also weasels produced in the silphion, which are very like those of Tartessos. Such are the wild animals which the land of the Libyans possesses, so far as we were able to discover by inquiries extended as much as possible.

193. Next to the Maxyan Libyans are the Zauekes, whose women drive their chariots for them to war.

194. Next to these are the Gyzantes, among whom honey is made in great quantity by bees, but in much greater quantity

still it is said to be made by men, who work at it as a trade. However that may be, these all smear themselves over with red ochre and eat monkeys, which are produced in very great numbers upon their mountains.

195. Opposite these, as the Carthaginians say, there lays an island called Kyrauis, two hundred furlongs in length but narrow, to which one may walk over from the mainland; and it is full of olives and vines. In it they say there is a pool, from which the native girls with birds' feathers smeared over with pitch bring up gold-dust out of the mud. Whether this is really so I do not know, but I write that which is reported; and nothing is impossible, for even in Zakynthos I saw myself pitch brought up out of a pool of water. There are there several pools and the largest of them measures seventy feet each way and is two fathoms in depth. Into this they plunge a pole with a myrtle-branch bound to it, and then with the branch of the myrtle they bring up pitch, which has the smell of asphalt, but in other respects it is superior to the pitch of Pieria. This they pour into a pit dug near the pool; and when they have collected a large quantity, then they pour it into the jars from the pit: and whatever thing falls into the pool goes under ground and reappears in the sea, which is distant about four furlongs from the pool. Thus then the report about the island lying near the coast of Libya is also probably enough true.

196. The Carthaginians say also this, namely that there is a place in Libya and men dwelling there, outside the Pillars of Heracles, to whom when they have come and have taken the merchandise forth from their ships, they set it in order along the beach and embark again in their ships, and after that they raise a smoke; and the natives of the country seeing the smoke come to the sea, and then they lay down gold as an equivalent for the merchandise and retire to a distance away from the merchandise. The Carthaginians upon that disembark and examine it, and if the gold is in their opinion sufficient for the value of the merchandise, they take it up and go their way; but if not, they embark again in their ships and sit there; and the

others approach and straightway add more gold to the former, until they satisfy them: and they say that neither party wrongs the other; for neither do the Carthaginians lay hands on the gold until it is made equal to the value of their merchandise, nor do the others lay hands on the merchandise until the Carthaginians have taken the gold.

197. These are the Libyan tribes whom we are able to name; and of these the greater number neither now pay any regard to the king of the Medes nor did they then. Thus much also I have to say about this land, namely that it is occupied by four races and no more, so far as we know; and of these races two are natives of the soil and the other two not so; for the Libyans and the Ethiopians are natives, the one race dwelling in the Northern parts of Libya and the other in the Southern, while the Phoenicians and the Hellenes are strangers.

198. I think moreover that (besides other things) in goodness of soil Libya does not very greatly excel as compared with Asia or Europe, except only the region of Kinyps, for the same name is given to the land as to the river. This region is equal to the best of lands in bringing forth the fruit of Demeter, nor does it at all resemble the rest of Libya; for it has black soil and is watered by springs, and neither has it fear of drought nor is it hurt by drinking too abundantly of rain; for rain there is in this part of Libya. Of the produce of the crops the same measures hold good here as for the Babylonian land. And that is good land also which the Euesperites occupy, for when it bears best it produces a hundred-fold, but the land in the region of Kinyps produces sometimes as much as three-hundred-fold.

199. Moreover the land of Kyrene, which is the highest land of the part of Libya which is occupied by nomads, has within its confines three seasons of harvest, at which we may marvel: for the parts by the sea-coasts first have their fruits ripe for reaping and for gathering the vintage; and when these have

been gathered in, the parts which lie above the sea-side places, those situated in the middle, which they call the hills, are ripe for the gathering in; and as soon as this middle crop has been gathered in, that in the highest part of the land comes to perfection and is ripe; so that by the time the first crop has been eaten and drunk up, the last is just coming in. Thus the harvest for the Kyrenians lasts eight months. Let so much as has been said suffice for these things.

ISLAND OF PANCHAEA BY EUHUMERUS; SUMMARIZED BY DIODORUS SICULUS

Diodorus, , Charles H. Oldfather, Charles L. Sherman, Russel M. Geer, Francis R. Walton, and C B. Welles. *Library of History*. London: W. Heinemann, 1933. Print.

41. But now that we have described the lands which lie to the west and those which extend toward the north, and also the islands in the ocean, we shall in turn discuss the islands in the ocean to the south which lie off that portion of Arabia which extends to the east and borders upon the country known as Cedrosia. Arabia contains many villages and notable cities, which in some cases are situated upon great mounds and in other instances are built upon hillocks or in plains; and the largest cities have royal residences of costly construction, possessing a multitude of inhabitants and ample estates. And the entire land of the Arabians abounds with domestic animals of every description, and it bears fruits as well and provides no lack of pasturage for the fatted animals; and many rivers flow through the land and irrigate a great portion of it, thus contributing to the full maturing of the fruits. Consequently that part of Arabia which holds the chief place for its fertility has received a name appropriate to it, being called Arabia the Blest.

On the farthest bounds of Arabia the Blest, where the ocean washes it, there lie opposite it a number of islands, of which there are three which merit a mention in history, one of them bearing the name Hiera or Sacred, on which it is not allowed to bury the dead, and another lying near it, seven stades distant, to which they take the bodies of the dead whom they see fit to inter. Now Hiera has no share in any other fruit, but it produces frankincense in such abundance as to suffice for the honors paid to the gods throughout the entire inhabited world; and it possesses also an exceptional quantity of myrrh and every variety of all the other kinds of incense of highly fragrant odor. The nature of frankincense and the preparing of it is like this: In size it is a small tree, and in appearance it resembles the white Egyptian Acacia, its leaves are like those of the willow, as it is called, the bloom it bears is in color like gold, and the frankincense which comes from it oozes forth in drops like tears. But the myrrh-tree is like the mastich-tree, although its leaves are more slender and grow thicker. It oozes myrrh when the earth is dug away from the roots, and if it is planted in fertile soil this takes place twice a year, in spring and in summer; the myrrh of the spring is red, because of the dew, but that of the summer is white. They also gather the fruit of the Christ's thorn, which they use both for meat and for drink and as a drug for the cure of dysentery.

42. The land of Hiera is divided among its inhabitants, and the king takes for himself the best land and likewise a tithe of the fruits which the island produces. The width of the island is reputed to be about two hundred stades. And the inhabitants of the island are known as Panchaeans, and these men take the frankincense and myrrh across to the mainland and sell it to Arab merchants, from whom others in turn purchase wares of this kind and convey them to Phoenician and Coelesyria and Egypt, and in the end merchants convey them from these countries throughout all the inhabited world. And there is yet another large island, thirty stades distant from the one we have mentioned, lying out in the ocean to the east and many stades in length; for men say that from its promontory which extends toward the east one can descry India, misty because of its great distance.

As for Panchaea itself, the island possesses many things which deserve to be recorded by history. It is inhabited by men who were sprung from the soil itself, called Panchaeans, and the foreigners there are Oceanites and Indians and Scythians and Cretans. There is also a notable city on the island, called

Panara, which enjoys unusual felicity; its citizens are called "suppliants of Zeus Triphylius," and they are the only inhabitants of the land of Panchaea who live under laws of their own making and have no king over them. Each year they elect three chief magistrates; these men have no authority over capital crimes, but render judgment in all any other matters; and the weightiest affairs they refer of their own accord to the priests.

Some sixty stades distant from the city of Panara is the temple of Zeus Triphylius, which lies out on a level plain and is especially admired for its antiquity, the costliness of its construction, and its favorable situation. 43. Thus, the plain lying around the temple is thickly covered with trees of every kind, not only such as bear fruit, but those also which possess the power of pleasing the eye; for the plain abounds with cypresses of enormous size and plane-trees and sweet-bay and myrtle, since the region is full of springs of water. Indeed, close to the sacred precinct there bursts forth from the earth a spring of sweet water of such size that it gives rise to a river on which boats may sail. And since the water is led off from the river to many parts of the plain and irrigates them, throughout the entire area of the plain there grow continuous forests of lofty trees, wherein a multitude of men pass their time in the summer season and a multitude of birds make their nests, birds of every kind and of various hues, which greatly delight the ear by their song; therein also is every kind of garden and many meadows with varied plants and flowers, so that there is a divine majesty in the prospect which makes the place appear worthy of the gods of the country. And there were palm trees there with mighty trunks, conspicuous for the fruits they bore, and many varieties of nut-bearing trees, which provide the natives of the place with the most abundant subsistence. And in addition to what we have mentioned, grape-vines were found there in great number and of every variety, which were trained to climb high and were variously intertwined so that they presented a pleasing sight and provided an enjoyment of the season without further ado.

44. The temple was a striking structure of white marble, two plethra in length and the width proportionate to the length; it was supported by large thick columns and decorated at intervals with reliefs of ingenious design; and there were also remarkable statues of the gods, exceptional in skill of execution and admired by men for their massiveness. Around about the temple the priests who served the gods had their dwellings, and the management of everything pertaining to the sacred precinct was in their hands. Leading from the temple an avenue had been constructed, four stades in length and a plethrum in width. On each side of the avenue are great bronze vessels which rest upon square bases, and at the end of the avenue the river we mentioned above has its sources, which pour forth in a turbulent stream. The water of the stream is exceedingly clear and sweet and the use of it is most conducive to the health of the body; and the river bears the name "Water of the Sun." The entire spring is surrounded by an expensive stone quay, which extends along each side of it four stades, and no man except the priests may set foot upon the place up to the edge of the quay. The plain lying below the temple has been made sacred to the gods, for a distance of two hundred stades, and the revenues which are derived from it are used to support the sacrifices.

Beyond the above-mentioned plain there is a lofty mountain which has been made sacred to the gods and is called the "Throne of Uranus" and also "Triphylian Olympus." For the myth relates that in ancient times, when Uranus was king of the inhabited earth, he took pleasure in tarrying in that place and in surveying from its lofty top both the heavens and the stars therein, and that at a later time it came to be called Triphylian Olympus because the men who dwelt about it were composed of three peoples; these, namely, were known as Panchaeans, Oceanites, and Doians, who were expelled at a later time by Ammon. For Ammon, men say, not only drove this nation into exile but also totally destroyed their cities, razing to the ground both Doia and Asterusia. And once a year, we are told, the priests hold a sacrifice in this mountain with great solemnity.

45. Beyond this mountain and throughout the rest of the land of Panchaeitis, the account continues, there is found a multitude of beasts of every description; for the land possesses many elephants and lions and leopards and gazelles and an unusual number of other wild animals which differ in their aspect and are of marvelous ferocity. This island also contains three notable cities, Hyracia, Dalis, and Oceanis. The whole country, moreover, is fruitful and possesses in particular a multitude of vines of every variety. The men are warlike and use chariots in battle after the ancient manner.

The entire body politic of the Panchaeans is divided into three castes: The first caste among them is that of the priests, to whom are assigned the artisans, the second consists of the farmers, and the third is that of the soldiers, to whom are added the herdsmen. The priests served as the leaders in all things, rendering the decisions in legal disputes and possessing the final authority in all other affairs which concerned the community; and the farmers, who are engaged in the tilling of the soil, bring the fruits into the common store, and the man among them who is thought to have practiced the best farming receives a special reward when the fruits are portioned out, the priests deciding who had been first, who second, and so in order to the tenth, this being done in order to spur on the rest. In the same manner the herdsmen also turn both the sacrificial animals and all others into the treasury of the state with all precision, some by number and some by weight. For, speaking generally, there is not a thing except a home and a garden which a man may possess for his own, but all the products and the revenues are taken over by the priests, who portion out with justice to each man his share, and to the priests alone is given two-fold.

The clothing of the Panchaeans is soft, because the wool of the sheep of the land is distinguished above all other for its softness; and they wear ornaments of gold, not only the women but the men as well, with collars of twisted gold about their necks, bracelets on their wrists, and rings hanging from their ears after the manner of the Persians. The same kind of shoes are worn by both sexes, and they are worked in more varied colors than is usual.

46. The soldiers receive a pay which is apportioned to them and in return protect the land by means of forts and posts fixed at intervals; for there is one section of the country which is infested with robber bands, composed of bold and lawless men who lie in wait for the farmer and war upon them. And as for the priests, they far excel the rest in luxury and in every other refinement and elegance of their manner of life; so, for instance, their robes are of linen and exceptionally sheer and soft, and at times they wear garments woven of the softest wool; furthermore, their headdress is interwoven with gold, their footgear consists of sandals which are of varied colors and ingeniously worked, and they wear the same gold ornaments as do the women, with the exception of the earrings. The first duties of the priests concerned with the services paid to the gods and with the hymns and praises which are accorded them, and in them they recite in song the achievements of the gods one after another and the benefactions they have bestowed upon mankind. According to the myth which the priests give, the gods had their origin in Crete, and were led by Zeus to Panchaea at the time when he sojourned among men and was king of the inhabited earth. In proof of this they cite their language, pointing out that most of the things they have about them still retain their Cretan names; and they add that the kinship which they have with the Cretans and the kindly regard they feel toward them are traditions they received from their ancestors, since this report is ever handed down from one generation to another. And it has been their practice, in corroboration of these claims, to point to inscriptions which, they said, were made by Zeus during the time he still sojourned among men and founded the temple.

The land possesses rich mines of gold, silver, copper, tin, and iron, but none of these metals is allowed to be taken from the island; nor may the priests for any reason whatsoever set foot outside of the hallowed land, and if one of them does so, whoever meets him is authorized to slay him. There are many great dedications of gold and of silver which have been made to the gods, since time has amassed the multitude of such offerings. The doorways of the temple are objects of wonder in their construction, being worked in silver and gold and ivory and citrus-wood. And there is the couch of the god, which is six cubits long and four wide and is entirely of gold and skillfully constructed in every detail of its workmanship. Similar to it both in size and in costliness in general is the table of the god which stands near the couch. And on the center of the couch stands a large gold stele which carries letters which the Egyptians call sacred, and the inscription recounts the deeds both of Uranus and of Zeus; and to them there were added by Hermes the deeds also of Artemis and of Apollo.

As regards the islands, then, which lie in the ocean opposite Arabia, we shall rest content with what has been said.

ENDNOTES

MLA (7th Edition)

---

[i] Lucian, , H W. Fowler, and F G. Fowler. *The Works of Lucian of Samosata: Complete with Exceptions Specified in the Preface*. Oxford: Clarendon Press, 1905. Print.
[ii] Herodotus, , and G C. Macaulay. *The History of Herodotus*. London: Macmillan and Co, 1890. Print.
[iii] Diogenes Laertius. Hicks, Robert D. *Diogenes Laertius: Lives of Eminent Philosophers*. New York: Harvard U. Press, 1925. Print.
[iv] Homer, , and A T. Murray. *The Iliad*. London: W. Heinemann, 1924. Print.
[v] Herodotus, , and G C. Macaulay. *The History of Herodotus*. London: Macmillan and Co, 1890. Print.
[vi] Thucydides, , Richard Crawley, and Richard Feetham. *Thucydides' Peloponnesian War*. London: J.M. Dent and Co, 1903. Print.
[vii] Herodotus, , and G C. Macaulay. *The History of Herodotus*. London: Macmillan and Co, 1890. Print.
[viii] Aelian, Claudius, and Thomas Stanley. *Claudius Ælianus His Various History*. London: Printed for Thomas Dring, 1665. Print.
[ix] **Pliny, , Philemon Holland, and Adam Islip. *The Historie of the World: Commonly Called the Natural Historie of C. Plinius Secundus*. London: Printed by Adam Islip, 1601. Print. Spelling modernized.:** Of Polypus or Pourcontrels, there be sundry kinds. They that keep near to the shore are bigger than those that haunt the deep. All of them help themselves with their fins and arms, like as we do with feet and hands: as for their tail, which is sharp and two-forked, it serves them in the act of generation. These Pourcontrels have a pipe in their back, by the help whereof they swim all over the

seas; and if they can shift, one while to the right side, and another while to the left. They swim awry or side-long with their head above, which is very hard and as it were puffed up, so long as they be alive. Moreover, they have certain hollow concavities dispersed within their claws or arms like to ventoses or cupping glasses, whereby they will stick too, and cleave fast, as it were by sucking, to anything; which they clasp and hold so fast (lying upward with their bellies) that it cannot be plucked from them. They never settle so low as the bottom of the water: and the greater they be, the less strong they are to clasp or hold anything. Of all soft fishes, they only go out of the water to dry land, especially into some rough place; for they cannot abide those that are plain and even. They live upon shell-fishes, and with their hairs or strings that they have, they will twine about their shells and crack them in pieces: and therefore a man may know where they lie and make their abode, by a number of shells that lie before their nest. And albeit otherwise it be a very brutish and senseless creature, so foolish withal, that it will swim and come to a man's hand; yet it seems after a sort to be witty and wise, and keeping of house and maintaining a family: for all that they can take, they carry home to their nest. When they have eaten the meat of the fishes, they throw the empty shells out of dores, and lie as it were in ambuscade behind, to watch and catch fishes that swim thither. They change their color eftsoones, and resemble the place where they be, and especially when they be afraid. That they gnaw and eat their own claws and arms, is a mere untruth; for they be the Congress that doe them that shrewd turn: but true it is, that they will grow again, like as the tail of snakes, adders, and lizards. But among the greatest wonders of Nature, is that fish, which of some is called Nautilos, of others Pompilos. This fish, for to come aloft above the water, turns upon his back, and raises or heaves himself up by little and little: and to the end he might swim with more ease, as disburdened of a sink, he discharges all the water within him at a pipe. After this, turning up his two foremost claws or arms, he displayed and stretched out between them, a membrane or skin of a wonderful thinness: this serves him instead of a sailed in the air above water: with the rest of his arms or claws, he rows and labors under water; and with his tail in the midst, he directs his course, and steers as it were with an helm. Thus holds he on and makes way in the sea, with a faire show of a foist or galley under sail. Now if he be afraid of anything in the way, he makes no more adoe but draws in water to balance his body, and so plunges himself down and sinks to the bottom.

[x] Thucydides, , Richard Crawley, and Richard Feetham. *Thucydides' Peloponnesian War.* London: J.M. Dent and Co, 1903. Print.

[xi] Augustine, , and Philip Schaff. *A Select Library of the Nicene and Post-Nicene Fathers of the Christian Church: Vol.* 2. New York: Christian literature Co, 1887. Print.

[xii] Herodotus, , and G C. Macaulay. *The History of Herodotus.* London: Macmillan and Co, 1890. Print.

[xiii] Lucian, , H W. Fowler, and F G. Fowler. *The Works of Lucian of Samosata: Complete with Exceptions Specified in the Preface.* Oxford: Clarendon Press, 1905. Print.

[xiv] Herodotus, , and G C. Macaulay. *The History of Herodotus.* London: Macmillan and Co, 1890. Print.

[xv] Pindar, ; Myers, Ernest J. *The Extant Odes of Pindar, Translated into English [in Prose], with an Introduction and Short Notes by E. Myers.* London, 1874. Print.

[xvi] **Lucian, , H W. Fowler, and F G. Fowler. *The Works of Lucian of Samosata: Complete with Exceptions Specified in the Preface.* Oxford: Clarendon Press, 1905. Print.**

Alexander ... Hannibal | Dialogues of the Dead 12:

Alexander. Hannibal. Minos. Scipio

Alex. Libyan, I claim precedence of you. I am the better

man.

Han. Pardon me.

Alex. Then let Minos decide.

Mi. Who are you both?

Alex. This is Hannibal, the Carthaginian: I am Alexander, the son of Philip.

Mi. . Bless me, a distinguished pair! And what is the quarrel about?

Alex. It is a question of precedence. He says he is the better general: and I maintain that neither Hannibal nor (I might almost add) any of my predecessors was my equal in strategy; all the world knows that.

Mi. Well, you shall each have your say in turn: the Libyan first.

Han. Fortunately for me, Minos, I have mastered Greek since I have been here; so that my adversary will not have even that advantage of me. Now I hold that the highest praise is due to those who have won their way to greatness from obscurity; who have clothed themselves in power, and shown themselves fit for dominion. I myself entered Spain with a handful of men, took service under my brother, and was found worthy of the supreme command. I conquered the Celtiberians, subdued Western Gaul, crossed the Alps, overran the valley of the Po, sacked town after town, made myself master of the plains, approached the bulwarks of the capital, and in one day slew such a host, that their finger-rings were measured by bushels, and the rivers were bridged by their bodies. And this I did, though I had never been called a son of Ammon; I never pretended to be a god, never related visions of my mother; I made no secret of the fact that I was mere flesh and blood. My rivals were the ablest generals in the world, commanding the best soldiers in the world; I warred not with Medes or Assyrians, who fly before they are pursued, and yield the victory to him that dares take it. Alexander, on the other hand, in increasing and

extending as he did the dominion which he had inherited from his father, was but following the impetus given to him by Fortune. And this conqueror had no sooner crushed his puny adversary by the victories of Issus and Arbela, than he forsook the traditions of his country, and lived the life of a Persian; accepting the prostrations of his subjects, assassinating his friends at his own table, or handing them over to the executioner. I in my command respected the freedom of my country, delayed not to obey her summons, when the enemy with their huge armament invaded Libya, laid aside the privileges of my office, and submitted to my sentence without a murmur. Yet I was a barbarian all unskilled in Greek culture; I could not recite Homer, nor had I enjoyed the advantages of Aristotle's instruction; I had to make a shift with such qualities as were mine by nature.- It is on these grounds that I claim the preeminence. My rival has indeed all the luster that attaches to the wearing of a diadem, and - I know not - for Macedonians such things may have charms: but I cannot think that this circumstance constitutes a higher claim than the courage and genius of one who owed nothing to Fortune, and everything to his own resolution.
Mi . Not bad, for a Libyan. - Well, Alexander, what do you say to that?
Alex . Silence, Minos, would be the best answer to such confident self-assertion. The tongue of Fame will suffice of itself to convince you that I was a great prince, and my opponent a petty adventurer. But I would have you consider the distance between us. Called to the throne while I was yet a boy, I quelled the disorders of my kingdom, and avenged my father's murder. By the destruction of Thebes, I inspired the Greeks with such awe, that they appointed me their commander-in-chief; and from that moment, scorning to confine myself to the kingdom that I inherited from my father, I extended my

gaze over the entire face of the earth, and thought it shame if I should govern less than the whole. With a small force I invaded Asia, gained a great victory on the Granicus, took Lydia, lonia, Phrygia,- in short, subdued all that was within my reach, before I commenced my march for Issus, where Darius was waiting for me at the head of his myriads. You know the sequel: yourselves can best say what was the number of the dead whom on one day I dispatched hither. The ferryman tells me that his boat would not hold them; most of them had to come across on rafts of their own construction. In these enterprises, I was ever at the head of my troops, ever courted danger. To say nothing of Tyre and Arbela, I penetrated into India, and carried my empire to the shores of Ocean; I captured elephants; I conquered Porus; I crossed the Tanais, and worsted the Scythians - no mean enemies - in a tremendous cavalry engagement. I heaped benefits upon my friends: I made my enemies taste my resentment. If men took me for a god, I cannot blame them; the vastness of my undertakings might excuse such a belief. But to conclude. I died a king: Hannibal, a fugitive at the court of the Bithynian Prusias - fitting end for villainy and cruelty. Of his Italian victories I say nothing; they were the fruit not of honest legitimate warfare, but of treachery, craft, and dissimulation. He taunts me with self-indulgence: my illustrious friend has surely forgotten the pleasant time he spent in Capua among the ladies, while the precious moments fleeted by. Had I not scorned the Western world, and turned my attention to the East, what would it have cost me to make the bloodless conquest of Italy, and Libya, and all, as far West as Gades? But nations that already cowered beneath a master were unworthy of my sword.- I have finished, Minos, and await your decision; of the many arguments I might have used, these shall suffice.

Sci. First, Minos let me speak.

Mi. And who are you, friend? And where do you come from?
Sci. I am Scipio, the Roman general, who destroyed Carthage, and gained great victories over the Libyans.
Mi. Well, and what have you to say?
Sci. That Alexander is my superior, and I am Hannibal's, having defeated him, and driven him to ignominious flight. What impudence is this, to contend with Alexander, to whom I, your conqueror, would not presume to compare myself!
Mi. Honestly spoken, Scipio, on my word! Very well, then: Alexander comes first, and you next; and I think we must say Hannibal third. And a very creditable third, too.

[xvii] Xenophon, , and Henry G. Dakyns. *The Works of Xenophon*. London: Macmillan and Co, 1890. Print.

[xviii] Homer, , George E. Dimock, and A T. Murray. *Odyssey*. Cambridge, MA: Harvard University Press, 1919. Print.

[xix] Homer, , George E. Dimock, and A T. Murray. *Odyssey*. Cambridge, MA: Harvard University Press, 1919. Print.

[xx] Aelian, Claudius, and Thomas Stanley. *Claudius Ælianus His Various History*. London: Printed for Thomas Dring, 1665. Print.

[xxi] Herodotus, , and G C. Macaulay. *The History of Herodotus*. London: Macmillan and Co, 1890. Print.

[xxii] Herodotus, , and G C. Macaulay. *The History of Herodotus*. London: Macmillan and Co, 1890. Print.

[xxiii] Plato, ; Benjamin Jowett. *Dialogues*. New York: C. Scribner's sons, 1871. Print.

[xxiv] Hesiod, , and Hugh G. Evelyn-White. *The Homeric Hyms: Homerica*. Cambridge (Mass.: Harvard University Press, 1914. Print.

[xxv] Herodotus, , and G C. Macaulay. *The History of Herodotus*. London: Macmillan and Co, 1890. Print.

[xxvi] Xenophon, , and Henry G. Dakyns. *The Works of*

Xenophon. London: Macmillan and Co, 1890. Print.

[xxvii] Hesiod, , and Hugh G. Evelyn-White. *The Homeric Hyms: Homerica*. Cambridge (Mass.: Harvard University Press, 1914. Print.

[xxviii] Lucian, , H W. Fowler, and F G. Fowler. *The Works of Lucian of Samosata: Complete with Exceptions Specified in the Preface*. Oxford: Clarendon Press, 1905. Print.

[xxix] Lucian, , H W. Fowler, and F G. Fowler. *The Works of Lucian of Samosata: Complete with Exceptions Specified in the Preface*. Oxford: Clarendon Press, 1905. Print.

[xxx] Plato, ; Benjamin Jowett. *Dialogues*. New York: C. Scribner's sons, 1871. Print.

[xxxi] Plato, ; Benjamin Jowett. *Dialogues*. New York: C. Scribner's sons, 1871. Print.

[xxxii] Homer, , George E. Dimock, and A T. Murray. *Odyssey*. Cambridge, MA: Harvard University Press, 1919. Print.

[xxxiii] Aelian, Claudius, and Thomas Stanley. *Claudius Ælianus His Various History*. London: Printed for Thomas Dring, 1665. Print.

[xxxiv] Homer, , George E. Dimock, and A T. Murray. *Odyssey*. Cambridge, MA: Harvard University Press, 1919. Print.

[xxxv] Plato, ; Benjamin Jowett. *Dialogues*. New York: C. Scribner's sons, 1871. Print.

[xxxvi] Homer, , George E. Dimock, and A T. Murray. *Odyssey*. Cambridge, MA: Harvard University Press, 1919. Print.

[xxxvii] Homer, , George E. Dimock, and A T. Murray. *Odyssey*. Cambridge, MA: Harvard University Press, 1919. Print.

[xxxviii] Homer, , George E. Dimock, and A T. Murray. *Odyssey*. Cambridge, MA: Harvard University Press, 1919. Print.

[xxxix] Herodotus, , and G C. Macaulay. *The History of Herodotus*. London: Macmillan and Co, 1890. Print.

[xl] Gellius, Aulus, John C. Rolfe, Aulus Gellius, and Aulus

Gellius. *The Attic Nights of Aulus Gellius*. London: Heinemann, 1927 (revised 1946). Print.
xli Herodotus, , and G C. Macaulay. *The History of Herodotus*. London: Macmillan and Co, 1890. Print.
xlii Homer, , George E. Dimock, and A T. Murray. *Odyssey*. Cambridge, MA: Harvard University Press, 1919. Print.
xliii Homer, , George E. Dimock, and A T. Murray. *Odyssey*. Cambridge, MA: Harvard University Press, 1919. Print.
xliv Plato, ; Benjamin Jowett. *Dialogues*. New York: C. Scribner's sons, 1871. Print.
xlv Aelian, Claudius, and Thomas Stanley. *Claudius Ælianus His Various History*. London: Printed for Thomas Dring, 1665. Print.

414 SUPLEMENT DE L'HISTOIRE

SUPLEMENT
DE L'HISTOIRE VERITABLE

Lucien ayant dit à la fin du Second Livre de cette Histoire, qu'il aloit décrire en suite les merveilles qu'il avoit veües aux Antipodes, & cela ne se trouvant point, soit que les Livres ayent esté perdus, ou autrement; il a pris envie à celuy qui a fait le precedent Dialogue, de se joüer à son exemple, en des avantures [illegible] tranges & inoüies. Mais comme il n'y a rien de si facile, que de feindre des choses qui n'ayent aucun fondement dans la Raison ni dans la Nature, il n'a pas creu le devoir imiter en ce point; & n'a rien dit, qui n'ait quelque [illegible] allegorique, ou quelque instruction [illegible] le plaisir.

LIVRE TROISIEME.

I. *Description de la Republique des Animaux. II. [illegible] mage qu'ils viennent rendre au Fenix. III. [illegible] Lucien aux Antipodes.* IV. *Bataille des [illegible] contre les Sauvages.* V. *Pacification par [illegible] de Lucien.*

I. *Description de la Republique des animaux.*

LE plus resolu demeura sans force & sans [illegible] ge, voyant nôtre Vaisseau brisé, & [illegible] rance du retour perdüe, mais aprés [illegible] consolez du mieux que nous pûmes, les [illegible] merent du feu, les autres se répandirent [illegible] la côte, ou entrerent plus avant dans le [illegible] le découvrir. Sur le soir, ceux qui [illegible] à la découverte, rapporterent que le pays [illegible] & remply de toutes sortes d'Animaux [illegible] leur estoient inconus, mais qu'ils [illegible]

VERITABLE, LIVRE III. 415

point veu d'hommes. Ce qui les avoit le plus étonnez, c'est qu'on voyoit d'un côté des Agneaux paître parmy des Loups; de l'autre des Faucons voler en la compagnie des Colombes; Icy des Cygnes se joüans avec des Serpens, & là des poissons nageans parmy des Castors & des Loutres. Sur ces entrefaites arrivent des Singes vêtus à la Grecque, qui nous vindrent faire commandement de la part du Roy de l'aler trouver; Ils portoient chacun sur le poin un Perroquet qui leur servoit de Trucheman, & parloit bon Grec; sans quoy l'on n'eût pû jamais rien entendre au jargon de ces Ambassadeurs. Cependant, obeïssans aux ordres du Prince, nous nous acheminons vers le lieu où il estoit, & aprenons d'eux en chemin, Que nous estions dans l'Isle des Animaux, qui dépendoit du vaste Empire des Fables; Qu'elle estoit environnée de celles des Geans, des Magiciens, des Pygmées, & autres semblables, qui relevoient toutes de la jurisdiction des Poëtes, dont l'Isle estoit assez proche. Que cét Empire estoit partagé en sept Comtez, gouvernées par autant de Comtes; qui sont les Contes pour rire, les Contes de la Cigogne, les Contes jaunes, les Contes violets, les Contes borgnes, les Contes à dormir debout, & les Contes de vieille, sans parler de plusieurs autres petits Contes de moindre importance, qui sont tous compris sous le nom des Contes de l'autre monde. Que parmy tous ces peuples, le plus grand crime estoit de conter deux fois une méme chose; Qu'on n'y estoit point introduit qu'on ne laissât son jugement à la porte, avec permission de le reprendre au retour; mais qu'on le retrouvoit presque toûjours ou égaré ou corrompu; Que la Republique des Animaux estoit gouvernée par le Fénix, & que celuy qui regnoit alors, avoit esté curieux de nous voir, parce qu'il ne faisoit que de naître, & n'avoit jamais veu d'hommes. Que sans cela, on ne nous auroit pas soufert plus long-tems dans l'Isle, parce qu'il leur estoit defen-

Tom. II. D4 du

Made in the USA
Monee, IL
29 December 2022